Murder
in the
Crypt

A Redmond and Haze Mystery
Book 1

By Irina Shapiro

Copyright

© 2020 by Irina Shapiro

All rights reserved. No part of this book may be reproduced in any form, except for quotations in printed reviews, without permission in writing from the author.

All characters are fictional. Any resemblances to actual people (except those who are actual historical figures) are purely coincidental.

Contents

Prologue 5
Chapter 1 7
Chapter 2 15
Chapter 3 20
Chapter 4 23
Chapter 5 37
Chapter 6 44
Chapter 7 54
Chapter 8 60
Chapter 9 64
Chapter 10 75
Chapter 11 92
Chapter 12 97
Chapter 13 103
Chapter 14 109
Chapter 15 112
Chapter 16 121
Chapter 17 126
Chapter 18 129
Chapter 19 138
Chapter 20 144
Chapter 21 148
Chapter 22 153
Chapter 23 163
Chapter 24 172
Chapter 25 177
Chapter 26 193

Chapter 27 204

Chapter 28 211

Chapter 29 225

Chapter 30 229

Chapter 31 237

Chapter 32 240

Epilogue 248

Notes.. 252

Excerpt from Murder at the Abbey.................................. 253

Prologue.. 253

Chapter 1 256

Chapter 2 260

Chapter 3 266

Prologue

Reverend Talbot walked the short distance from the vicarage and stepped inside his church. The familiar smells of wood polish, beeswax candles, and a hint of mustiness assailed him, and he felt a glorious sense of peace envelop him. This church was his home and had been since he'd come here as a young vicar more than twenty years ago. He lovingly ran a finger along the smooth wood of the altar, smiling reverently at the heavy cross that stood on the embroidered altar cloth. Gentle summer sun shone through the stained-glass window, illuminating the chancel in a rainbow-colored beam, setting the cross alight as if God himself smiled upon him.

The reverend's brow furrowed in displeasure when he noticed something smeared on the base of the cross, something brownish and repugnant. His gaze traveled downward, following the splatter of stains on the stone floor. It didn't take long for Reverend Talbot to understand what he was looking at. Blood. And it led to the crypt.

Taking a deep breath and asking the Lord for courage, Reverend Talbot followed the bloodstains like a trail of crumbs, descending into the murky bowels of the church. There was no gas lighting in the crypt, so he reached for the matches that were always kept next to two tall pillar candles and lit the wicks, flooding the crypt with flickering candlelight. At first glance, everything appeared normal, the tombs lining the walls as silent and dignified as their esteemed occupants, but the blood led to the furthest tomb, that of Sir Percival Talbot, Reverend Talbot's revered crusader ancestor, and ended there. The reverend picked up one of the candles and inched closer to the tomb, terrified of what he'd find. His eyes opened wide in amazement when he noticed that the lid had been shifted and a small opening allowed a glimpse into the upper left-hand corner of the sarcophagus.

Holding the candle so close to his face he nearly singed his bushy eyebrows, he leaned forward and peered into the shadowy confines of the stone coffin. He expected to see the gleam of bone beneath the helmet Sir Percival had been buried in sometime in the fourteenth century, but what he saw was a headful of dark hair and the pale cheek of a young man, whose forehead rested against the helmet as if he were gazing deep into the knight's hollow eye sockets. The reverend dropped the candle, let out a strangled cry, and scurried from the crypt, running down the path between the gravestones and through the lychgate until he spotted a boy walking across the green.

"You there," Reverend Talbot cried. He knew the lad, but the name escaped him in his panic. "Get the constable right quick. There's been a murder."

Chapter 1

Sunday, June 3, 1866

The waning light of a summer afternoon enveloped the valley in a golden haze. Although cooler than in New York, the weather was pleasantly warm, and the somnolent village of Birch Hill appeared no different from the other villages they'd passed through on their way from Liverpool. Captain Jason Redmond looked out the carriage window, eager to finally reach their destination. The steamship from New York had taken close to three weeks to cross the ocean, followed by days in a hired carriage engaged in Liverpool to transport him and Micah to Essex, which was halfway across the country. After being confined to the primitive wooden carriage and jolted until his teeth rattled, he was at the end of his patience and ready to face whatever awaited him at the end of the lane.

At last, the manor house came into view, and he leaned forward, eager to see his father's childhood home. The house was bigger than he'd expected. Built of red brick, the Georgian-style manor looked relatively modern, its symmetry pleasing to the eye, unlike some of the Tudor buildings he'd seen that seemed to lean on each other for support like old men.

"Is that it? Is that your house?" Micah cried as he leaned across Jason to look out the window, his blue eyes round with excitement.

"I believe it is," Jason replied, amused by the boy's enthusiasm.

"Are there horses?"

"I should think so," Jason replied noncommittally. "I suppose we'll find out soon enough."

The hired carriage rolled down the treelined drive and pulled up before the front door. Jason alighted but made no move to approach the house. He stood still, listening to the silence that was interrupted only by birdsong and the rustling of leaves in the gentle breeze, and taking in the elegant lines of the ancestral home he hardly knew anything about. Micah, on the other hand, was vibrating with impatience, his skinny legs practically doing a jig.

"Can we go inside? It sure looks grand, Captain. Your grandsire must've been one rich dotard."

Jason almost laughed out loud at Micah's description. He'd never met his grandfather but didn't imagine for one moment that Lord Giles Redmond would have appreciated being referred to as a *dotard*, especially by a copper-haired Irish boy from rural Maryland. He had no idea where Micah had heard the term.

The door opened, and an elderly gentleman peered out, staring at Jason as if he'd just seen an apparition. "May I help you, sir?" he inquired.

"Good afternoon. I'm Captain Jason Redmond," Jason replied. He took the letter from Mr. Worth, his grandfather's solicitor, out of his pocket and held it out to the old man, in case he felt it awkward to ask for proof of Jason's identity. The man scanned the letter, and his face broke into a joyous smile.

"Goodness me," he exclaimed. "You must be Master Geoffrey's boy. Never thought I'd see the day." He colored at the impropriety of such an address and instantly pulled himself up, as if on parade. "I do apologize, sir. You took me by surprise, is all. I'm Dodson, the butler," the man said with all the dignity he could muster. "Please, come in. You must be tired after your journey. Can I offer you some refreshment?" Dodson asked as he led them into a drawing room decorated in butter yellow and cream.

Jason looked around, trying to imagine his father in this room, but he couldn't. The room was beautifully appointed but lacked charm and modernity of style, something Geoffrey Redmond had encouraged in his own home in Washington Square. At least it wasn't overly decorated with stuffed birds, porcelain knickknacks, and other Victorian paraphernalia that seemed popular with the English.

"I'm sorry, sir, but the house has been shut up for over a year, the staff dismissed. It's just myself, Mrs. Dodson, both cook and housekeeper at the moment, and Joe, the head groom. When Mr. Worth failed to receive a response from Master Geoffrey after his lordship passed…" Dodson's voice trailed off as he waited for an explanation.

"My father died nearly three years ago," Jason said softly. "And I was otherwise engaged."

"Oh, I'm so sorry, your lordship," Dodson exclaimed.

The immediate change of address wasn't lost on Jason. With his father gone, he was the new Lord Redmond, the heir to the Redmond estate, a position he'd never expected to find himself in, at least not this soon.

"Please, call me *Captain*," Jason said. Having been born and raised in America, he didn't feel comfortable with noble titles.

"As you wish, your lord—Captain. Were you in the war?" Dodson asked, making the connection between Jason's rank and the recent events in the United States.

"Yes, I was. Fought for the North."

Dodson nodded wisely. "A terrible business, that. A terrible business. You must be glad it's over." Having offered what he believed to be an appropriate platitude, Dodson turned to more practical matters. "I'll instruct Mrs. Dodson to prepare rooms and send Joe to the inn to fetch some supper. There's nothing ready, as we weren't expecting you. Had you written…"

"I'm sorry. It was a spur-of-the-moment decision to come," Jason explained. "Don't trouble yourself. If there's bread and cheese and something to drink, Micah and I will be quite content. We're used to simple fare. I would like some hot water, if possible."

"Of course, your lor—eh—Captain. I'll have Joe bring up hot water for you both."

"Micah would like to be in a room next to mine," Jason said, noticing Micah's pale face. His freckles stood out on his nose, making him look somehow younger and more vulnerable.

"Certainly. His lordship never mentioned he had a great-grandson," Dodson said, gazing at Micah with interest.

"Micah is not my son," Jason replied. "He's my companion."

"I see. I meant no offense, sir."

"None taken."

Jason was amused by Dodson's confusion. It was clear he was trying to work out the relationship between his new master and the boy, who looked to be about nine years old. Micah was eleven, but a year in Andersonville Prison had stunted his growth and peeled whatever extra flesh he had off his bones. He'd gained some of the weight back since the prison was liberated, but it would take time for him to thrive. They had survived their imprisonment, just barely, but their health had been severely compromised by the brutal and inhumane conditions of the Confederate prison. The superintendent of the prison, Major Wirz, had been arrested and executed on a charge of crimes against humanity after the war ended, but that was a small comfort to the widows and children of the men who'd died of starvation, exposure, and disease under his command. Having nearly starved to death, Micah always needed to know where his next meal was coming from for fear of not getting enough to eat, and Jason made sure he ate several hearty meals and healthful snacks in between.

"I'll just see to the rooms and reopen the dining room," Dodson muttered.

"No need. A tray in my room, if you please."

"Yes, Captain. Would you like to see something of the house?"

"Perhaps later."

"As you wish, sir," Dodson said, and hurried from the room.

Two hours later, having bathed and changed into clean clothes, Jason and Micah enjoyed a supper of sliced pork, cheese, and bread, taken with a rather good claret for Jason and a glass of milk for Micah.

"No," Jason said firmly when Micah eyed the bottle lovingly.

"I won't be able to sleep," Micah complained.

"You will. Just try to relax and think pleasant thoughts."

This bit of advice was ridiculous in the face of the nightmares Micah still suffered from, but Jason couldn't very well keep feeding the boy laudanum. He'd have happily taken some himself if it helped him sleep through the night and not wake up drenched in cold sweat as he dreamed of the horrors of the prison, but it was high time they both learned to deal with the past. Jason hoped that the new surroundings would help heal the scars that refused to fade.

"So, this is all yours now?" Micah asked, taking in the luxurious bedroom hung with rich velvet curtains in deep blue and wallpapered in pale blue silk patterned with silvery flowers and hummingbirds. Soft gaslight from matching sconces bathed the room in a warm glow.

"It is."

"Your father turned his back on such splendor?" Micah asked, his gaze traveling to the lacquered Chinese cabinet that stood between the two windows. "Why?"

"He and his father fell out," Jason explained.

"Over what?"

"Over my father's choice of bride. My mother was American, and although she came from a wealthy family, she didn't have the pedigree my grandfather wanted for his only son."

"What's a pedigree?" Micah asked. Having come from a farm in Maryland, such trivialities were lost on him.

"Lineage. My mother didn't come from a titled family. Her father was a banker."

"Did your grandsire cut your father off, then?" Micah asked, determined to get the whole story out.

"He threatened to, but he didn't need to. My father followed my mother to New York when she left for home after her family's visit to England, and they married shortly after he arrived. He never set foot in England again, nor did he ever ask his father for money. He went to work for his father-in-law and did quite well for himself."

"Did he ever speak to his father again?" Micah asked as he reached for another slice of bread and covered it liberally with pork.

"After nearly a decade of silence, my father finally wrote to the old man, and he replied. He missed his son and was happy to learn he was a grandfather. They maintained a correspondence until my parents died." It still hurt to say it out loud, and Jason rarely spoke of the accident that had claimed his parents' lives.

"What'd they die of?" Micah asked tactlessly.

"They died in a railway crash three years ago."

"Do you miss them?"

"Yes, very much. I wish I had been able to attend their funeral," Jason said sadly. "By the time I heard the news, they were long gone."

"I'm sorry, Captain," Micah said. "I suppose it's rough losing your parents at any age."

"It is that," Jason agreed. "Now, stop asking questions and go to bed. I will be right here should you need me."

Micah gave him a searching look clearly meant to ascertain whether Jason would permit him to sleep in his bed, but Jason shook his head. Micah had slept with him for months after they had arrived in New York, having gotten used to sleeping by Jason's side after Micah's father had died at Andersonville, but Jason had drawn the line when they boarded the steamship for England. Micah had to start taking steps toward independence.

"There's nothing to be frightened of. You're safe, Micah."

Micah nodded. "I know. I'll be all right. I do hope they'll have something good for breakfast," he said, his thoughts turning to his stomach as they often did when he was anxious. "Sausages would be nice."

"I'm sure Mrs. Dodson will give us a splendid breakfast. Now, off with you."

"Goodnight, Captain," Micah said, and left the room, closing the door softly behind him.

Jason poured himself another glass of wine and gazed out the window at the gathering darkness. He wasn't ready to go to bed, but he wasn't in the mood to read. He set the glass down and walked down the corridor, stopping in front of the bedroom that had been his grandfather's. He wasn't sure what he expected to find, but he pushed open the door and walked in. The room was large and luxurious, with a heavily carved bed and dresser made of dark wood that gleamed in the moonlight streaming through the window. The bed hangings were maroon velvet that echoed the deep reds in the Turkish rug on the floor.

Jason thought he might get some sense of the man by standing in his private sanctum, but he felt nothing save emptiness and a desire to leave. He was about to go when he noticed a dark rectangle on the bedside table. Approaching the bed, he lifted the photograph off the stand and took it to the window, where he could study it in the moonlight. His heart clenched with grief when he saw his mother's smiling face and his father's kind eyes. His gaze traveled to the boy standing next to his father. He must have been around seven then, still a child. His dark hair fell into his face and his gray eyes stared into the camera as he waited for the photographer's flash, afraid he'd blink. A scab on his knee was just visible below the hem of his short pants and his shoes were a bit scuffed. He smiled at the memory. How happy he'd been then, how loved.

It had been his parents' greatest sorrow that they weren't blessed with more children. It was only as Jason got older and developed an interest in medicine that he'd realized his mother had suffered several miscarriages, but as a boy, he'd thought she was simply too delicate to have more babies and he'd reveled in her undivided love. His parents had begged him not to join the Union Army when the war broke out, but as fate would have it, they were the ones who had died, and now he was in England, standing in the bedroom of the grandfather he'd never met, looking at his seven-year-old self as tears of loss stung his eyes and a fox screamed somewhere out in the night, echoing his own loneliness.

Jason was about to replace the photograph on the nightstand but thought better of it and took it back to his room, setting it next to his own unfamiliar bed. When he was finally ready for sleep, he felt better knowing that his parents would be watching over him and hoped he'd finally sleep through the night, grateful for the oblivion only sleep could provide.

Chapter 2

Monday, June 4

Jason woke up with a start, surprised to see sunlight streaming through the window. Mrs. Dodson had drawn the heavy curtains when she'd prepared the room last night, but Jason had pulled them open, preferring to see the nighttime sky if he woke during the night. He rarely slept past dawn, but according to the pocket watch he'd left on the nightstand, it was just past ten.

He sat up and looked around at the unfamiliar room, slowly recalling that he'd finished the bottle of claret, which probably explained why his head was fuzzy and how he'd managed to sleep well into the morning. The sound that had woken him reverberated through the house. It was the iron knocker being struck again and again. Jason heard raised voices, then Dodson's heavy tread on the stairs. He knocked on the bedroom door and poked his head in.

"I'm sorry to disturb you, Captain, but there's someone who wishes to speak with you urgently."

"Give me a moment to get dressed," Jason replied, already swinging his legs out of bed.

Dodson glanced at the open curtains and Jason's clothes carelessly tossed across a chair but said nothing. He had begun to retreat when Jason called after him.

"Dodson, is there any coffee?"

"Coffee, sir?"

"Yes. I need a cup of coffee."

"Eh, I'll see if we can find some, your lord—Captain," He shrugged in exasperation and left the room.

Having seen to his personal needs, Jason hastily dressed and presented himself downstairs. He assumed he was about to be confronted by Mr. Worth. He knew no one in England, so the lawyer would be the only person who might have something to say to him, given his unexpected arrival. Surely there were papers to sign, his grandfather's wishes to be apprised of, and general estate business to attend to. Jason was in no mood to deal with any of those matters, but he wasn't in the habit of turning visitors away by pretending not to be at home. Hoping the meeting wouldn't take long, he entered the drawing room, where his visitor was waiting.

A man stood with his back to the room, his hands clasped behind his back as he gazed out the window. He turned at the sound of Jason's footsteps, but didn't smile or extend his hand in greeting. Instead, he tilted his head to the side as he took Jason's measure, his eyes narrowing as if he found Jason wanting.

Jason took a moment to study the man in return. He was around his own age—late twenties, maybe thirty—with neatly brushed dark-brown hair and intelligent brown eyes behind round spectacles, which gave him a studious appearance. He wore a gray tweed suit and a somber tie, the only flaw in his appearance the dusty shoes that could use a good polish.

"How can I help you?" Jason asked when the man failed to introduce himself.

"My name is Daniel Haze, and I'm the parish constable."

"Pleasure to meet you. Captain Jason Redmond. Won't you have a seat?" Jason invited.

The constable sat down but didn't make himself comfortable. His posture was stiff, his shoulders squared as he faced Jason, who sat in the wingchair opposite. Jason waited patiently for the man to speak.

"The body of a young man was discovered early this morning," Constable Haze said.

"I'm sorry to hear that."

"I'm making inquiries into his death."

"I see," Jason said, wishing the man would get to the point.

"What time did you arrive at Redmond Hall yesterday?" the constable asked.

"Around five," Jason replied.

"And did you leave the house again last night?"

"No, I did not."

"What about your young companion?"

Word travels fast, Jason thought as he sat forward, sensing the constable's unexplained antagonism toward him. "Micah was with me until he went to bed around nine. What's this about, Constable? Are you suggesting we had something to do with the death of this young man?"

"Hours after you arrived, a man was murdered. Given the proximity of the two events, I would be derelict in my duty if I didn't ask, since they might be connected."

"Is that your professional opinion, or the ill-conceived assumption of a man grasping at straws?" Jason asked tartly, and instantly regretted his outburst. The man was only doing his job.

The constable winced and moderated his tone. "I'm not accusing you of anything, my lord."

It certainly sounded like he was, but Jason decided to try a different tack. "What reason would I have had to kill this man?" Jason asked, striving for calm. "I know no one in these parts, and I came here directly from Liverpool, where I arrived three days ago from New York."

"Is there anyone who can verify that?"

"I suppose you can check with the White Star steamship line and track down the coachman I hired to bring us here. Mr. and Mrs. Dodson were both here when we arrived, as well as Joe, who brought in our luggage. They can all attest to the fact that Micah and I never left the house yesterday evening."

"I will do that," the constable replied tersely.

"Who is this man, anyway?" Jason asked, intrigued despite his initial irritation.

The constable's taciturn expression turned to one of embarrassment. "I don't know."

"He's not local?"

"No. I've never seen him before."

"So, you have absolutely nothing to go on save the fact that my friend and I arrived in Birch Hill yesterday?"

"I do not, *your lordship*," the man said with exaggerated emphasis on the title.

"And how did this man die?"

"I've yet to find out. The doctor has been summoned, but he appears to be indisposed, so an examination of the body will have to wait."

"What makes you believe this man was murdered?" Jason asked, his professional curiosity getting the better of him. He'd seen more corpses in his twenty-eight years than he cared to count, but suspicious death had always held a special interest for him because of the clues it left behind. The body had much to tell someone who was ready to listen and knew how to interpret the information.

"His body was discovered in one of the tombs in the crypt of the church. I doubt he climbed in there of his own accord and pulled the lid closed before dying. There are easier ways to end one's life."

"Are there any marks on his body?"

"Are you a doctor, sir?" Constable Haze asked, his irritation bubbling to the surface as he sprang to his feet. He didn't seem to appreciate the suspect questioning him instead of the other way around.

"As it happens, I am," Jason said, standing as well.

The constable's eyebrows lifted in surprise. "Are you, indeed? I was given to believe you were a military man."

"I was an infantry captain, but I'm also a trained surgeon."

"Which side did you fight on?" Daniel Haze asked with ill-disguised interest.

"I fought for the North."

"Was that because you believe slavery to be a moral wrong or because that happened to be where you were from?"

"Slavery has no place in the modern world," Jason replied patiently before his mind returned to the murder. "Constable, I would be happy to examine the body if you would permit it."

Constable Haze smiled, his eyes twinkling with amusement. "Well, seeing as you have an alibi for the time of the murder and as you're offering your services, I'll be glad to accept your help, my lord."

"Please, call me Captain Redmond," Jason said.

The constable shrugged. "I'll call you helpful if you can tell me anything about this man's death. Dr. Miller is a good man, but he's a country doctor more suited to setting broken bones and delivering babies. We don't have a police surgeon here, like they do in London," the man said wistfully.

"Is there a police station near here?"

Daniel Haze laughed bitterly. "The nearest police station is in Brentwood, but it's still in its infancy. The Metropolitan Police Service has been in existence in London for some years, but the concept of a trained, organized police force has yet to spread to the rest of England. In Birch Hill, I'm all there is."

"I see. Would you like to join me for a cup of coffee, Constable?" Jason asked politely. "I was just about to have some."

"No, thank you. I will question the staff while you enjoy your coffee. Shall we meet outside in about ten minutes?"

"I will see you there."

Chapter 3

Daniel stepped outside into the pleasant warmth of the June morning after confirming with Mr. and Mrs. Dodson that Jason Redmond had told him the truth. He felt a right fool. He hadn't realized the newcomers to the village were the new Lord Redmond and his companion, who was only a child, when he'd come banging on the door. He'd heard only that a hired carriage had been spotted in the vicinity of Redmond Hall, news he'd paid little attention to until the body was discovered by the vicar this morning. Until a few minutes ago, when Dodson set him straight on the identity of the hall's new residents, the strangers had been the obvious suspects, and in his desire to prove himself, Daniel had practically accused Lord Redmond of murder and made an utter ass of himself.

Having rounded the side of the building, he made for the stables to question the groom. He didn't hold out much hope of learning anything from Joe Marin. Joe had a reputation for being better with horses than he was with people and had worked on the Redmond estate since he was a boy. Daniel had known him and his brother, John, all his life. In fact, he knew everyone in Birch Hill, having grown up in a hamlet just outside the village. He'd played with all the boys who were now men and had fallen in love at the tender age of twelve with a ten-year-old girl named Sarah. Sarah was now his wife, but she wasn't the girl he'd known, nor even the woman he'd married.

Daniel felt the familiar pang of grief as he crossed the yard toward the stables. He knew what had happened wasn't his fault; he hadn't even been there at the time of the accident, but Sarah had blamed him, and he'd had no choice but to acquiesce to her wishes and return to Birch Hill from London, where they had settled shortly after their marriage. He'd had to give up his dream of becoming a police detective. At the time of the accident, Daniel had been a peeler, or a bobby, as some liked to call them—a policeman on the Metropolitan Police Service. He'd loved his job and wore the blue uniform proudly, reporting to his post at the Whitechapel station early each morning with a spring in his step and a burning desire to make a difference. He'd worked hard and paid attention, learning the craft of policing not only from his colleagues and superiors, but also from Detective Colin Franks, who would become something of a friend and mentor. He'd have been a dedicated detective, had he ever got the chance, but the Almighty had a different plan for him, and for Sarah.

For the past three years, they had resided with his widowed mother-in-law, and Daniel held the title of Parish Constable. He was grateful to have been offered the position when the old constable finally saw fit to retire from his duties, but the job entailed mostly searching for lost sheep, investigating minor theft, and occasionally breaking up a fight, if he happened to be in the vicinity of the brawl. There hadn't been a murder in Birch Hill for as long as he could remember, at least not one that had been properly investigated. People died all the time, but for the most part, it was either of natural causes or from accidents that might have been caused deliberately but were treated as misadventure by the local magistrate, who wasn't overly concerned with the disputes of the lower orders.

And now a murder had been committed on his patch, and for the first time in years, Daniel felt a tingle of excitement. At thirty, he was too old to ever be a peeler again, the cutoff age being twenty-seven, but perhaps if he were to prove capable, in time, he might apply to the Essex constabulary and perhaps have a chance to start again as a junior detective. Sarah wouldn't like that; she wanted to remain in Birch Hill, but he'd try to persuade her. Maybe once they had a child, he thought, and instantly realized that having a baby would make Sarah even more resolute to remain in the sticks. But he wanted children, and he wanted Sarah to be happy. At this stage, it was all hypothetical, since relations between him and Sarah had been strained since their return to the village, so he turned his attention back to the matter at hand as he pushed open the door to the stables.

He liked the earthy smell of horses and hay and glanced in admiration at the pair of chestnuts that stood in their stalls, their coats glossy and their manes and tails thick and coppery. Joe was mucking out an empty stall but stopped when he saw Daniel.

"Hallo there, Daniel," Joe said, baring uneven teeth.

"Hello, Joe," Daniel answered. He wished Joe would call him by his proper title, but just then, the formalities weren't important. "Joe, what time did Lord Redmond arrive at Redmond Hall last night?"

"Fivish," Joe replied. "Why?"

"Did you see either him or the boy leave the house at any time after that?"

"Nah. Stayed in all night, they did. Why do ye ask?"

"A man was murdered."

Joe's eyebrows rose in surprise, but he didn't comment or inquire as to the identity of the victim, going back to mucking out the stall with remarkable indifference.

Chapter 4

Jason had been standing by the window, looking out over the gently sloping lawn that stretched toward the parkland, when Mrs. Dodson brought in the coffee accompanied by a beaker of milk and a bowl of sugar. "I'm sorry, Captain, but this was all we had. Just enough to make the one pot. Dodson and I favor tea," she said. "But I'll be sure to order some from Brentwood straight away, seeing as you have a taste for it."

"Thank you, Mrs. Dodson. Would you be kind enough to prepare breakfast for Micah? He was hoping for some sausages."

"I will see to it, my lord," Mrs. Dodson said, reverting to using the title. "The young gentleman is still asleep, I believe."

"Good. Let him rest."

Jason accepted a cup of coffee from Mrs. Dodson and added a splash of milk and one teaspoon of sugar. It was watery and tasted stale, but he gulped it down anyway and stepped out into the foyer, where Dodson was waiting with Jason's coat and hat. Jason turned at the sound of running footsteps. Micah appeared at the top of the stairs. He was still in his nightshirt, his skinny ankles sticking out from beneath the hem, his hair tousled, and his eyes wide with worry.

"Where are you going? Can I come too?" he cried.

"I'll be back shortly," Jason said patiently. He was all Micah had in the world, so the boy's anxiety was understandable, especially since he was now even further from his Maryland home. "In the meantime, you can enjoy your breakfast and then have a look at the horses. I'll expect a full report by the time I return."

Micah's face relaxed at the mention of horses. The boy had a great fondness for animals and often talked of the animals they'd had on his family's farm before the war. His sister, Mary, had done the milking and seen to the sheep, but Micah had looked after the horses and a particularly stubborn donkey he'd named Horace, a chore he'd enjoyed. He missed the undemanding companionship of animals. It would do him good to get back to something he loved, Jason thought as he smiled at him reassuringly.

"All right," Micah agreed, his gaze no longer filled with panic. "I'll go after breakfast." He made to come down the stairs.

"I think you'd better get dressed first," Jason said, stopping him. Micah colored slightly, then retreated to his room.

Constable Haze was already waiting outside. Jason had expected to see some sort of conveyance, but the constable appeared to have come on foot and meant for them to walk to the church.

"Were you able to confirm our whereabouts to your satisfaction, Constable?" Jason asked as he joined the constable on the drive.

Constable Haze's face turned a mottled shade of pink. "Your lordship," he began. "I mean, Captain, please forgive my rudeness earlier. I was out of line. I never meant to insinuate…" He coughed into his hand to hide his obvious embarrassment. "It was clumsily done," he finally said, having found the right words to express what he wished to say.

"You were only doing your duty," Jason replied, feeling sympathy for the man. "Shall we go?"

"Eh, yes. The church is less than a mile from here."

"Where is the corpse?" Jason asked as they fell into step.

"I left it under the watchful eye of the vicar. He was the one who discovered the body."

"And how exactly did he discover the body if it was in a tomb?" Jason asked, his mind turning to practicalities.

Haze glanced at Jason from beneath the brim of his bowler hat, as if surprised by the question. "The vicar noticed bloodstains on the floor leading to the steps to the crypt. He found the lid of one of the tombs slightly askew and looked inside. He expected to see skeletal remains, but what he saw instead was the body of a man, lying face down, his forehead resting against the helmet of Sir Percival Talbot."

"Who was?"

"Who was a knight during the last Crusade and the liege lord of all you see."

"Careless," Jason muttered to himself.

"I beg your pardon?"

"Whoever tried to dispose of the body was careless," Jason explained. "Why bother to hide the corpse in a tomb no one is likely to open if you're going to leave bloodstains on the floor and fail to shut the lid properly?"

"Those are very good questions, Captain," Constable Haze replied, nodding in agreement. "Why, indeed."

"Either the killer was pressed for time, or it was too dark to see," Jason mused. "Have you checked if anything has been stolen from the tomb? Perhaps the victim had tried to rob the grave and was injured in the process. Or he might have been murdered by his partner, who had no desire to share the proceeds from the theft."

"According to Reverend Talbot, nothing was taken," Constable Haze replied. "You're certain it was a man who's responsible?" he asked, cocking his head like a dog who'd spotted a squirrel.

"Do you think a woman, even a strong one, could have pushed aside the stone lid of the tomb and hefted the body inside?" Jason replied.

Constable Haze carefully considered his answer. "The victim might have been lured to the crypt on some pretext, then killed there. Perhaps he even helped his killer to open the tomb, believing there was something of value inside. The killer might have meant to do it all along, or perhaps an argument broke out and things got heated."

"And the blood in the church?"

"The blood could have belonged to either man. Perhaps one of them was already injured when they met."

"Yes, that's a plausible theory," Jason replied. "Let's see if it holds up."

"How do you propose to do that?"

"The body will tell us much about how the man died and whether he died before or after being placed in the tomb."

"Will it, indeed?" Constable Haze asked, clearly surprised.

"I believe so."

"You've handled your share of dead bodies, haven't you?" Constable Haze asked softly. "I've read about your war in the papers. Wouldn't wish that on any man, having to kill one's countrymen. Families divided, brother fighting against brother. Makes it all so much more personal. Never wanted to be a soldier myself. Don't have the stomach for it."

"Yes, Constable, I've seen the kind of carnage that makes a man question everything he believes about his fellow man. It also makes one doubt the existence of God."

Constable Haze sucked in his breath at this statement but didn't comment, either because he was too shocked by the sentiment or because they had reached the village green and his thoughts had returned to the matter at hand. The church was just across, its gray square tower rising proudly against a cloudless blue sky. Jason followed the constable through a lichen-covered lychgate, and down a path that bisected the graveyard and led to the church porch. Every church he'd seen since arriving in England seemed ancient, Jason thought as he took in the Norman-style building before him. Having been brought up in New York, he was used to things that were new and modern, but in England, time seemed to stand still, the sleepy villages remaining unchanged for generations, quaint with their thatched-roof cottages, half-timbered taverns, and grand manor houses that sat on acres of lush parkland, the few ruling the many for centuries with the help of Parliament and the Church.

Jason kept his thoughts to himself as he entered the church by a thick iron-studded door and followed the constable down a stone nave. Their footsteps echoed in the silence of the building, only the saints adorning the stained-glass windows watching their progress, albeit without much interest.

"Show me where the blood begins," Jason said as they neared the rood screen.

"Just here."

Jason looked down at the floor, then, instead of going toward the steps to the crypt, he walked slowly around the altar. "There's some here," he observed as he stared at the worn stone blocks. He glanced up at the window behind the altar, which was facing east and would have caught the first rays of the rising sun at the time the vicar must have arrived at the church. The light that filtered through the window would have shone on the altar and the floor directly in front of it, drawing the vicar's eye to the stains. Had the vicar arrived later, once the sun had risen higher in the sky, or had the day been overcast, he might have taken the brown smudges for dirt and never have descended to the crypt, leaving the body undiscovered until the smell of putrefaction wafted up the stairs. If the door to the crypt had remained firmly closed, the body might not have been discovered for weeks, months even, making it impossible to learn anything from the victim, which was probably what the killer had intended when he'd decided to dispose of the body in such a creative way.

Constable Haze followed Jason's gaze and nodded sagely. "There's blood on the base of the cross," he said, lifting it to examine the heavy base. "Think this is the murder weapon?"

Jason shook his head. "Unlikely. Had the victim been killed with this cross, there'd be a lot more blood. Given that there's just a smudge on the base and a splatter of stains leading away from the altar, I'd say the cross was used to stun rather than to kill."

"Shall we go down to the crypt?" Constable Haze asked.

"Lead the way." Jason followed Constable Haze down the narrow flight of stone steps.

Two tall pillar candles were the only source of light in the crypt, their mellow light flickering on the walls and barely illuminating the tombs that lined three of the walls. Jason could see how the killer might have thought he'd closed the lid all the way, his senses lulled into false security by the deep shadows that shrouded the coffins. They looked ancient, the stone faces of the deceased worn away after slumbering for centuries in the musty underbelly of the church. For a moment, Jason felt panic brought on by being confined in this windowless stone box, but quickly got hold of himself. No one was holding him against his will, and the door was wide open.

The vicar sat on a low stone bench by the far wall. Jason had expected him to look as old as his church, but the man was no more than forty-five, with thinning dark hair, a fleshy pink face, and eyes so dark they looked like empty holes in the dim light of the crypt. The vicar's lips had been moving, possibly in prayer, but he finished shortly after they arrived and stood to greet them.

"Reverend Talbot, this is Captain Jason Redmond of Redmond Hall," Constable Haze said. He kept his voice low, as if fearful of disturbing the dead.

"Lord Redmond's grandson?" the vicar asked, coming forward, his hand outstretched. "A pleasure to meet you, sir. Your grandfather spoke of you often, especially during the last weeks of his illness. It had been his fondest wish that he'd meet you in person. He'd be pleased to know you've come home at last."

Birch Hill wasn't home, but Jason refrained from pointing that out. The vicar was just being welcoming, a gesture that couldn't have been easy for him given that his gaze kept straying to the knight's tomb, his hands clasped before him so tightly the knuckles were white with tension.

"May I see the body?" Jason asked.

Reverend Talbot looked to Constable Haze, clearly confused by Jason's presence.

"Captain Redmond is a surgeon," the constable said. "He will examine the body in lieu of Dr. Miller. He will be respectful. Won't you, Captain?" he asked, cuing Jason to answer in the affirmative.

"You will not perform a postmortem," the vicar said. "I won't allow it. Desecrating a body goes against God and the teachings of the Church."

"The police surgeons in London perform autopsies all the time," Constable Haze replied petulantly. "They have the full support of the Church."

"I won't allow it," Reverend Talbot repeated stubbornly.

"I will do my best to determine the cause of death without a postmortem," Jason replied, more to pacify the vicar than because he fully agreed to his demand. If he couldn't learn what he needed to from examining the body, he'd find a way to get around the vicar's edict. "Now, can I see the body?" he repeated.

The vicar pointed to a tomb along the eastern wall of the crypt. Jason lifted one of the tall candleholders and brought the candle closer to the coffin. It didn't give off nearly enough light, but it was all he had to hand, so it'd have to do. The stone lid was slightly ajar, revealing a gap of about two inches at the head. Jason peered inside. Even with poor lighting, he could make out the head of the man. He had curling dark hair, and the firm pale cheek and thick lashes were those of a young man, probably no older than twenty. Had he not been lying face down in a tomb, he might have been asleep. Jason reached in and pressed two fingers to the man's neck just to be sure he was dead and not just unconscious. There was no pulse.

"We need to get him out," Jason said, turning to the constable. "Is there something to lay the body on?"

"There's a blanket in the vestry," Reverend Talbot said. "I'll go fetch it."

"Yes, please," Constable Haze replied absentmindedly. "What do you think?" he asked, turning to Jason.

"I think it's too soon to say anything definite. I need to examine him fully."

"Should you be doing that here? This is a church, after all, and someone might come down here and see him in a state of undress."

"Have you a better idea?" Jason replied. "Where will you take the body after you've finished with it?"

"There's a woman in the village, Mrs. Etty, who lays out the dead. We can take him to her."

Jason shook his head. "I would prefer to examine him before he's moved. You can stand guard and make sure no one disturbs us."

"All right. Is there anything you need?"

"Light. Is there a lantern? Two would be better."

"I'll see to it. Anything else?"

"Not at the moment, but I will need several items should an autopsy become necessary."

"An autopsy?" The constable nearly choked on the word. "But you promised Reverend Talbot."

"If I can't ascertain how he was killed just by looking at him, then yes, an autopsy would tell us more. The vicar need never know."

"Oh, he'd know," Constable Haze replied. "Mrs. Etty would tell him. Have you ever performed one?" Haze asked, his curiosity piqued.

"Yes, of course."

"Do you not find it gruesome?" Constable Haze asked. "I've never seen an autopsy done, but I heard it's not for the faint of heart."

"No, it's not, but sometimes it's necessary. It's the best way to learn about what happened to a body. It's like a road map of a person's existence."

Constable Haze was about to ask something else when the vicar came down with an old blanket. He didn't offer to help, but judging by his stance, he wasn't about to leave either.

"Captain Redmond needs lanterns," the constable said. "Do you have any at the vicarage?"

"Yes. Ask my daughter. She'll show you where," Reverend Talbot replied. He wasn't about to leave his post.

"Help me lift him out and then you can go for the lanterns," Jason said. "I'll need to undress him before I can proceed."

The vicar winced but said nothing, taking up his perch on the bench again. At least he didn't suggest the victim be examined while fully dressed.

Both men removed their coats and hats and tossed them onto a neighboring tomb before approaching the open tomb. They couldn't move the lid sideways since the tomb was positioned against the wall, but they managed to push it backward, making an opening large enough to lift out the man by holding him beneath the arms. Once his torso was fully out of the tomb, Constable Haze grabbed him by the legs and helped Jason lower the man onto the blanket on the floor. His head shifted marginally to the side and his hand appeared to move, making Reverend Talbot start in surprise. He leaned forward, staring at the man's bared teeth, then cried out in alarm when a hissing sound filled the crypt.

"What was that?" Reverend Talbot asked, his eyes wide with fear. "Are you sure he's dead? Could he be a victim of possession?"

"That was just gas escaping the body, Reverend," Jason explained patiently.

"What about that grin?"

"It's not a grin, Reverend. It's a grimace. I suspect he was in pain at the time of death."

"Eh, perhaps I'd better leave you to it," Reverend Talbot said, rising to his feet. "Duties to attend to."

"Of course," Jason replied, his lip twitching with amusement. For a vicar, Reverend Talbot was surprisingly squeamish.

"I'll get you those lanterns," Constable Haze said, and followed the vicar up the stairs.

Left alone, Jason went about undressing the victim, which wasn't an easy task given the degree of rigor mortis, but he managed it without tearing the clothes. He checked his pockets, then folded his clothes neatly and laid them on the bench. They might be needed for the burial.

Constable Haze appeared a few minutes later, carrying two oil lanterns. "Will these do?"

"Yes. Thank you."

"Mind if I watch?" he asked.

"Not at all."

"Well?" Constable Haze said as he leaned over Jason's shoulder and peered at the dead man.

"Well what?"

"What do you think?" Haze asked.

"I think he's dead. Give me a few minutes to perform an examination."

"Sorry. I'm just curious, I suppose," Haze explained.

Jason nodded. He envied the man. Jason didn't care to recall all the mangled, bloodied corpses that had lain strewn on a battlefield after each engagement with the enemy. Nor did he wish to remember the emaciated, flea-ridden men who'd died in his arms at the prison, their last words directed to those they'd loved and would never see again.

"What's a peeler?" Jason asked absentmindedly, his attention on the body before him. Constable Haze had used the term during their walk to the church, but Jason hadn't questioned him at the time, not wishing to interrupt unnecessarily. He assumed it wasn't someone who peeled potatoes.

"A policeman. A bobby. What do they call them in America?"

"Policemen. Coppers," Jason replied. "How long were you on the force?"

"Only four years. My wife and I had to leave London. For personal reasons."

This didn't warrant a reply, so Jason focused his attention on the corpse. The young man's skin glowed white in the light of the lanterns. He was thin but not malnourished, and his limbs were firm and well-defined. He'd worked for a living and had probably done lots of walking, judging by his muscular thighs and calves. His hands were clean, the fingernails gently rounded, not broken or ragged, with no dirt trapped underneath. His hair must have been recently washed and had a luster that came from eating regularly and well. There was a gash at the base of the hairline that must have bled profusely but didn't look deep enough to have been the cause of death.

A dark reddish-blue bruise covered most of the victim's chest and extended almost as far as the navel. After checking the advancement of rigor mortis to determine the time of death, Jason rolled the man onto his stomach. His back and legs were unblemished except for a narrow wound between the third and fourth rib on the left side. Having examined the wound, Jason turned the body over again and left the man on his back.

"So, what do you reckon?" Constable Haze asked again, unable to contain himself any longer.

Jason wiped his hands on his handkerchief and rose to his feet, turning to face Constable Haze. "The victim has been dead for at least twelve hours, so I would put the time of death at around midnight. The bloodstains we saw are from the cut on his forehead."

"Is that what killed him?" Haze asked.

"No. The blow probably knocked him senseless but didn't kill him."

"What did?"

"Do you see this bruise on his chest? This is what's known as livor mortis," Jason explained. "It's when the blood pools in the lowest part of the body after the heart stops beating. Since the victim was lying on his front, the blood flowed downward after his death. The fatal wound was administered to the back with a sharp, narrow blade. Given the entry point, I'd hazard to guess that it pierced the heart and caused a significant amount of internal bleeding. Had he been laid on his back, the tomb would have been awash with blood, but since he was already lying on his belly, the wound didn't bleed much externally."

"Are you saying that he was knocked out, then laid in the tomb and killed afterwards?"

"Given the absence of blood near the tomb or inside it, I would think that he was murdered once already in the tomb and lying face down. I think he might have come around just before he died, which would explain the grimace of pain on his face."

"Was it a knife, do you think?" Constable Haze asked.

"The wound is too narrow to have been made by a knife. More like a dagger," Jason replied.

"Poor sod. God rest his soul. I'm really impressed by how much you were able to discern just by looking at him."

Jason smiled, pleased to have been able to help. "I can also tell you that he wasn't from a wealthy family, and the motive for murder wasn't robbery."

"They teach you how to spot that in medical school?" Haze joked.

"No, just simple powers of observation. His clothes are of decent quality, but his coat is frayed at the cuffs and the soles of his shoes are worn. Also, there's money in his purse and his pocket watch hasn't been taken."

Jason pointed out the watch he'd found in the pocket of the young man's coat, which was lying next to his clothes. "This is an expensive watch, but it doesn't look new. Either it was passed down from an older relative or he bought it secondhand."

"Well, aren't you clever?" Constable Haze said caustically.

"I like to think so," Jason replied, grinning at the wide-eyed policeman. He felt pity for the young man on the floor, but he was beyond anyone's help. The only thing Jason could do was to solve the mystery of his murder and help Constable Haze bring the culprit to justice.

"What now?" Jason asked as he struggled to re-dress the dead man. Constable Haze squatted beside the corpse and did his best to help fold the stiffened limbs into sleeves and trouser legs.

"I don't know," Haze admitted. "Your observations are helpful, but without a name, I can't begin to hope to trace his movements."

"Have you asked at the inn?" Jason inquired as he stuffed the man's feet into his shoes.

The constable shook his head. "I'm not on the best terms with the publican. He mistrusts me since I brought him up on charges of purchasing smuggled goods. He was able to pay the fine, but we've barely said a word to one another since. He won't tell me the truth out of pure spite."

"I take it you don't drink at the Red Stag?" Jason had noticed the tavern when the carriage passed through the village on the way to the hall. He thought it looked welcoming, if a tad old-fashioned, but he'd come to expect that from a country pub.

"It's the only tavern in the village, so I do have a jar of ale now and then, but I don't linger."

"Why not let me try?" Jason suggested.

"What makes you think Brody will answer your questions? He's a surly fellow; take my word for it."

Jason got to his feet and adjusted his cuffs. "Why don't you see to the body, and I'll see to Brody, after which I will return to the hall. Micah will be missing me."

"Shall I call on you later today?" Constable Haze asked as he folded the blanket over the dead man, making sure to cover his face.

"You will find me at home," Jason replied somewhat imperiously, and made for the stairs.

"You're beginning to sound like a lord already," the constable called after him, giving Jason a much-needed chuckle.

In the space of an hour, they'd gone from suspicion and wariness to the sort of camaraderie that reminded Jason of his time in the army. He missed the rapport the men tended to establish after a few days of forced togetherness and the humor they relied on to mask their uncertainty and fear.

Stepping into the well-lit body of the church, Jason wondered if the constable was afraid of not being able to solve the crime. Whom did he answer to, and who paid him? Jason wasn't familiar with the English justice system, but he meant to educate himself, especially since he intended to keep a close eye on the investigation, if only to keep his restless mind occupied with something other than questions about the future.

Chapter 5

After leaving the church, Jason crossed the green to the Red Stag. Word of the murder wouldn't have made the rounds yet, since no one knew what had happened except for the vicar, Jason, and the constable. The boy Reverend Talbot had sent to fetch the constable hadn't been furnished with any details, partly because the vicar had been too shocked to speak of what he had seen and partly because he hadn't wanted every nosey villager to descend on the church to see the corpse for themselves. Jason hoped to question the publican before the man realized anything was amiss, unless he was involved and had something to hide.

Jason entered the Red Stag and took a table in the corner, sitting with his back to the wall, a habit he'd acquired in prison, where it was dangerous to turn one's back on other prisoners or guards. He removed his top hat, peeled off his gloves, and leaned back in the chair, taking a moment to familiarize himself with the place.

The dining room, which was low-ceilinged and dark-beamed, was unpleasantly dim even at that time of the day despite the faint light streaming through the mullioned windows, but there was a surprising number of patrons. Some had come in for their midday meal, while others were nursing tankards of ale or whatever else the tavern served up, looking for all the world like they had no other place to be. Several men were smoking, gray wisps curling from the bowls of their pipes and swirling upward toward the ceiling like mist.

The polished bar that ran along the side wall was manned by what Jason assumed to be the publican, a rugged-looking man of about forty who looked like he might be the boxing champion of the county. His shirtsleeves strained over his muscled arms as he filled tankard after tankard, and his shrewd gaze scanned the room, immediately alighting on Jason and pegging him as a newcomer. He caught the eye of a young woman who'd just come out from the back with two plates of stew and tilted his head in Jason's direction, silently instructing her to serve him.

She delivered the plates and sauntered over to his table. "Good day to ye, sir," she said, dimpling at him. "What can I get ye?"

"What's your name?" Jason asked politely.

"Moll. Moll Brody."

"A pint of your best ale, Moll, and something to eat. What would you recommend?" Jason asked, smiling up at her. She was pretty, in a sensual kind of way, her knowing gaze taking his measure and finding him to be worthy of her interest.

"Ye're not from around here, are ye?" Moll said, having evidently noticed his American accent.

"No, I'm from New York."

"Cor, that's on the other side of the world, ain't it," she said, cocking her head and smiling into his eyes. "I wouldn't object to hearing 'bout it sometime, if ye're staying for a spell. We could get better acquainted." The look she gave him left Jason in no doubt of what she meant, and he felt a sudden and irrational desire to take her up on her offer, until he caught the publican's narrowed gaze. He had no wish to get on the wrong side of the man.

"I don't think your father would like that," Jason replied.

The young woman laughed. "Oh, he don't mind. And he's not my father. He's my uncle."

Jason wasn't quite sure which part of what was on offer her uncle wouldn't mind, the conversation or what was sure to come afterwards. The girl licked her lips and arched her back, offering Jason an eyeful of her creamy breasts. He tried valiantly to suppress the stirring in his blood. It'd been a long time since he'd found a woman attractive, but he wasn't in the market for what Moll seemed to be offering, nor would it be wise to become entangled with the village honeypot.

"I plan to stay a while, so perhaps we'll get a chance to talk some more," Jason said neutrally.

Moll pouted prettily, then returned to her duties. "We offer traditional English fare here. There's mutton stew, and the steak and ale pies just came out of the oven," she said. "They're piping hot and delicious."

"If you made them, they're bound to be," Jason replied.

"I didn't make them, but I helped."

"I'll have two."

"Ye must have some appetite on ye," she purred, her gaze fixed on his mouth, her lips slightly parted.

"I'm ravenous," Jason replied, unable to resist her brazen charm.

"Don't worry, guv. I'll take care of ye."

Moll giggled and went to fetch the ale. Jason sat back and watched her, amused by his reaction to her. He couldn't recall the last time he'd flirted with a woman. He could barely get up the strength to crawl out of bed in the morning after returning to New York after his release, much less muster admiration for the opposite sex. There had been several attractive women on the steamship, but Jason had had no desire to get embroiled in an onboard romance. He wasn't coming to England to find a wife. He meant to claim his inheritance, make a decision regarding its disposal, and return home. Flirting with Moll was a bit of harmless fun, and she obviously took it in good stride.

Setting the pewter mug on the table, Moll gave him a seductive half-smile. "I'll just go and get those pies, guv."

"Don't rush off just yet," Jason said as he took a sip of the cool beer, savoring its rich flavor. "Tell me, do you have rooms to let?"

Moll's smile turned into a pout. "We do, but there are only two, and they're both engaged at the moment."

"Who by?" Jason asked.

"Two young ladies, their aunt, and a ladies' maid. The aunt has caught a chill, poor dear, so they stopped over for a few days to give her time to rest. I can't even offer ye the loft above the stable.

Their coachman is biding there until 'is mistress is well enough to continue the journey."

"It wasn't a room I was after," Jason explained. "I am looking for a friend who said he'd be staying in the village," he lied.

"Who is 'e, then, yer friend?"

Jason described the man found in the crypt. Moll looked thoughtful for a moment.

"'E did come in 'ere, now ye mention it, asking for a room, but Uncle Davy turned 'im away on account of the rooms already being taken. 'E were a pleasant fellow. Liked pies," she added, her lips lifting at the corners.

"Would you know where he went?" Jason asked.

"Uncle Davy told 'im to try Mrs. Harris. She's room to spare since 'er daughter wed, and the extra money wouldn't come amiss. I reckon 'e went there."

"Did you see him again after that?" Jason asked.

"Oh, aye. 'E came in once or twice."

"Did he seem worried at all?" Jason asked. Moll seemed like an observant girl, so it was worth a try.

Moll shrugged. "'E weren't chatty, not like ye," she answered with an impish smile. "Looked pensive, 'e did, like something were weighing on 'is mind."

"Moll, quit blathering and get ye to work," the publican yelled, putting an instant end to the conversation. Moll fled, coming back a few minutes later with the steaming pies. She deposited the plate on the table, smiled apologetically, and went to attend to the other customers.

The pies really were delicious, and Jason enjoyed his meal immensely. Having paid, he stepped outside, only to come face to face with Constable Haze, who was walking past.

"Ah, Captain, I trust you learned something at the tavern?" the constable asked.

"As a matter of fact, I have. Are you familiar with Mrs. Harris?"

"Yes, of course. She lives on the outskirts of the village."

"According to Moll Brody, the victim came into the tavern asking for a room a few days ago, but since both rooms were already occupied, he was directed to try Mrs. Harris, who apparently has a room to let. Is Davy Brody a violent man?" Jason asked, recalling the man's bulging biceps.

"Why do you ask?"

"His niece is rather, eh…friendly. Perhaps the victim saw an opportunity and seized it."

Constable Haze laughed out loud. "If Davy Brody were to stab every man who tried it on with Moll, there'd be no one left in the village but women and children. He turns a blind eye to her flirting because it brings in the customers, but sadly, I don't think he cares enough to sully his hands on her behalf. Moll often pushes the bounds of propriety, but she's a good sort and knows where to draw the line. However, I will question the occupants of the rooms. They're strangers to the village and might have something to do with the murder."

Jason shook his head. "I doubt it. According to Moll, there are four women and their coachman. The women wouldn't have the strength to lift a senseless man and deposit him in the tomb."

"They would if the coachman were to help them."

"According to Moll, the women only stopped here because their aunt fell ill. It wasn't a planned stop on their journey, and the young man arrived a day later. You should, of course, question them, but I'd like to speak to Mrs. Harris first."

"I will interview Mrs. Harris," the constable replied tersely. "I thank you for your help, but you need trouble yourself no longer."

"I don't mind," Jason replied.

Constable Haze stopped and faced him. "Captain, I'm the constable, and I must be the one to conduct this investigation."

"Of course," Jason replied contritely.

Constable Haze tipped his hat and walked on. He was right, of course. It was time Jason returned to Redmond Hall, but his interest was piqued, and he longed to hear what Mrs. Harris had to say. In fact, this was the most engaged he'd felt in a long time, his mind turning over the possibilities and sorting through plausible scenarios, and after examining the victim, he had a right to know who the man had been. Haze owed him that much.

"Where are you going?" Constable Haze asked as Jason fell into step with him.

"With you. I hear Mrs. Harris has a room to let, and I'd like to inquire about her rates."

"Why? Are you looking for a place to stay?" the constable asked, taken aback.

"I might be."

Constable Haze's serious face broke into a smile of amusement. "You are tenacious; I'll give you that."

"I want to know what happened to that young man. Whoever killed him knew what they were doing."

"Why do you say that?" the constable asked.

"Because they knew exactly where to stick the dagger to pierce the heart. The entry wound was neat and precise. The person knew something of anatomy."

"Most people who live in farming communities know something of anatomy," Constable Haze replied.

"They stabbed him once he was already in the tomb, facing downward, so as to avoid leaving a pool of blood at the scene."

"Anyone who's ever butchered a carcass would know which way the blood would flow," Constable Haze argued.

"Yes, they would, but what reason would some farmer have to kill this man?" Jason asked.

"Perhaps he'd dishonored his daughter."

"Or his wife? Revenge is always a powerful motive."

Haze nodded in agreement. "I think you have a future in policing, my lord, should you find yourself looking for employment."

"I'll keep that in mind."

Chapter 6

The walk took no more than ten minutes. Mrs. Harris's house was the last in a row of low stone cottages with steeply pitched roofs. The facade showed signs of neglect, and the tiny front garden was choked with weeds. Constable Haze knocked on the door and it was opened almost immediately by a woman whose frothy gray hair fought valiantly to escape from its pins. She was so thin, a strong wind could have blown her over, and she had the pasty complexion of someone who spent most of her time indoors.

"Good day to you, Mrs. Harris," the constable said, smiling warmly.

"Good day, Constable," she replied, eyeing Jason with suspicion.

"This is Captain Redmond," Constable Haze said without giving Mrs. Harris any reason for Jason's presence.

"Captain," Mrs. Harris acknowledged him. Jason gave her a curt bow.

"Mrs. Harris, have you a lodger staying with you at the present?" Haze asked.

"That I do, Constable."

"Is he in?"

"Is 'e in some sort of trouble?" Mrs. Harris demanded, her eyes narrowing in suspicion.

"He might be," the constable replied vaguely. "Is he in, Mrs. Harris?"

"I haven't seen 'im yet this morning. I knocked on 'is door, but 'e didn't stir. Missed 'is breakfast, 'e did."

"Are you sure he's still in his room?" Constable Haze asked.

"Well, where else would 'e be? I haven't heard 'im leave, and the door was bolted from the inside."

"What about the back door?" the constable asked.

Mrs. Harris looked momentarily confused. "I never checked."

"Do you normally lock the back door?" the constable persisted.

"Never needed to."

"Can you describe the lodger, Mrs. Harris?"

"Quiet, well mannered," she replied warily.

"I meant his appearance," Constable Haze clarified.

"Oh, I see. Well," Mrs. Harris said thoughtfully, "I reckon ye could say 'e's handsome."

Jason looked down at his boots to hide his smile of amusement. He could almost sense Haze's mounting frustration.

"Mrs. Harris, what color is his hair?"

"Dark brown, I s'pose."

"And his eyes?"

"I hadn't really noticed. Blue?"

"Do you know his name?" Constable Haze asked, growing impatient.

"Oh, yes. Alexander McDougal."

"Is he a Scotsman?" Constable Haze asked, clearly surprised.

"'E didn't sound Scotch," Mrs. Harris replied, bristling. "Sounded like a normal person to me."

"I wasn't implying that he wasn't a normal person, Mrs. Harris, only that he might have come from Scotland."

Mrs. Harris shook her head. "From London, 'e were. Seven Dials. Or so 'e told me."

"May I see his room?"

Mrs. Harris blocked the door. "No, ye may not. I pride myself on offering my lodgers complete privacy and discretion. Ye can't go rifling through 'is things."

Constable Haze exhaled loudly and looked heavenward, as if praying for patience. "Mrs. Harris, a young man, who was very possibly Alexander McDougal, was found dead this morning. I must ascertain whether the victim was indeed your lodger."

"Well, why didn't ye say so?" Mrs. Harris demanded. "Let me see 'im, and I'll tell ye if it's 'im. What easier way is there to ass-ertain?" she asked, tripping over the unfamiliar word.

"I suppose you'd best come with me, then," the constable said. "The body is with Mrs. Etty."

"Now, just hold your horses, Constable," Mrs. Harris snapped. "I've bread baking in the oven, and soup on the boil."

"Perhaps I can examine the room while you attend to your chores," Constable Haze suggested.

"I told ye, I'm not letting ye in unless I'm sure Mr. McDougal ain't coming back. Wait 'ere," she said, and slammed the door in Constable Haze's face.

"This might take a while," the constable said irritably.

"I'll leave you to it, then," Jason said, tipping his hat. "I would appreciate it if you'd let me know if the victim is indeed Alexander McDougal."

Without waiting for a reply, Jason headed back the way they'd come. He had nothing to gain by hanging around. He briefly considered returning to the Red Stag to interview the coachman, but thought he'd be overstepping, so instead, he found the lane that led to Redmond Hall and proceeded to walk at a brisk pace, suddenly eager to get back.

It was a pleasant walk, the silence broken only by birdsong and the buzzing of insects. Jason stopped and closed his eyes for a moment, allowing the peace to wash over him. This was the first time in years he'd felt so serene. There were no sounds of carriage traffic, no blasting of guns, no cries of wounded men and dying horses, or the barking of prison guards. Just blessed silence, which, of course, was perfect for thinking.

Jason opened his eyes and resumed his walk, slowing his pace to enjoy the bucolic idyll around him. He knew little of life in an English village, but it seemed likely Mrs. Harris's lodger was the victim, and if he was, what had brought him to a place like Birch Hill? What would draw a young man from London to this remote spot? He'd been in the village for a few days, at least, which meant he must have met with someone. But whom? Jason forced his questions to the back of his mind when he saw Micah sitting on a fallen log beside the road. He looked pale and worried, his fingers plucking at a loose button on his coat.

"Where have you been?" Micah exclaimed when he spotted Jason.

"I'm sorry," Jason said. "It took longer than I expected. What are you doing here?"

"Waiting for you," Micah replied petulantly.

"Come. Let's go back to the house, and you can tell me about your morning."

"I don't like kippers," Micah said.

"I'm not a fan of them myself."

"The sausages were tasty," Micah said, brightening up.

"Did you see the horses?" Jason asked.

Micah nodded enthusiastically. "There are only two. Chestnuts," he said, as if that explained everything. Having lived his whole life in New York, Jason didn't know much about horseflesh. He could ride, of course, but to him, as long as a horse had four legs, it'd do.

"Are chestnuts not to your liking?"

"They are fine beasts," Micah replied, sounding knowledgeable beyond his years. "They could use some exercise, though," he added, smiling up at Jason.

"And you'd like to be the one to ride them," Jason replied.

"Can I?"

"I don't see why not, as long as the groom comes with you."

Micah pouted. "I wanted to go on my own."

"And you will, once you've gotten to know the horses. Besides, there are two, so they can both get the exercise they need."

"Fine," Micah muttered. "You missed luncheon."

"I had something at the tavern in the village. Have you eaten?"

Micah nodded. "I had boiled beef. Then I left."

"Why's that?"

"Because the place is a madhouse."

"How do you mean?" Jason asked. They were nearing the house, and he was surprised to notice that the sleepy, forlorn look the house had worn only yesterday had vanished.

"Mr. Dodson put the call out, and at least a dozen people showed up. They're cleaning, airing out, polishing the silver, and filling the pantry with supplies. Seems *his lordship* has come," Micah said with an impish smile. "I had no idea you were so posh."

"Neither did I," Jason replied. He should have told Dodson last night that he didn't mean to stay. Now all these people would think they'd have steady employment, when in fact, they'd be cast out again in a few weeks, a few months at most. He'd have to speak to the butler about his plans In the meantime, he'd be willing to retain a few extra people, just so the Dodsons wouldn't feel overwhelmed. He'd leave the decision to the butler, who'd know best what sort of help was needed most.

"Ah, your lord—Captain," Dodson said when Jason and Micah walked into the house. The foyer smelled of wood polish, and a vase with fresh flowers had been placed on a small round table in the center. The floor gleamed, and the doors to the other rooms were open, the white sheets that had covered the furniture gone now that the new master had arrived.

"This arrived while you were out." Dodson held out a silver salver with great ceremony, inviting Jason to take the letter that rested on its polished surface. Jason picked up the missive and looked at the name in some confusion.

"It's an invitation," Dodson explained. "From Mrs. Chadwick."

"And who is Mrs. Chadwick?" Jason asked, perplexed.

"Mrs. Caroline Chadwick is the mistress of Chadwick Manor."

"And?" Jason prompted. He knew that English butlers were notoriously tight-lipped, but he needed help navigating the social mores of the society he found himself in. "Anything you say to me, Dodson, is in complete confidence. I really could use your help."

The butler sighed but nodded in understanding. "The Chadwicks are by far the wealthiest family in the county. New money. They started out by buying up coal mines, then invested heavily in the railways."

"Is that so?" Jason asked, amused by Dodson's sour expression. Gossiping did not come easily to him. "So, what would someone with such deep pockets want with me?"

"What the Chadwicks don't have is a title, and that's something Mrs. Chadwick covets above all else."

"I see," Jason replied, and tore open the envelope. The message inside was brief.

My Dear Lord Redmond,

I was so glad to hear of your arrival. Your grandfather was a good friend to our family, and I hope you will be as well. Please do us the honor of joining us for dinner tomorrow night so that we can properly welcome you to our close-knit community.

Warm regards,

Caroline Chadwick

Jason looked at Dodson, who seemed fascinated with something just beyond Jason's shoulder. "It seems Mrs. Chadwick would like to welcome me to her close-knit circle. Who is she referring to?"

Dodson looked uncomfortable, especially since two maids, who hadn't been there the day before, appeared in the foyer, brushes and buckets in their hands. He waited until they left before answering Jason's question.

"She is referring to Squire Talbot and the vicar," Dodson replied. "The village is part of the Talbot estate, and the squire is also the local magistrate. The vicar is Squire Talbot's cousin."

"That's a happy coincidence," Jason said, assuming the vicar had been assigned to the parish by the bishop or whoever oversaw such things.

"It's not a coincidence, Captain. Squire Talbot gave the living to his cousin."

"Sorry, I don't understand."

"It's in the gift of the squire to fill the post of the parson since he owns the church and the rectory."

"I've much to learn about the way things are done here, don't I?"

"Indeed, you do, Captain, especially about the ruthless ambition of women with daughters of marriageable age. And Mrs. Chadwick has two."

"Are you saying she's already got me pegged as a potential husband for one of them?"

Dodson suddenly smiled, revealing uneven teeth. "I'm not sure if you realize it, sir, but you are one of the most eligible bachelors in the county."

Micah giggled behind Jason's back, but stopped immediately when Jason turned to give him a narrow-eyed stare. "I have no interest in getting married," Jason said, more to himself than to Micah or Dodson.

"I've no doubt Mrs. Chadwick will do her utmost to change your mind."

"I'll need your help, Dodson," Jason said, dismissing Mrs. Chadwick's motives from his mind and focusing on practicalities instead. "I'll need to dress appropriately and learn the proper form of address." This wasn't New York, where everyone was addressed as Mr., Mrs., or Miss. There were rules, and Jason didn't care to embarrass himself at his first social function.

"Not to worry, Captain," Dodson answered solemnly. "I will tell you everything you need to know."

"Good. Now, how about a game of chess, Micah?" Jason asked, turning to the boy. "There's a chess set in the library."

Micah nodded enthusiastically. He loved the game and was becoming quite good at it. Jason had taught him to play after they'd returned from Georgia and spent most evenings at home, still too weak and heartsick to face anyone.

Having made his opening move, Micah sat back and studied Jason. "So, are you going to this dinner party?"

"Yes. I'm sorry you can't come with me," Jason added. The invitation hadn't included Micah, and he didn't think a boy his age would ever be included, even if Micah were his son.

The boy shrugged. "I don't want to go to some fancy dinner," he replied sullenly.

"I'll tell you all about it when I get home."

Micah's face paled. "I knew it," he muttered under his breath.

"You knew what?"

"That you like it here. You called it home."

Jason smiled gently at the boy. "Micah, this place is our home for as long as we choose to stay, but I told you we'd go back to our real home, and I meant it."

"I don't have a real home," Micah snapped. "My parents are dead. My brother is dead. And I don't even know where Mary is," he wailed, tears welling in his eyes.

"We will find Mary. I promise."

"She's probably dead too." Micah sniffled miserably. "And now you're going to go to this party, meet Mrs. what's-her-name's daughter and fall in love, and then you'll want to stay here forever."

"I promise not to fall in love," Jason replied gently.

He meant it too. He wasn't ready to love anyone, much less some English miss who couldn't possibly relate to what he'd been through. Then again, the American miss he'd loved hadn't much cared either, getting engaged to his friend Mark Baxter, who'd chosen not to join up, as soon as word of Jason's imprisonment reached New York. Cecilia said she'd believed him to be dead, but even had he died in that prison, surely, had she loved him, she'd have taken a little time to mourn before marrying another. By the time Jason returned to Washington Square more than a year later, Cecelia was married to Mark and expecting her first child. He wished her well and hoped to God never to lay eyes on her or Mark again. He supposed he'd dodged a bullet when Cecilia left him, but he wasn't ready to think of marriage or family. Micah was his family now and would remain in his care until Jason managed to track down his sister.

"Tell me about the man in the crypt," Micah invited, looking a bit shamefaced. If he was embarrassed by his outburst, he had no reason to be. He was a little boy who was missing his family and worrying about the future.

Looking at Micah's sweet round face, Jason still couldn't believe his father had taken him to war. Micah had been a drummer boy, and a good one. The soldiers who'd served in his regiment and had been taken prisoner along with Micah, his brother, and his father had treated the boy with respect, as if he were one of the men. And he was. He was braver than some of the men Jason had served with. But had Micah been his son, Jason would never have allowed him anywhere near a battlefield. He'd

52

have left him at home, where he'd be safe from bullets and cannon fire, and where he'd have the chance to grow up without ever seeing the carnage firsthand or knowing the cruelty of men, who, drunk on limitless power, treated their fellow men worse than he'd treat any beast.

Jason gave Micah two good games but made sure to lose both times to make the boy feel better. Once Micah was in somewhat better spirits, Jason suggested, "What do you say we walk down to the river?"

Micah shrugged. "All right."

"We can find a good fishing spot," Jason said, knowing that would win Micah over instantly.

"Really? Do they have fishing poles here?"

"We'll ask Dodson. And if they don't, we'll make some ourselves. But first, let's scout the area."

Micah jumped to his feet, ready to go. The spark of excitement in his eyes gave Jason a warm feeling he hardly recognized anymore. Joy.

Chapter 7

Daniel Haze sprang to his feet when Mrs. Harris finally came to fetch him. He'd waited more than half an hour for her to finish making her soup, only to be told that it was dinnertime and she needed to eat before accompanying him to Mrs. Etty's house. She settled with her bowl of soup and slice of buttered bread, taking her time and savoring her meal as if an irate constable weren't sitting in her tiny parlor. The soup smelled good, and Daniel wished he'd had time to have breakfast before rushing off to the church that morning. His stomach growled, and he resolved to go into the Red Stag after he was finished with Mrs. Harris to have a pint and a pie, and damn Davy Brody if he didn't like it.

At last, Mrs. Harris finished, untied her apron, and presented herself in the parlor, ready to go. They walked the short distance to Mrs. Etty's house and were admitted immediately. Estelle Etty was a no-nonsense woman in her sixties who'd been laying out the dead since she was a child and assisted her mother and grandmother in the task. Death didn't frighten her, nor did she mind the unpleasant task of washing the dead and preparing them for burial. She took pride in her work and cared for each body as if the person had been someone she'd loved. She kept her 'clients' in a specially prepared shed out back, furnished with a long pine table and a shelf for the tools of her trade.

"Mrs. Etty, Mrs. Harris is here to identify the body," Daniel said. "We think he might be her lodger."

"Right, then. Follow me," Mrs. Etty said briskly. She led them through the house and out the back door toward the shed, where she lit an oil lamp. The shutters were firmly closed in order to keep the shed cool and the body fresh. The smell of death hung over the place.

"Well, there ye are, then," Mrs. Etty said, pulling down the sheet that covered the man's face. "That 'im, Sally?" she asked Mrs. Harris.

Mrs. Harris's hand flew to her mouth, and she let out a mournful wail. She nodded, her frizzy gray hair moving around her head like the downy tufts of a dandelion. "It is," she moaned. "Oh, poor lad. What had 'e done to meet with such an end?" she cried, tears sliding down her pale cheeks.

"Get a hold of yerself, Sally," Mrs. Etty said, pulling the sheet over the man's face. "I'll take good care of 'im," she added, her tone reassuring.

Mrs. Harris nodded, sniffled loudly, and followed Daniel out of the shed.

"I'll need to have a look at his room," Daniel reminded her.

"Come back later, Constable," Mrs. Harris mumbled. "I need me a lie-down."

"Don't touch anything in the room," Daniel warned her.

"I won't go near it," she promised, and rushed off.

"Thank you, Mrs. Etty," Daniel said.

"I hope ye don't expect to leave 'im 'ere for too long, Constable. Mr. Dawes 'as been poorly since Friday. Dropped like a stone while weeding 'is garden and 'asn't woken since. I reckon I'll be needing the shed soon."

"I will speak to the magistrate and ask him to set a date for the inquest."

"Ye do that. There's only so long a body will keep in this weather," she reminded him.

Taking his leave, Daniel walked back toward the Red Stag. It had grown considerably warmer since he'd left his house that morning, and he was thirsty. He crossed to the other side of the road to walk in the shade and considered what he'd learned so far. He now had the victim's name and knew how he had been killed, which was an excellent result for several hours of investigative work. Solid policing. He'd now have something to present to Squire Talbot when he went to see him later today. Of course, Captain Redmond deserved some credit. Jason Redmond seemed knowledgeable and was probably highly skilled with a scalpel. His elegant hands had moved over the body with confidence and experience—feeling, probing, and assessing without a moment's hesitation. Going to question the new lord of Redmond Hall had proved to be less of a mistake than he'd initially thought.

A smile tugged at the corners of Daniel's lips. When he'd heard from Dodson that the new lord was an American, he hadn't been at all sure what to expect. He'd come across a few Americans in London in the line of duty, but they had been mostly sailors and merchants—brash, ill-mannered men who spoke with an odd accent and thought all Englishmen were hapless fuddy-duddies. Captain Redmond was nothing like those men. He was obviously well educated and well bred, and he had an inborn elegance that reminded Daniel of Redmond's late grandfather. He was also quite direct, something Daniel found appealing and off-putting in equal measure. He couldn't help wondering what Captain Redmond's experience in the war had been.

The American Civil War had been the bloodiest, most brutal conflict the Americans had experienced since the Revolutionary War, the mention of which still made most Englishmen cringe with shame. Some were glad the Americans had finally turned on their own, but Daniel secretly admired the colonists, as some persisted in referring to them. They were smart, hardworking, and courageous, and what he found most admirable was that they weren't afraid of new ideas or sweeping change. They were rebels in the best sense of the word, and he had to admit—only to himself, of course—that he was pleased as punch to have met one such man.

Daniel's reverie was interrupted by the sight of an elegant coach pulling up to the entrance of the Red Stag. Its pale-yellow exterior gleamed in the morning sun, and the wheels were completely devoid of mud, a testament to the coach being recently and thoroughly cleaned. The conveyance had to belong to the ladies who were currently staying at the Red Stag and would only have been brought out if they were ready to depart. Daniel lengthened his stride and called out to the coachman, who'd jumped off the box and was about to open the carriage door.

"Oi!" Daniel cried. "A word, if you please, sir."

The coachman looked abashed at being hailed in such a manner but let go of the door and faced Daniel. He was a thickset man in his fifties with thick graying muttonchops and a ruddy complexion. Where some men might have instantly adopted a belligerent manner, the coachman simply waited for Daniel to approach, a bland look on his face.

"How can I be of service to you, sir?" he asked pleasantly. His speech was slightly more cultured than that of the average working man, which surprised Daniel.

"I'm Constable Haze, and I would like to ask you a few questions," Daniel said, hoping the man wouldn't go out of his way to be difficult.

"Of course, sir."

"What is your name?"

"Harley Lewis, sir."

"Mr. Lewis, do you know anyone called Alexander McDougal?"

"No, sir."

"What about your mistress?"

"What about her, sir?" Mr. Lewis asked, looking confused.

"Has she ever mentioned the name?"

Mr. Lewis scratched his chin thoughtfully. "I have three mistresses, sir, which is more than any man should have to endure," he said with a rueful smile. "I've never heard any of them mention a Mr. McDougal, but then again, they don't discuss their acquaintances with the likes of me. I will tell you that they don't have many gentlemen calling."

"What about tradesmen?"

"Tradesmen conduct their business with the housekeeper, Mrs. Coyle."

"How did you come to be in Birch Hill?"

"We were traveling home to London when Mrs. Storey took ill," Mr. Lewis explained. "We've been here since Tuesday afternoon."

"Where were you coming from?"

"Mrs. Storey's widowed sister lives near Coventry, sir. We were her guests since early May."

"Did you summon a doctor for your mistress?" Daniel asked.

"Yes, sir. Dr. Miller was called in, and he said it was naught but a chill. He recommended a few days in bed and copious amounts of beef tea."

"And Mrs. Storey's nieces. What are their names?"

"Violet and Verity Shipman. They're the daughters of Mrs. Storey's late brother, Reverend Shipman."

"What can you tell me about them?"

The coachman shrugged helplessly. He was about to answer when the ladies in question erupted from the Red Stag in a flurry of petticoats. Mrs. Storey appeared to be in her late sixties or early seventies, a birdlike woman with a sharp face and inquisitive eyes. She was dressed in a somber navy gown with a cream-colored fichu that matched the trim on her bonnet. Her two nieces had to be in their early thirties. They were both skeletally thin and whey-faced, and wore matching traveling gowns in dove-gray, a color that did not suit them in the least. They seemed beside themselves with anxiety, clucking like hens whose feathers had been ruffled and talking over each other in their highly excitable state. A maidservant of middle years followed, her arms draped with several carry-on items. Her face was strained, and she looked like she was at the end of her tether, especially when one of the nieces let go of the door and it nearly hit the poor woman in the face.

"We're ready to depart, Lewis," Mrs. Storey announced, giving Daniel a hard stare.

Police procedure demanded that Daniel question all four women, but in this instance, he had to follow his gut instinct, which told him he'd be wasting his time. The old lady looked too frail to harm anyone, and the nieces would probably get the vapors if they so much as saw a drop of blood. The likelihood of them killing a man and stuffing him into an occupied tomb was about as high as the two sailing to Crimea to nurse the wounded alongside Florence Nightingale during the disaster that had been the Crimean War. The maid was probably too harassed by the three women to get a moment's peace during her endless days, and the coachman had seemed genuine when he'd said that he'd never heard of Alexander McDougal. As he'd stated, the stop in Birch Hill hadn't been planned, and if they had known Alexander McDougal from London, the chances of them meeting in Birch Hill accidentally after a month in Coventry seemed slim, unless Alexander McDougal had intentionally planned to meet them for some reason Daniel had yet to discover.

Daniel watched as the women were handed into the coach, chattering excitedly as they settled themselves and speculating as to the chance of rain, as if a summer shower might be as catastrophic as the eruption of Mount Vesuvius. The maid handed them their hand luggage and climbed onto the box, exhaling sharply and allowing her shoulders to sag with relief. She'd probably take the chance of getting drenched rather than ride inside the carriage with her nearly hysterical mistresses.

"If there's nothing else, sir," Mr. Lewis said once he shut the door on the mayhem inside.

"If you would just give me Mrs. Storey's London address," Daniel said, feeling the need to retain some sort of control over the proceedings. He didn't think he'd be calling on Mrs. Storey or her nieces, but he'd take the address just in case.

Mr. Lewis told him what he wanted to know and heaved himself onto the box, taking up the reins and clucking his tongue. The horses moved at a dignified pace. Daniel pushed open the door to the Red Stag and went in to get some well-deserved sustenance.

Chapter 8

Jason walked slowly on purpose, giving Micah a chance to explore. He liked watching him darting to and fro, standing on the bank of the river and looking into the distance, and just generally behaving like a carefree boy. Micah had grown up in a place like this, so the time he'd spent with Jason in New York City had been difficult for him. He wasn't accustomed to being surrounded by buildings and shops, nor did he like the constant stream of carriages that rolled past Washington Square, their wheels rattling over the cobblestone streets and the clip-clop of hooves keeping him awake. Micah longed for land and sky, and his family. Jason couldn't give him the latter, but he was glad to see him enjoying himself at last.

"Here!" Micah exclaimed. "This is the perfect spot."

"I think you're right," Jason agreed. To him, the Ingrebourne River looked more like a creek, but as long as there were fish in it, it would do. "Let's earmark this spot and we will come back as soon as we have fishing gear. I think you'd better start digging for worms," Jason added. "We'll need lots."

"I'll start tomorrow morning," Micah promised.

"Did you want to start back?" Jason asked.

"No, let's walk a little more. I like it here," Micah said. "It reminds me of home."

"All right. Lead the way."

They walked a little while longer, heading toward the village and the ancient stone bridge that spanned the narrow river. Jason was surprised to see Constable Haze standing by the bridge, skimming pebbles across the water with a practiced hand. He looked surprised when he saw the two of them.

"Good afternoon, Constable Haze," Jason said.

"Oh, hello," Constable Haze replied. "And this must be—"

"Micah Donovan. Pleased to meet you, sir," Micah said solemnly.

"The pleasure is all mine," Constable Haze replied, smiling as though amused by Micah's formality. "Are you two out for a walk?"

"We were scouting a good spot for fishing," Micah volunteered. "Do you fish, Mr. Haze?"

"I haven't in a long time, but I do enjoy it. I like this spot best. This is where I come to think when I have something on my mind," he explained.

"Was Mrs. Harris able to identify the victim?" Jason asked as he picked up a pebble and let it loose. It plopped into the water, making Micah smirk at his lack of skill.

"She was. The victim was Alexander McDougal."

"Surely confirming his identity is a step in the right direction," Jason remarked, wondering why Constable Haze looked so glum.

The constable shook his head. "Once Mrs. Harris calmed down, and it took some time, she let me in the house so I could look through Mr. McDougal's belongings. Unfortunately, someone got to them before I did."

"Did they break in during the night?" Jason asked.

"Either during the night or once Mrs. Harris left the house with me. They took everything, even his dirty linen."

Jason picked up another stone and let it fly. The stone skimmed the water twice, then sank. "Does Mrs. Harris remember what he had with him? She must have cleaned his room while he was out."

"The only thing she recalls him having was evening clothes. He asked her to press the tailcoat and trousers for him as soon as possible."

Jason gaped at Constable Haze. "Why would a working-class young man need evening clothes in a place like Birch Hill?"

"I couldn't begin to guess."

"Perhaps Mrs. Chadwick invited him to dinner too," Micah said as he concentrated on finding the perfect pebble.

Constable Haze chuckled. "I highly doubt that, Micah. Mrs. Chadwick is very selective about who graces her dinner table." The constable then focused his attention on Jason. "So, she's invited you to dinner, has she?"

"Tomorrow evening," Jason replied. It wasn't until the constable had asked him that he'd realized how much he didn't want to go, but it would be rude to refuse. The least he could do was meet his neighbors, but it'd been a long time since he'd gone out into society, especially to mix with people he didn't know, and he suddenly felt like a small boy who worried he'd know no one at a party and would feel out of place. He immediately dismissed the thought, angry for allowing such childish fears to get the better of him. He was a grown man, a soldier, for God's sake; he could face a roomful of people he didn't know and hold his own.

"She certainly didn't waste any time. I would be grateful if you would relay any gossip that might pertain to the murder," Constable Haze said.

"Do you think the murder is an appropriate topic of conversation at a dinner party?" It would be in New York, but Jason assumed the British were more reserved, at least in polite company.

"This is a small village, Captain. Very little of interest happens here. People will be talking about this murder for years to come, decades even. And the upper classes are no different than the common folk when it comes to a gory tale. They love a tragedy, as long as it doesn't affect them directly."

"I'll be sure to let you know if I learn anything that might be of use," Jason promised. "And what about you? What's your next step?"

The constable looked thoughtful. "I was a policeman for several years before returning to Birch Hill, but I never investigated a murder on my own, so I don't have a point of reference, but I think I must go to London. Alexander McDougal might have family, who, even if they're unable to shed any light on what he was doing in Birch Hill, deserve to know what happened to him and make arrangements for his burial."

"I'd be most interested to learn what you discover," Jason said.

"I will call on you Wednesday morning," Constable Haze replied.

Jason nodded in agreement, then glanced at Micah, who appeared to be getting restless. "I think we'd best be getting back. It's nearly time for supper."

"Good evening to you both," Constable Haze said, tipping his hat. "I'd best be off too." With that, he walked away, a solitary figure heading into the purpling twilight.

Chapter 9

Tuesday, June 5

Daniel rose early the following morning, washed, dressed, and let himself out of the house. The air was cool and fresh, and gauzy swirls of mist hovered over the fields and enshrouded the trees, making them appear like ghostly giants marching across the ancient landscape. Daniel walked to the fork in the road and stopped to wait. Jacob Hurley had promised to collect him on his way to the market at Brentwood and deliver him to the train station.

He'd told Sarah he was going to London today, but her only response had been a pursing of the lips and a curt nod of acknowledgement. They hadn't been to London since coming back to Birch Hill. In fact, they hadn't done many things since leaving London, like sharing a bed. It'd been three years, but Sarah couldn't seem to shrug off the soul-crushing grief that seemed to envelop her like the ghoulish mist. She'd been happy once, carefree, but now she was an empty husk of the woman he'd known, a ghost of the girl he'd loved.

A familiar pain squeezed Daniel's heart. He'd been so lonely, so desperate to climb out of the chasm Felix's death had opened between him and Sarah. Would they live this way for the rest of their lives, two people inhabiting the same space, sharing a name, and pretending they were a couple when they went to church or attended the village fete, but went their separate ways as soon as they returned home? Would she never allow him to touch her again, even to take her hand? Would she deny them the opportunity to have another child in the future?

Daniel pushed away his sad thoughts when Jacob's wagon materialized out of the mist, the creaking of the wheels unbearably loud in the hushed stillness of the morning.

Daniel climbed onto the bench and took a seat next to Jacob. "Good morning," he said, but all he received in greeting was a grunt. Jacob was a taciturn man inclined to remain silent rather than make small talk, which was just fine with Daniel. Despite the grim nature of his errand, he felt a stirring of excitement as the wagon jolted down the narrow lane toward the road that would take them into Brentwood. These days, he didn't have much call to travel to London, or anywhere else, for that matter, so the prospect of the journey lifted his sagging spirits.

When they arrived in Brentwood, Daniel thanked Jacob for the ride, then went into the station to check the timetable. The next London-bound train wasn't due to arrive for another forty minutes, so he purchased a ticket for a third-class carriage and proceeded to a nearby tearoom, where he ordered a pot of tea and some toast. The toast came with orange marmalade and fresh butter, and he enjoyed his breakfast immensely, feeling more like a little boy going on an adventure than a constable going about police business.

Having finished, he left the tearoom, purchased a newspaper, and returned to the station, where he stood patiently on the platform until he saw the plume of smoke in the distance that announced the approach of the train.

Daniel found an empty compartment, took a seat by the window, and waited for the train to pull out of the station before unfolding his newspaper. He read for a few minutes, but his thoughts kept straying to Captain Redmond. He didn't like to jump to conclusions, especially ones based on such short acquaintance, but the captain did not appear to relish his new position as lord of the manor. If anything, he seemed encumbered by it. Perhaps he simply needed time to become accustomed to his new life and position in society. A year from now, the man who'd treated Daniel as his equal would probably look down his nose and pretend they'd never faced each other over a dead body or debated possible motives for the murder. Or would he? There was something unexpectedly relatable about the captain, and the raw intensity Daniel had seen in his eyes had not come from leading a cushy life.

Daniel watched fields and villages slide by the window. The early morning mist had burned off and brilliant sunshine flooded the compartment, making him feel rather warm in his tweed suit. Daniel unbuttoned his coat and removed his hat. Thankfully, no one had joined him in the compartment at the last minute, so he could afford to make himself a little more comfortable. Newspaper forgotten, he returned to his speculation.

Who was the boy, and how had he come to be the captain's ward? Most people would assume that Micah was the captain's illegitimate son, but there was nothing in Micah's freckled face or copper hair to suggest he was in any way related to Jason Redmond. Perhaps he was the son of a friend, or even a faithful servant. Captain Redmond seemed like a kind man, one who'd take his responsibilities seriously, but then again, what did Daniel know? He knew nothing of the life Jason Redmond had led before coming to Birch Hill, nor could he presume to guess at his motives.

The scenery changed as the train approached London, green pastures giving way to ramshackle housing and soot-belching chimneys. Daniel buttoned his coat, put on his hat, and got to his feet once the train arrived in Charing Cross station and the doors began to slam up and down the length of the train as passengers disembarked and headed for the station exits. Normally, Daniel would have walked, but he was eager to get on with the investigation. He hailed a passing hansom cab and asked to be taken to Seven Dials.

Daniel sat back and looked around, keen to immerse himself in the sights and sounds of the city. London hadn't changed much since he'd last been there. Elegant carriages shared the road with ungainly brewery drays and vegetable-piled wagons, and crossing sweeps darted into the intersections to clean the horse droppings with their brooms, their shoes covered in muck. Peddlers and costermongers called out their wares, and the tall hats of uniformed bobbies stood out from the crowd, their brass buttons reflecting the sunshine and their wooden truncheons slapping against their thighs.

The surroundings became seedier as the hansom approached Seven Dials. Daniel hadn't spent much time in that area of London when he'd walked his beat, but Seven Dials was notorious, so much so that Charles Dickens, Daniel's favorite author, had mentioned it several times in his writings in the most unflattering terms. It had been one of London's most unsavory neighborhoods for decades, but over the last few years, Seven Dials had deteriorated even further, the narrow streets and dark alleyways becoming a cesspool of humanity, the inhabitants defeated by poverty and mowed down by disease.

The driver deposited him on the edge of the circular space, where the seven main streets that gave the slum its name converged. At one time, there had been a column with six sundials, one for each of the six roads that were originally planned before a seventh was added, but the column had long since been removed, torn down by an angry mob, or so the story went, and the plaza had lost its genteel elegance. At the apex of each intersection was a pub, the streets beyond murky even at this time of day.

Daniel decided to start with the pubs. They were just beginning to open, so he walked into the one closest to him and asked after Alexander McDougal. Having no luck, he went to the next, and the next, until a surly barman at the Pale Horse, whose head seemed to be attached directly to his shoulders without the benefit of a neck, admitted that he was acquainted with the young man.

"Oh, aye, 'e drinks in 'ere from time to time, guv. What d 'ye want with 'im?"

"Would you know where he lives?" Daniel asked, deliberately refraining from speaking of Alexander in the past tense.

"Mrs. Glynn's lodging 'ouse. 'Tis over yonder," he said, waving his hand in the general direction of northwest. "Just continue down Mercer Street and ask someone for Mrs. Glynn's establishment. They'll be sure to direct ye. For a small consideration," he added, showing tobacco-stained teeth punctuated by several gaps.

Daniel thanked the barkeep and exited the pub, turning into Mercer Street, which smelled of decaying rubbish and spilled ale. The stench intensified as he advanced deeper into Seven Dials, as did the oppressive miasma of extreme poverty. Some of the buildings appeared deserted, while others had been converted into warehouses and workshops. Ragged children darted from place to place, their dirty faces pale and thin, their eyes dull, and their hair lank and greasy.

"Need 'elp, mister?" a boy who looked about ten asked. He may have been older, but it was hard to tell. "I'll take ye wherever ye need to go." He held out his grubby hand.

Daniel had just opened his mouth to reply when he spotted a girl of about twelve or thirteen standing in a doorway. She was very thin, her body not yet that of a woman, and wore a tatty lowcut gown that must have belonged to someone with a more generous bosom. The girl eyed him with an expression that gave him the chills. *No child should look at a man like that*, Daniel thought as he instinctively tried to avert his gaze.

"If ye're not in a rush, my sister, Annie, would be 'appy to entertain ye," the boy said, grinning lewdly. "She'll do whatever ye like," he added, and made a hand gesture to demonstrate what he meant.

Annie licked her lips, her gaze fixed on Daniel's groin, and Daniel shuddered with pity and shock. Annie was nothing more than a tarted-up child, a little girl who should be at her lessons, not soliciting punters in a filthy alley.

"Eh, no thank you," Daniel muttered, and hurried along. He eventually stopped, unsure if he had passed Mrs. Glynn's lodging house. There were several workers standing outside a workshop, having a smoke, so he asked them for directions. The men stopped talking and stared at Daniel, their expressions feral, as if they were considering whether to direct him or cosh him over the head and steal his purse.

"That 'ouse there," one of them said, extending a hand and pointing to a rundown building on the opposite side of the street.

Daniel thanked him and went on his way, feeling the stares of the men piercing his back like daggers. There were plenty of people out in the street, but he was the only one who was well dressed, and well fed, most likely. Seven Dials was the den of petty thieves, pox-ridden whores, and good people who were simply too poor to dwell anyplace else. Daniel didn't judge them; he felt sorry for them. Just about everything in life was an accident of birth. He'd been lucky enough to be born into a well-to-do family, the only son of a school master, but how easily he could have been born to a prostitute, or a navvy, who might have gotten maimed or killed while laying train tracks across England, leaving his wife and children to starve without his wage.

Depressed by these grim thoughts, Daniel knocked on the door. A plump woman, possibly in her fifties, opened the door and smiled in welcome. He hadn't expected that.

"What can I do for ye, my dove?" she cooed.

Daniel fervently hoped the man hadn't directed him to a brothel for a lark. "I'm looking for the lodgings of Alexander McDougal."

"Ye found them," the woman answered. "Alex is not in. 'E's gone away for a few days."

"Does he have any family?"

Mrs. Glynn shook her head. "No. 'Is mother, God rest her soul, passed three months ago. Lovely woman, she was. A real lady."

"Mrs. Glynn, can I come inside?" Daniel asked, sensing this woman would be his only source of information and not wishing to ask his questions on the doorstep. "My name is Daniel Haze, and I'm a parish constable from a village called Birch Hill in Essex. It's very important that I speak to you."

"Come on, then," she said, and stepped aside to let him pass. The dim corridor smelled of decay, but the small parlor Mrs. Glynn invited him into was clean and tidy. There were lace curtains at the window, yellowed but still whole, and antimacassars on the two chairs facing the hearth.

"Sit yerself down. Can I offer ye a dish of tea, love?" she asked kindly. "Ye look a bit peaky."

"Thank you, no," Daniel said. He'd have loved a cup but wasn't sure the cups would be clean or the water untainted by sewage.

"Suit yerself." Mrs. Glynn sat across from him, her dark eyes wide with curiosity. "'Ow can I 'elp ye, then?"

"Mrs. Glynn, Alexander McDougal was found dead yesterday morning. He was murdered."

Mrs. Glynn's hand flew to her ample bosom, and she gasped in shock. "Was 'e set upon by footpaths, the poor lamb?"

"No, I don't believe so. This wasn't a random killing."

"Where?" she whispered. "Was it in that village ye mentioned?"

"Yes. I was hoping to inform his family and to interview someone who knew him in the hope of gleaning something that might lead me to his killer."

"Alex 'ad no family left. It were 'im and 'is mum for as long as I've known 'em."

"And how long was that?"

"Oh, going on eight years, I'd say. Margaret never spoke of it, but she must 'ave fallen on 'ard times after 'er man died and was too proud to go back to 'er family. She worked as a seamstress in a dress shop, but it weren't enough to support 'er and the boy."

"And where was her family?" Daniel asked.

"Scotch, she were."

"Was her husband English?"

"Must 'a been. I gathered from what she said that she met 'im in Scotland and followed 'im to London."

"Do you happen to know his name?" Daniel asked.

Mrs. Glynn looked thoughtful for a moment. "Yes. Bartholomew McDougal. 'E were a bank clerk in the city. Alex was the spit of 'im, she used to say."

"And what of his family?"

Mrs. Glynn shook her head. "I don't rightly know. Margaret didn't like to speak of 'im. Still grieving, she were, when she came 'ere with Alex. 'Tis 'ard enough to lose yer husband without losing yer home too."

"And what of Alex? Did he have employment? How old was he?" Daniel asked as an afterthought.

"Just turned twenty in May. 'E worked in a second-'and shop, down New Bond Street. Fletcher's Thrift Shop's the name."

"Can you think of any reason Alex would have traveled to Essex, Mrs. Glynn? Birch Hill, specifically."

"I don't rightly know. 'E did seem excited 'bout somethin'."

"What?"

She shrugged. "'E didn't say, and I didn't ask. I pride myself on not stickin' my nose where it don't belong."

"Very commendable, to be sure," Daniel said, wishing that in this case she'd have been more inquisitive. "Mrs. Glynn, might I see his room?"

"I s'pose there's no 'arm in it now, is there?"

She heaved herself to her feet and beckoned for him to follow. They went up the stairs to the third floor, and Mrs. Glynn used one of the keys from her keyring to unlock the chamber. It was a rectangular room with one narrow window facing the street. There was a neatly made bed, a small writing desk and chair, and a chest of drawers. Every effort had been made to make the room pretty, despite the ugliness beyond its walls. There was a framed picture of the sea hanging above the bed, a plant that could use watering on the desk, and a lace doily covering the top of the chest of drawers.

"I'll leave ye to it," Mrs. Glynn said. "Let me know when ye're finished in 'ere."

"Thank you. I will."

Daniel waited for Mrs. Glynn to leave before opening the drawers of the desk. There were a few sheets of paper, a small bottle of ink, and a pair of scissors. The dresser contained some smallclothes, two clean shirts, and an extra blanket, and there was a tweed suit of reasonably good quality hanging on a hanger on the back of the door. Daniel didn't find anything that might have belonged to Mrs. McDougal. Alex must have sold his mother's things in the shop where he worked, or maybe he'd exchanged them for the evening clothes he'd brought to Birch Hill or the pocket watch, unless it had belonged to his father.

A small leather-covered Bible lay on a three-legged stool next to the bed. Daniel picked it up and opened it to the flyleaf, which proclaimed it to be the property of Margaret McDougal. The volume had been printed in Glasgow in 1824, and Daniel thought it might be a Catholic Bible, although he'd never actually seen one. He leafed through the book, curious to note that some passages were carefully underlined. At first glance, most of them related to forgiveness and accepting the will of God. Halfway through the volume, he came across several folded pieces of paper. They were newspaper clippings, brittle and yellowed with age, but still legible. The oldest one was the announcement of Mr. Robert Chadwick's marriage to the Honorable Caroline Browning, dated March 15, 1845, and three birth announcements, one for each of the Chadwick children. The last clipping was newer, the paper not as old. It was the obituary for Mr. Robert Chadwick, dated April 1865. Daniel checked the rest of the Bible but found nothing else of interest. He took the book and left the forlorn little room, closing the door softly behind him.

"May I take this?" Daniel asked once he rejoined Mrs. Glynn in her parlor.

"Well, it's no use to me, is it?"

"Thank you. What will happen to Alex's things?" Daniel asked, but he already knew the answer. Mrs. Glynn would clear out the room as soon as possible and dispose of Alex's belongings, most likely selling them to a rag shop. She'd pocket the money and let the room to someone else.

"There's rent owing on the room," Mrs. Glynn said, confirming Daniel's suspicions. "And I've got to let it soon. It's my livelihood, ye see."

"Yes, of course. I'll let myself out," he said, eager to leave.

"Constable, I wonder if I could beg a favor of ye," Mrs. Glynn said, her eyes moist with emotion. "Will ye write to me and let me know when Alex's funeral will be? I'd like to be there for 'im. And for Margaret."

Daniel nodded, glad she cared enough to make the effort. "He won't be buried until after the inquest, and the funeral will most likely be held in Birch Hill, as he has no one to claim his body."

Mrs. Glynn nodded sadly. "I'd gladly claim it if I 'ad the means to bury 'im, proper like. Like a son to me, Alex was," she said. "Same age my own boy would 'ave been had 'e lived. My Bertie died of consumption when 'e were thirteen," she added in a barely audible whisper.

"I'm very sorry for your loss, Mrs. Glynn," Daniel said, and meant it.

"Thank ye, Mr. Haze. Ye find Alex's killer, and when ye do, ye make sure 'e swings."

That's not an easy undertaking, Daniel thought as he stepped into the street. He supposed he knew a little more than he had that morning, but still not enough to have any idea why Alexander McDougal had decided to travel to Birch Hill. The Chadwick family resided in Birch Hill, which was the only connection he could make based on the clippings he'd found, but the Bible had belonged to Margaret, who'd been deceased for several months. Perhaps they had nothing to do with her son's visit to the village at all.

The day had grown warmer while Daniel was at Mrs. Glynn's, and the stinking heaps of refuse steamed in the sun, filling the streets with their noxious odor. Daniel kept his arms pressed to his sides to avoid getting his pockets picked by the numerous urchins who eyed him with interest, and avoided the leering gazes of the prostitutes who were bleary-eyed from lack of sleep but already skulking in doorways in the hope of bagging a punter.

Frustrated and depressed, Daniel walked at a brisk pace until Seven Dials and its misery were far behind him, then found a pleasant-looking chophouse near Trafalgar Square where he could have his dinner before setting off for home.

Chapter 10

The evening was warm and pleasant, the rose-colored orb of the sun still perched above the jagged line of trees in a lavender sky when Jason walked down the steps toward the waiting carriage. The chestnuts were perfectly matched, their bodies lithe and elegant, and the curricle, painted a sleek black, had maroon trim that perfectly accented the color of the wheels. The hood of the carriage was drawn back on account of the fine weather. Jason nodded in appreciation. It seemed his grandfather had enjoyed traveling in style. There was also a brougham in the carriage house, a closed coach best suited to cold or inclement weather. Joe, dressed in a well-cut frock coat and top hat for the occasion, stood next to the carriage, ready to take his seat on the box as soon as Jason was ready to leave. He opened the door as Jason approached.

"Good evening, Joe," Jason said.

"Good evening, your lordship."

Jason climbed into the carriage and leaned back, ensconced by the buttery comfort of the tufted leather seat. He looked up at the house and raised a hand in a wave, receiving an answering wave from Micah, who stood at his bedroom window, looking a bit forlorn. The gesture hadn't been lost on Joe, who smiled up at the boy before taking his place.

As the carriage rolled through the gates, Jason braced himself for the evening ahead. He wasn't an antisocial person by nature, but tonight, he'd be the entertainment, the exotic beast the locals had come to see. The English viewed Americans with suspicion and thought them to be uncultured, unmannered, and generally rough around the edges, whereas Americans saw England's upper crust as an elitist group who valiantly clung to the past, looked down their noses at anyone who didn't share their arcane values, and would generally do well to remove the stick from their collective ass.

It would have been churlish to refuse Mrs. Chadwick's invitation, but truth be told, Jason would much rather have spent the evening playing chess with Micah. He had no plans to remain in England permanently, so meeting his neighbors wasn't an investment in the future; however, he was curious to learn something of his father's life as a young man and discover why he'd crossed the ocean in search of a happier life when he'd clearly led a privileged existence in his native England.

"My lord, if I might beg your indulgence for a moment," Joe suddenly said, startling Jason out of his reverie.

"Of course. What is it, Joe?"

"I was wondering if you might permit young Micah to accompany me to my brother's house tomorrow. My brother is the gamekeeper at the Chadwick estate and has a lad 'bout Micah's age. I thought they might get on. I hope you don't think me impertinent for asking," Joe added, his manner ingratiating, "but I thought the young gentleman could use company his own age."

Some small part of Jason wanted to refuse Joe and tell him to mind his own business, but deep down he acknowledged that the man was right. Micah had spent the past few years in the company of adults, first at the prison and then while recuperating at Jason's parents' house, Jason's house now. He'd met several children his age during the ocean crossing but hadn't seemed to crave their company after the first few days of the voyage. Jason didn't press him to socialize. Micah had endured something most adults couldn't begin to fathom. Emotionally, he was no longer a child and couldn't hope to establish a camaraderie with boys whose most frightening experience had been a reprimand from their parents or some minor punishment for bad behavior. Micah had seen battle, death, and the kind of human suffering that had tipped many a grown man over the edge and into full-blown madness.

"If Micah wishes to accompany you, I have no objection," Jason said. "It'd be nice for him to have a friend his own age."

"Thank you, my lord," Joe replied, his shoulders slumping with obvious relief at not being put in his place for suggesting Micah fraternize with the help.

Jason looked around with interest as the carriage passed through the gates of Chadwick Manor. The parkland was extensive, the lawns that stretched away from the house immaculate. The house itself was of Palladian design, a three-storied building of eye-pleasing symmetry, adorned with dual external staircases that led to the portico and rows of tall windows that caught the mellow rays of the early evening sun. Joe deposited Jason before the house and continued toward the stables, where he'd wait for his master.

The door was opened by a footman dressed in a blue and silver livery as soon as Jason reached the top of the steps. The footman took Jason's hat and gloves and retreated, leaving him with the butler, who led Jason toward the beautifully appointed parlor where the guests were assembled. Jason plastered a genial smile onto his face as the butler announced him in a booming voice.

"Lord Redmond of Redmond Hall."

"My dear Lord Redmond, what a pleasure it is to make your acquaintance."

The woman who came forward to greet him had to be the hostess, Mrs. Chadwick. She was around forty, possibly a few years older, with a high forehead and sharp cheekbones accentuated by auburn locks that were swept back from her face, thickly lashed wide blue eyes, and full lips that stretched prettily into a smile of welcome. Her somber gown, fashioned of dusky purple silk, proclaimed her to still be in mourning for her husband, who'd passed away just over a year ago. Jason was grateful to Dodson for explaining British mourning rituals to him since, as an American, he never would have made the connection between wearing shades of purple and mourning.

"I prefer to be addressed as Captain Redmond," Jason said stiffly.

Mrs. Chadwick laughed merrily. "Devilishly handsome and wonderfully humble. I like you already, Captain. Allow me to introduce you to everyone," she continued. "But first, let's get you a drink."

The footman who'd been standing against the wall was instantly at Jason's side, holding out a small tray bearing a glass of champagne. Jason accepted the drink, even though he wasn't overly fond of champagne and would have preferred something stronger, then turned back to his hostess.

"I'm Caroline Chadwick, in case you haven't already figured that out," she said with a coy smile, "and these are my children, Harry, Arabella, and Lucinda."

"Mr. Chadwick," Jason said to the young man. "Ladies."

Harry was a handsome young man of about twenty. He puffed out his chest and drawled a greeting as if he were a man twice his age. Arabella had to be eighteen or nineteen. She resembled her mother but lacked Mrs. Chadwick's lush beauty. Her hair was a pale red, almost fair, and her eyes, although blue like her mother's, were a lighter shade and not at all enhanced by the nearly colorless lashes and brows, and she was a bit plump. Lucinda's heart-shaped face was framed by dark curls, and her aquamarine eyes sparkled with mischief as she smiled at Jason and held out her gloved hand. She was taller and thinner than her sister and moved with the grace of a dancer. She was the youngest of the three and clearly the most spirited. Both girls also wore gowns of purple to commemorate their late father. Jason smiled back, feeling sympathetic toward these young women who were on the threshold of adulthood and therefore under increasing pressure to make a good match.

Next, Caroline led him toward an older man who stood by the hearth, his bearing rigid and proud. He was in his late sixties or early seventies and whippet-thin, his silver hair a sharp contrast to skin that was tanned leather-brown. As their eyes met, Jason couldn't help noticing a slight yellowing of the whites around the piercing blue irises and a greenish tinge beneath the golden tan. The man was leaning heavily on his stick, the thin wrist that protruded from the cuff of his coat discolored by an ugly bruise.

"Captain, may I present my father-in-law, Colonel Chadwick," Caroline said, her tone deferential. She smiled brightly, but her smile lacked warmth, and a spark of irritation flared deep in the old man's gaze before he directed his attention to the newcomer.

Jason bowed from the neck. "Colonel."

The colonel bowed stiffly, his gaze never leaving Jason's face. "A military man, are you? I'd be interested to hear about your service. I'm retired now, naturally, but I spent my youth in India. Wonderful place. Utterly wasted on the ignorant wretches who live there. Have you ever been to India, sir?"

"No, Colonel. I did my military service in the United States."

"Of course, I forgot your father skedaddled to America and abandoned his duty to queen and country," the colonel said gruffly.

Jason highly doubted the colonel had forgotten, but the remark was meant to insult the memory of Jason's father and it had hit home.

"Colonel! Really," Caroline Chadwick exclaimed, clearly embarrassed by her father-in-law's rudeness.

Acknowledging how arrogant he'd sounded, the colonel smiled, his eyes narrowing as he studied Jason. "I do apologize, Captain. Your grandfather was a close friend for many years. I suppose I'm still angry on his behalf. He never did recover from the loss of his only son. Talked about him incessantly. He always thought Geoffrey would come back, but America proved to be too tempting a mistress."

Jason ignored the dig. It wasn't America his father had fallen in love with, but an American, and she hadn't been his mistress, but his wife. Lord Redmond had bullied and belittled his son for marrying beneath him, but Jason's parents had been happy and in love, a memory that comforted him when he thought of their untimely deaths. At least they'd died together. It was a small comfort, but he knew that if one of them had survived the train wreck, they would have been broken beyond repair.

"Yes, my father loved his adopted country," Jason replied, pinning the colonel with his gaze. "He enjoyed things that were exciting and modern and was always open to new ideas."

The colonel took his meaning, and his mouth tightened with anger. "Clearly the idea of duty and honor were too outdated for him," he said tartly.

Jason glared at the colonel, annoyed with the man for placing him in such an awkward position. He was dutybound to defend his father, but a confrontation would embarrass his hostess and ruin the party she'd planned in his honor. Instead, Jason smiled politely and inclined his head in the merest of bows. "It comforts me to know you were a loyal friend to my grandfather at a time when he was in need of support."

The colonel seemed confused by the sentiment, but inclined his head in return, accepting that the verbal duel was over for the time being.

Seizing on the lull in the conversation, Caroline Chadwick slid her arm through Jason's and led him away from her father-in-law, who was still sizing him up.

"I believe you've already met Reverend Talbot," Mrs. Chadwick said as she led Jason around the room. "And this is his daughter, Miss Katherine Talbot."

"Your servant, ma'am," Jason said, bowing to the young woman. She smiled shyly at him, her bespectacled dark eyes warm as she met his gaze.

She looked like she was about to say something when the door opened and the butler announced Squire Talbot and his family, who swept into the room as if they owned the place.

"Captain Redmond, may I present Squire and Mrs. Talbot, their son Oliver, and their charming daughter Imogen," Mrs. Chadwick said.

Jason bowed from the neck, then kissed the hands of the ladies, all the while taking their measure.

The squire was a stocky man with a balding pate and a ruddy complexion that contrasted sharply with his black hair and coal-black eyes. His wife was pretty in an English rose sort of way: fair, blue-eyed, and rosy-cheeked. She must have been quite beautiful in her day, but there was an air of dejection about her. The son was in his early twenties and showed signs of aging into a replica of his father. His hair was already beginning to thin in the front, and his dark eyes seemed to miss little as he surveyed the room. Imogen had to be seventeen or eighteen, pretty like her mother, and judging by the look in her eyes, intimidated by the assembled company. Perhaps she was younger than he assumed. He wasn't sure at what age young ladies were introduced into society or if the rules varied when visiting friends.

"Squire Talbot's family is descended from a great knight who settled in this area in the fourteenth century. His tomb is in the crypt. Oh," Mrs. Chadwick said, her hand flying to her mouth. "Forgive me. I spoke without thinking. That poor young man," she said. "Why, it's barbarous what happened to him. Absolutely barbarous. I couldn't sleep a wink after I found out about the murder. I thought someone would break in and kill us all in our beds."

"My dear lady, you have nothing to fear," Squire Talbot said. "This matter will be quickly resolved."

"The squire is our local magistrate," Mrs. Chadwick explained, gazing up at him as if he were the local deity instead.

"You seem awfully certain of the outcome, sir," Jason said, marveling at the man's conviction.

"I am. Constable Haze is a tenacious fellow. He'll get to the bottom of this business in short order."

"I was led to believe that this is the first crime of this nature to occur in Birch Hill," Jason said. "Apprehending a killer requires a bit more gumption than finding a lost sheep."

He wasn't sure why he was arguing with the squire, but he felt the man was putting undue expectation on Constable Haze. Jason had great confidence in the man's abilities, but not every crime got solved, not even by an organized, efficient police force. Constable Haze was only one man, who, by his own admission, had virtually no experience working a murder case.

"My dear Captain," the squire said, dripping condescension, "the killer was clearly an outsider. No one in this parish is capable of committing such an atrocity. I've known everyone in Birch Hill since I was a small boy. They're good, Godfearing people. Salt of the earth. Not a single one of them would kill a man in cold blood, especially not in the house of the Lord."

"But someone did," Jason countered. "According to Constable Haze, there were no strangers in the village besides Mrs. Storey, her nieces, and me."

"Well, there you have it," Squire Talbot said, shaking his head as if Jason had just stumbled upon an indisputable truth. "The man was killed by Mrs. Storey's coachman. The two had probably met in London before coming here and had some score to settle. The dregs of society, people like that. Probably argued over a gambling debt or a woman. You know how it is. And now one's dead and the other gone, so, in all fairness, this case is no longer our problem."

"Are you suggesting the crime should go unpunished?" Jason asked, shocked by the magistrate's lack of interest in seeing justice done. "What if your assumption is wrong and the killer strikes again?" he added for good measure.

"I don't believe it would be wise to continue this conversation in front of the ladies, Captain," Squire Talbot said, glaring at Jason. Indeed, Imogen Talbot and Arabella Chadwick looked like they were about to swoon, while Lucinda eyed them with obvious derision.

"I beg your pardon, ladies," Jason said, chastised. He should have known better, and despite the merit of his argument, he was clearly in the wrong.

"No harm done, my dear fellow," Squire Talbot said, brightening up. "You Americans are a brash bunch. Outspoken. I rather admire that," he admitted. "Takes courage to speak one's mind. You do remind me of your father," he observed. "Geoffrey and I were the best of chums in our younger years. We got into some scrapes, didn't we, Victor?" he said, addressing his cousin, who nodded but didn't join the conversation. "Victor wasn't really a part of our circle. Too pious by half, but Geoffrey and I were practically inseparable. How is the old rascal?"

"My parents died in a railway accident," Jason said, his voice catching despite his best effort not to give in to emotion.

"Oh, I am sorry," the squire said, patting Jason's arm in a paternal manner. "I assumed you'd come in your father's stead, given how keen he was to remain in America and cling to his self-imposed ordinariness. Your grandfather thought he'd come back to claim his birthright once the appeal of the exotic started to wane, but Geoffrey was always as stubborn as a mule."

"My dear, you mustn't speak ill of the dead," his wife chastised him. "I'm deeply sorry for your loss, my lord. I didn't know your father, not having lived here before my marriage, but I'm sure he was a very fine man, and your dear mama a wonderful woman."

"Thank you," Jason replied stiffly. He was desperate to change the subject, but the next question made him even more uncomfortable.

"Tell us about the war, Lord Redmond. Terrible business that, countrymen fighting against one another. Thankfully, we learned our lesson with our own Civil War and haven't turned our guns on one another since. I do hope it was worth it," the squire said with a sarcastic grin. "Leave well enough alone, I always say. If the South wanted to maintain its way of life, why not let them? Most of those poor buggers they owned were probably better off anyway. It's not such a bad life, is it?" he asked, looking from one guest to another. "They have a roof over their heads, food, someone to care for them in their old age. Of course, they must work hard, but show me a common man who doesn't if he wishes to feed his family. Surely the issue was not worth the slaughter, but you Americans are a righteous lot, aren't you? 'All men are created equal'," the squire quoted from the Declaration of Independence and burst out laughing. "I think not. There will always be those who rule and those who need to be ruled. It's the way of the world. Thankfully, my boy understands that and won't run away from his responsibilities. Will you, Olly?"

"No, father. I look forward to taking up the reins of the estate," Oliver replied smoothly.

Squire Talbot let out a bark of laughter. "You just hold on there, my boy. I'm not in my dotage yet, and you still have much to learn. Your only responsibility now is to find a suitable wife." His gaze strayed to the Chadwick girls, making Mrs. Chadwick's eyes sparkle with obvious delight. Oliver ignored the hint.

Squire Talbot pulled a cigar from his front pocket and beckoned the footman over to give him a light. The footman instantly extracted a box of matches from his pocket and held a lit match to the cigar, remaining still until the flame came dangerously close to his fingers. Jason, who detested cigar smoke, excused himself and walked over to the window, which was open to let in the fragrant summer air.

"It will diminish in time," a voice at his elbow said. He turned to find himself looking down at Katherine Talbot. She wasn't pretty in the conventional sense, but he found her considerably more appealing than Mrs. Chadwick, who exuded raw sexuality, even in her bereaved state. Miss Talbot, who barely came to his shoulder, had chestnut-brown hair that was parted in the center and pulled into a neat chignon at the nape, and her fine brown eyes were magnified by the round spectacles she wore. They gave her a bookish appearance that most men of his ilk would find off-putting, but Jason found it endearing.

"What will?" he asked, realizing he still hadn't replied to her observation.

"The grief," she said. "My sister died three years ago. She was my dearest companion and closest confidante. Our mother died when we were quite young, so it was just us two against the world."

"What of your father?"

"Father is more interested in the spiritual well-being of others," Miss Talbot replied, her voice low.

"I'm sorry for your loss," Jason said, touched by the sadness in her eyes.

"Life can be cruel, but I think you already know that, given what you must have witnessed during the war."

"Yes, it can," Jason agreed. "And terribly unfair."

"Being away from you must have been difficult for your son," Katherine Talbot said.

"Micah is not my son; he's my ward. He was orphaned during the war, and I promised his father as he lay dying that I would look after his boy."

"But you're fond of him?" Katherine asked.

"Very. He's the bravest, smartest, kindest boy I've ever met. If ever I have a son, I hope he'll be just like Micah."

Jason was taken aback by the shimmer of tears behind the lenses of Miss Talbot's spectacles. "Your devotion to him does you credit," she said primly, trying hard to mask her true feelings. Jason wasn't sure precisely what they were, but some part of him suddenly wanted to comfort her. Jason was about to offer some inane platitude when the butler appeared in the doorway to announce that dinner was served.

"Captain, will you lead me into dinner?" Mrs. Chadwick asked, smiling beguilingly at Jason and offering her arm. Jason smiled apologetically at Katherine Talbot and took the proffered arm.

"Grandpapa," Lucinda said as she approached her grandfather purposefully. Dodson had said that there was a prescribed order to the way the guests went into dinner, with the master of the house leading the most prominent female guest, which in this case would be Squire Talbot's wife, but it seemed the colonel needed a partner he could lean on. The colonel slid his arm through Lucinda's, blessing her with a smile of such devotion that it redeemed him in Jason's eyes by a good measure. He clearly doted on his granddaughter, and she on him.

After Lucinda and the colonel came the squire and his wife, followed by Reverend Talbot and his daughter, and Harry and Imogen. Oliver and Arabella brought up the rear. Jason couldn't help but be amused by the orderly procession. It was as if they were on parade or part of a wedding.

Dinner was an informal affair, with the squire holding forth on various subjects and Mrs. Chadwick agreeing with his every word as if he were some oracle of truth. Seated between Lucinda and Miss Talbot, Oliver went out of his way to snub the vicar's daughter, who was left to converse with Harry Chadwick. The young man appeared bored, especially when Miss Talbot mentioned a book she was reading. The vicar ate heartily but spoke little, deferring to his cousin whenever his opinion was asked, and leaving Lucinda and Imogen, who were on either side of him, stranded for conversation.

Jason was seated between Mrs. Chadwick and Arabella, a decision Mrs. Chadwick had clearly made with some forethought. Arabella blushed violently whenever Jason so much as looked at her and tried to smile at him when she caught her mother's gimlet stare, the smile more a grimace of misery than the tool of seduction it was meant to be. Jason felt sorry for the poor girl and tried his best to engage her in conversation to make her feel more at ease.

"Do you enjoy reading, Miss Chadwick?" Jason asked, his gaze straying to Miss Talbot, who appeared to be paying attention to their conversation.

"Not really," Arabella muttered apologetically. "I like to paint."

"Do you?" Jason asked, seizing on the topic like a drowning man hauling himself onto a bit of flotsam. "What do you paint?"

"I like to paint flowers. I have my easel set up in the conservatory. It's lovely there," Arabella said, finally offering a genuine smile.

"And what are your favorite flowers?" Jason asked, glad he'd thrown the poor girl a lifeline.

"I like roses and orchids best, but I'd happily paint any flower. I just like nature."

Lucinda scoffed across the table. "She likes nature so much she won't even paint outdoors."

Mrs. Chadwick threw Lucinda a warning look, but the girl wasn't about to be silenced.

"I like riding. Do you ride, Captain Redmond? I bet you do," Lucinda said, smiling at him beguilingly. "You can join me for a ride any day, if you dare."

"Lucinda!" Mrs. Chadwick exclaimed.

"And I don't ride sidesaddle either," Lucinda continued. "I like to ride astride, like a man, and wear britches. Does that shock you, Captain?" Lucinda's blue eyes danced with merriment, her color high.

"Not at all, Miss Chadwick," Jason replied, grinning at her despite Mrs. Chadwick's displeasure. "I think all ladies should ride astride and wear britches. It would make riding so much more pleasurable for them."

"And for us," Oliver Talbot chimed in.

"Do ladies wear britches in America?" Imogen Talbot asked, clearly scandalized. Mrs. Talbot looked positively appalled by the direction the conversation had taken.

"Not as a rule, but a lady of my acquaintance did and said it was most comfortable."

"Does she wear them still?" Lucinda asked.

"I really couldn't say. I haven't seen her in a long while," Jason confessed. He had no idea why he'd brought up Cecelia. Perhaps because he'd suddenly remembered the fun they'd had together before he joined up and left her, asking Mark to look in on her from time to time to make sure she was well.

"See, Mama. Captain Redmond doesn't think his lady friend is a hoyden for wearing britches," Lucinda said with a pout.

"Captain Redmond is being polite," Mrs. Chadwick hissed.

"Let her be, Caroline," Colonel Chadwick said, pinning his daughter-in-law with a stern stare. "It's just youthful high spirits, nothing more."

Mrs. Chadwick allowed the matter to drop and addressed Reverend Talbot. "How are the plans for the church fete coming along, vicar? If you need any help, the girls would be happy to lend a hand." She glared at Lucinda, who stared back defiantly.

"Very well, Mrs. Chadwick. Very well. If the girls would like to help, they can apply to Katherine. She'll find them something to do," Reverend Talbot responded. "Always such an undertaking," he complained. "So much to do. Thank God for dear Katherine. I don't know what I would do without her help." Katherine Talbot colored slightly but said nothing.

"We should have an archery competition," Lucinda said.

"Not like you would be allowed to enter," her brother said, smiling nastily at her. "Competitions are for men."

"I'm a way better archer than you are," Lucinda retorted, clearly stung.

"We would have an archery competition for ladies, but unfortunately there aren't enough ladies interested," Katherine Talbot said in a conciliatory manner.

"It's not much of a competition if there's only one participant," Reverend Talbot agreed.

"We all know you're an excellent archer, Lucinda," the colonel said, smiling at his granddaughter. "You would be the clear winner."

Jason was grateful when the plates were cleared, and dessert was finally brought out. He longed for a cup of coffee, but none was offered. Instead, individual servings of something white and pasty were brought out, the quivering mound garnished with strawberries.

"Blancmange," Mrs. Chadwick explained upon seeing Jason's confusion. "Do they not serve it in America?"

"I've never had the pleasure of trying it, but it looks delicious," Jason replied politely.

Everyone *oohed* with delight, except the colonel, who'd hardly eaten during the meal and seemed to remain upright in his chair by sheer force of will. Jason had no doubt the man was ill. Cirrhosis of the liver, if he had to guess, and quite advanced if the symptoms he displayed were anything to go by. He didn't think the man would last out the year and wondered if the colonel was aware of the severity of his condition.

"I saw him, you know," Arabella suddenly said, her voice barely above a whisper.

"I'm sorry?" Jason asked, caught completely off guard.

"The man who was murdered. He came here on Tuesday."

"How do you know it was him?" Jason asked, wondering if Arabella was simply vying for attention or trying to shock him.

"Well, it had to be him, didn't it? He wasn't a tradesman, since he had tried to gain admittance by the front door, and he hadn't been carrying anything except a rather handsome walking stick. He looked like a gentleman, even though his coat was a bit shabby," Arabella added. "It was definitely him." She seemed eager to prove her point.

Jason was instantly engaged, his full attention directed toward Arabella. Her description matched that of the victim closely enough to make her claim plausible. "Did you speak to him?"

"Of course not. I saw him from the window of the morning room. He seemed nervous."

"Whom did he come to see?" Jason asked, keeping his voice low so Mrs. Chadwick, who was regaling the company with some anecdote, wouldn't hear.

"I don't know. Llewelyn, that's our butler," she clarified for Jason's benefit, "didn't let him in. He sent him to the tradesman's entrance. I lost sight of him once he rounded the corner."

"Could he have come to speak to one of the servants?"

Arabella shrugged. "No idea. No one mentioned his visit afterward. I don't suppose it was important. He looked nice, though," she added with a sigh. "He had a kind face."

Yes, he did, Jason thought, *and he was young.* He'd had his whole life ahead of him before someone had decided to cut it short.

"Did Lucinda see him as well?" he asked, wondering if Arabella might have invented seeing the murdered young man to appear more interesting.

"No, Lucinda was fenc—reading," she instantly corrected herself. "She likes reading."

Lucinda glared at her from across the table.

"I'm sorry. I shouldn't have said anything," Arabella muttered. "I don't suppose it matters much now."

"It matters," Jason assured her.

He was about to ask Arabella if she could recall anything else when water-filled bowls were brought out and placed before each guest. Having washed her hands, Mrs. Chadwick signaled Mrs. Talbot with an almost imperceptible nod, then rose and invited the ladies to retire to the drawing room, leaving the men to enjoy brandy and cigars. Jason wished he could make his excuses and leave, but it'd be rude, so he sat through another half hour of mind-numbing conversation, learning more about agriculture than he'd ever wished to know. The evening finally broke up when the colonel stood and wished everyone a good night. Jason had to admire the man's stamina. He looked exhausted and frail, but his back was ramrod straight and his shoulders squared as he walked from the dining room, leaning heavily on his cane.

"Thank you for a lovely evening," Jason said to Mrs. Chadwick, who'd come out to the foyer to see her guests off. "It was a pleasure to meet you all."

Mrs. Chadwick smiled up at him, her gaze warm on his face. "The pleasure was ours, Captain, and I hope we'll meet again very soon." She looked like she wanted to say something more but didn't. To push too hard would be bad form.

"As do I," Jason replied, and kissed her gloved hand before taking his leave.

He climbed into the carriage, leaned back, and allowed the fragrant caress of the summer night to cool his flushed face. He had to tread carefully, since he'd recognized the calculating gleam in Caroline Chadwick's eyes. She wanted him for Arabella and would strategize like a general going into battle, intent on getting her daughter the title that had eluded her.

Jason chuckled, startling Joe, who sat on the box, shoulders hunched with fatigue after cooling his heels for hours while waiting for him to emerge. Arabella was a sweet girl, but Jason wasn't interested. Had he been ten years younger, he might have found himself smitten with Lucinda, attracted by her lovely face and indomitable spirit. Cecilia had been spirited and fun, he recalled wistfully. And changeable, and easily bored, and not devoted enough to wait for him. And still he missed her and the life they would have built together.

Chapter 11

Jason threw off the counterpane and strode to the window, pulling it open. A three-quarter moon floated in a sky strewn with stars, the tiny dots shimmering like shards of broken glass. A gentle breeze moved through the trees beyond the lawn, caressing Jason's face with cool fingers. He was hot, restless, and thirsty.

Pulling on his trousers, he left the room and headed toward the main staircase, his bare feet slapping against the polished wood steps. Pale shafts of moonlight illuminated his way as he reached the foyer, entered the servants' quarters through the green baize door, and descended another flight of stairs to the basement kitchen. He'd thought he'd find it deserted, but an oil lamp burned bright on the wooden table and a dainty steaming teapot was positioned before Mrs. Dodson, who was clad in a flowery dressing gown, her pale hair loose about her shoulders.

"Captain," she exclaimed, as surprised to see him as he was to see her. "What's amiss?" She took in his untucked shirt and bare feet and looked away as if the sight of him were indecent.

"I came down for a glass of water," Jason explained. "I didn't mean to disturb you. What time is it?" he asked, wondering if it was nearly morning and Mrs. Dodson was about to embark on her daily routine.

"Just gone two. Would you care for a cup?"

Jason shook his head. "I'm too hot for tea."

"Come and sit down," Mrs. Dodson invited. She got up and poured Jason a glass of water that she set before him. "I often come down here in the night," she said.

"Trouble sleeping?"

"Dodson snorts like a prize heifer. Keeps me awake. How was the dinner? Did you enjoy the food?" she asked, her eyes sparkling with curiosity.

Jason shrugged. "It was all right, I suppose."

Mrs. Dodson smiled sheepishly. "I used to work at Chadwick Manor. Started out as a scullion at fourteen. Their cook, Elsie, was a friend of mine, but we fell out after I left. She fancied Dodson, but it was me he wanted," she said proudly.

Jason grinned. She was as coy as a young girl. "Her food wasn't nearly as good as yours, Mrs. D," Jason said, making her glow with pleasure. "And that blancmange—" He made a face of disgust, and she laughed.

"I do enjoy cooking for Micah. He's always so appreciative, and so hungry for more. It's as if he's afraid he won't get enough."

"Micah has known true hunger, the type of hunger that drives you mad with desperation. It'll take him time to learn to pace himself."

"The poor mite," Mrs. Dodson said. "He's lucky to have you, Captain. I can see you care for him. I'm sure he'll never forget your kindness."

"I'm not doing it to be kind," Jason replied. "I feel responsible for him, and I will look after him until he's ready to be independent. Why does everyone act as if I'm some paragon of virtue for taking in an orphaned boy?" he asked, feeling a bit defensive.

"Because you are. Not many men in your position would bother about some orphan. In fact, many don't even care about their own spawn. Why, half the people in this village are descended from the Talbots. The Talbot men always took what they wanted and damn the consequences. If the child was born on the wrong side of the blanket, well, it had nothing to do with them, not even if the child lived in abject poverty and went to bed hungry more often than not."

"A man should take responsibility for a life he's created," Jason said fiercely.

"Children are a gift from God," Mrs. Dodson said, her eyes misting with tears. "Dodson and I were never blessed with a living child," she said sadly. "But at least the pain of our loss never drove us apart, like some folk we know."

Jason cocked his head but remained quiet. Most people tended to speak when there was a void in the conversation simply to fill the awkward silence, and Mrs. Dodson was no different.

"Daniel Haze was always such a happy boy. Bright as a newly minted penny," she said, shaking her head. "I haven't seen him up close in an age. Not much reason for our paths to cross. I do see him and Sarah at church sometimes, but they always sit on the other side and toward the back. Seeing him yesterday…" Her voice trailed off, and she took a sip of her tea.

"Did something happen to him during his childhood?" Jason asked. He didn't normally gossip, but he was curious about the man.

Mrs. Dodson sighed loudly and shook her head. "Daniel and Sarah moved to London shortly after they wed. It was Daniel's dream to join the police. He was so keen, and his mother was so proud when he joined the service," she said, smiling at the memory. "She went to visit them in London and got to see him in his uniform. So smart he looked, so authoritative, she said. He was making a name for himself, courting a promotion. It was only a matter of time until he became a detective. But then it all went horribly wrong."

"How?" Jason asked. Mrs. Dodson clearly wanted to tell him, but she was going to do it at her own pace and in her own good time. Jason wondered how she knew so much about Daniel Haze, but then the answer was obvious. Mrs. Dodson had been born and bred in Birch Hill, as were most of the people who lived and worked here. Their families went back generations, and everyone knew each other's business, like it or not. It took real talent to keep a secret in a place like this.

"Their boy," Mrs. Dodson whispered. "Their beautiful boy, Felix. I saw him once when they came back to visit. So precious he was, so angelic. He looked just like Daniel when he was a little lad. Fair curls, wide brown eyes." Mrs. Dodson's voice trailed off again and she bowed her head, as if praying. "Sarah was alone with the child most days while Daniel was working. She liked to take him to the park. It was their routine. He had a little toy sailboat, you see," she said, as if that explained everything.

"Did he drown?" Jason asked softly.

Mrs. Dodson shook her head. "He dropped the sailboat while they were crossing the street in front of their house, but Sarah didn't see. He became upset, broke free of his mother's hand, and darted into the street to pick it up. He was run over by a carriage that was going too fast to stop."

Jason felt as if Mrs. Dodson had punched him in the gut. He couldn't think of a worse death for a small child. The agony he endured must have been unimaginable. "Did he die instantly?" Jason asked, hoping against hope the child hadn't suffered, but Mrs. Dodson instantly dispelled that notion.

"No, he didn't. After he passed, poor Sarah was mad with grief. She blamed herself, and she blamed Daniel for bringing them to London. She refused to remain and demanded that Felix be buried here, in Birch Hill. His death broke them," Mrs. Dodson said, nodding miserably.

Jason sat in silence, his head bowed, his fingers wrapped around the cool glass. He'd seen tragedy, but the death of the little boy touched him in ways he couldn't begin to explain.

"How old was he?" he asked at last, his voice hoarse with feeling.

"Nearly three. Oh, I shouldn't have told you," Mrs. Dodson exclaimed, rising to her feet. "I do hate to gossip, but seeing Daniel upset me and made me think of that poor boy the vicar found in the crypt. He was someone's son, wasn't he?" she said sadly. "It doesn't matter how old they are. They're still someone's children, even when they're grown."

"Yes, they are," Jason agreed. His own parents might have feared for him at the time of their accident. They'd died not knowing that he'd survived the war, which made their passing even harder to bear.

Jason stood and nodded to Mrs. Dodson before leaving the kitchen. He was no longer hot or restless. He felt bone-weary and fell into a deep sleep as soon as he climbed into bed.

Chapter 12

Wednesday, June 6

Jason was shaving when Henley, his newly appointed valet, came to announce Constable Haze. "That man doesn't keep civil hours," Henley grumbled as he handed Jason a towel, a scowl on his face.

Jason thought Henley was not annoyed with Constable Haze but rather with Jason for refusing to allow Henley to shave him. He wasn't accustomed to being waited upon hand and foot and was perfectly capable of washing and dressing on his own. He'd informed Dodson that he had no need of a valet but had agreed to allow the man to stay on for at least a month or until he found a different position. Or until Jason had completed his business and left for New York.

"Please tell him I'll be down directly," Jason said as he dressed in the clothes Henley had laid out for him.

"Of course, sir." Henley looked downright depressed, hanging his head in dejection, when Jason tied his own tie.

Jason shrugged on his coat and cursed the idiocy of having to remain fully dressed in one's own home, but it seemed unacceptable that he should come down in shirtsleeves. Allowing Mrs. Dodson to catch a glimpse of his bare chest had been scandalous enough. Jason buttoned the coat, adjusted the shirt cuffs, and ran a brush through his hair before going downstairs to see the constable. Daniel Haze was waiting for him in the drawing room.

"Good morning, Captain," the constable said, coming forward to greet Jason.

"Good morning," Jason replied warmly. A part of him wished Mrs. Dodson hadn't told him about little Felix, but knowing about the tragedy made him want to help the constable all the more. It was the least he could do. "Have you breakfasted?" he asked.

"Eh, yes. Some hours ago. I'm an early riser."

"Then please join me. I always think better after my morning coffee."

"Thank you, Captain. I'd be delighted."

Jason led the constable into the dining room, where several chafing dishes were arrayed on the sideboard. "Please, help yourself. There's always so much more than Micah and I need," Jason said. He helped himself to some eggs, bacon, and grilled tomato.

Constable Haze took a plate and filled it with eggs, bacon, kippers, and mushrooms before taking a seat at the table. A maid Jason hadn't met before brought in a pot of coffee and two racks of toast and poured coffee for both men.

"How was the dinner party?"

Jason rolled his eyes heavenward. "I'm not good at keeping myself in check when I violently oppose the opinions of my dinner companions."

Constable Haze nodded. "I take it you met Squire Talbot, then?"

"Yes. It seems the man owns the entire village. It's positively medieval."

"It really is," Constable Haze agreed. "He's a benevolent master. Most of the time."

"How is he as a magistrate?"

"Not as harsh as you might expect."

"I'm glad to hear it," Jason said.

"Were you able to learn anything?" the constable asked as he tucked into his breakfast.

"Not really. The murder was discussed in the most general of terms, and then the subject was dropped. The only item of interest is that Arabella Chadwick saw Alexander McDougal at Chadwick Manor on Tuesday. She said he tried to gain admittance, but the butler sent him to the tradesman's entrance. He must have come to see one of the servants."

"I'll have to ask Mrs. Chadwick for permission to interview the staff."

"Have your inquiries proved more fruitful?" Jason asked.

"More fruitful than yours, but not by much. Alexander McDougal lived with his mother until her death. According to Mrs. Glynn, the landlady, Margaret McDougal was a widow who'd fallen on hard times after the death of her husband. Alexander worked in a second-hand shop, where he might have obtained the evening clothes and the pocket watch. The only things I found that tied him to Birch Hill were several clippings hidden between the pages of his mother's Bible that pertained to the Chadwick family. There was the marriage announcement of Robert Chadwick and Caroline Browning, the birth announcements for their children, and the obituary for Robert Chadwick."

Jason dabbed at his mouth with a napkin and leaned back in his chair, taking a sip of his coffee before commenting. "Might she have been a poor relation of some sort?"

"Mrs. Glynn said the woman was Scottish. Neither Mr. Chadwick nor his wife are of Scottish descent as far as I know."

"Have you formed a theory?" Jason asked.

"I think Mrs. McDougal might have been employed by Robert Chadwick or his father before her marriage. Perhaps she'd been in love with her employer and followed his life from a safe distance."

"That doesn't explain why her son decided to come to Birch Hill and was promptly murdered. This wasn't an opportunistic killing," Jason theorized.

"It might have been," Constable Haze argued. "I agree that the meeting between Alexander McDougal and the killer was probably prearranged, but it seems that the killer used whatever was to hand to attack McDougal. The meeting didn't go as planned, so he became angry, hit McDougal with the cross, then dragged him down to the crypt, where he used a dagger he'd already had on his person to finish the job. It's entirely possible that killing McDougal had never been the plan."

"What would Alexander McDougal have to discuss with someone from Birch Hill, assuming the person he met with was indeed local?"

"Perhaps Margaret McDougal met with some misfortune while in Chadwick's employ, and her son wanted retribution," Constable Haze suggested.

"What sort of misfortune are you referring to?"

"She might have been unjustly dismissed and denied a character reference, which would make it highly difficult for her to obtain another position, or perhaps she'd fallen pregnant."

"By the master of the house?" Jason asked.

"She wouldn't be the first. Robert Chadwick was, by all accounts, devoted to his wife, but Colonel Chadwick has been widowed for a long time and has a reputation for making free with the female staff. Perhaps he got her with child and tossed her out on her ear. Or it could have been a member of the staff, the butler or a footman, or even a groom. There are plenty of men in any wealthy household."

"Assuming your theory is correct, why would Alexander McDougal come now?" Jason reached for the coffeepot and refilled his cup, holding out the pot to Constable Haze, who shook his head.

"He might have wished to meet his father."

"Or blackmail him."

"That's a possibility as well. He told Mrs. Glynn he expected an imminent change in his circumstances," Haze said.

"A change in circumstances requires more than a one-time payment from an old family retainer."

"Indeed, it does. But what if he'd come to see the colonel?"

"The colonel is seriously ill, Constable. He barely sat through dinner last night and only picked at his food. Even if he's Alexander McDougal's father, he couldn't have dragged the young man to the crypt, pushed open the stone lid, and lifted the man into the tomb before pulling the lid closed again. I also doubt he could have entered Mrs. Harris's house unnoticed and searched Alexander's room. The man is very frail. He did have a bruise on his wrist, but cirrhosis of the liver causes the skin to bruise easily. The bruise could have been caused by something as simple as lifting himself out of the tub."

Constable Haze nodded. "I think you're right. In either case, we're getting ahead of ourselves. First, I need to find out if Margaret McDougal ever set foot in Chadwick Hall."

"Then I think you have some servants to interview," Jason said, pushing away his empty plate.

"What about you?" Constable Haze asked. "What are your plans for the day?"

"I have something far less pleasant to attend to," Jason said with a grimace of distaste. "A meeting with the estate agent. I know nothing about running an estate, and the worst part is that I have little interest in learning."

"You'll have to, now you're lord of the manor," Constable Haze said as he rose to take his leave.

"I'm not sure that I do."

Constable Haze instantly took Jason's meaning. "You mean to return to America," he said. It wasn't a question but an erudite guess.

"It's where I belong. And I must think of Micah."

"I think that boy will be happy anywhere as long as he's with you," Constable Haze observed.

"Micah has an older sister. When I took him to his family's farm in Maryland, the farm had been burned to the ground and Mary was gone. Micah won't rest until he finds out what happened to Mary. She's the only family he's got left."

Constable Haze shook his head. "She won't be easy to find, assuming she's still alive."

"I must try," Jason said as he escorted the constable to the door of the dining room. "I owe him that much. I've hired a man to look into the matter."

"Then best of luck in your search," Constable Haze said as he accepted his hat and walking stick from Dodson. "And thank you for breakfast."

Chapter 13

Having left Redmond Hall, Daniel set off for Chadwick Manor. It was almost five miles away, but the walk would do him good and give him time to think. It wouldn't do to arrive too early anyway, as the rich kept their own hours. By the time he finally walked up the drive, it was close to noon, and he was no closer to having a viable theory. Perhaps the Chadwicks or their staff would be able to shed some light. Daniel hoped Mrs. Chadwick was up and ready to receive visitors.

"Good day. I'd like to speak to Mrs. Chadwick," Daniel said when Llewelyn, the butler, opened the door to his knock.

"Mrs. Chadwick is not at home to visitors," Llewelyn intoned.

"Then I'll speak to the colonel," Daniel said impatiently.

"The colonel is not at home to visitors either."

"I'm here on official business, not for a dish of tea and cucumber sandwiches."

"All the same," the butler replied, unfazed by Daniel's irritation.

"Then I would like to interview the servants," Daniel persisted. If turned away, he had no idea how to proceed with the investigation, since his only connection was the clippings pertaining to the Chadwick family.

"I'm afraid I can't allow that," Llewelyn said, his smug expression infuriating. "Not without express permission from the lady of the house."

"Then I will interview you," Daniel replied, his tone brooking no argument. "Surely you can allow *that*," he said tartly.

Llewelyn gave a slight nod. "You may ask me whatever you wish, Constable. Let's talk somewhere more private, shall we?"

The butler led Daniel out of the foyer and through the baize door that separated the servants' quarters from the rest of the house. They walked down a narrow corridor, past the kitchen, and toward a small, windowless room that was the butler's pantry. There was a desk with a hardback chair, a cane chair for visitors, a shelf with neatly arranged ledgers, and a strip of wood next to the door with hooks for various keys that probably opened everything from cabinets to attic rooms.

Llewelyn gestured to the visitor's chair and took the chair behind the desk. Here, he was the master. "How can I help you, Constable?"

Daniel decided to start from afar. He had no way of confirming that Alexander McDougal had really come to the house, nor did he have any way of knowing if McDougal had been his mother's real name. It was most likely her married name, or even an alias she'd chosen for herself when she left the Chadwicks' employ.

"Mr. Llewelyn, how long have you worked here?"

"Nigh on thirty years."

"Were you always the butler?"

"I started as second footman and worked my way up."

"So, when you started at Chadwick Manor, it was Colonel Simon Chadwick who was your master?"

"That's correct. And he's still my master," Llewellyn corrected Daniel, who acknowledged the truth of that. Mrs. Chadwick might be lady of the house since the colonel was widowed, but it was the old man who was master of the house and would remain so until his death, when Harry Chadwick would inherit the estate.

"Was the colonel always here?" Daniel asked.

Llewellyn's brows lifted in surprise. "No, he wasn't always here," he snapped. "He was in the army, man. He spent years away from his family. And he often stayed at the London house when back in England. He detested living in the country in his younger days. Found it too dull."

"And now?"

"And now he prefers to live here, on account of his health," Lewellyn spat out.

Daniel nodded. Lewellyn wouldn't tell him any more on that score, but he'd confirmed what Captain Redmond had said about the colonel's illness.

"Were there ever any Scottish members of staff?" Daniel asked, hoping against hope it would be as easy as finding out that Margaret McDougal had worked at Chadwick Manor during Llewelyn's tenure.

"No, never."

Deflated, Daniel continued. "What about visiting servants? Any Scottish ladies' maids or valets that came to the house with their masters?"

Llewelyn took a moment to consider the question. He nodded. "Yes, there was one Scotch valet who came several times. McDonald, his name was. He served Lord Buxton, who was a close associate of the colonel in his army days."

"But no female servants?"

"Not that I can recall. Have you a name?"

"McDougal," Daniel plunged in.

Lewellyn's face tightened with understanding. "No one by that name worked here during my time."

"What about someone named Margaret?"

Daniel thought he saw a hint of a smile on Lewellyn's otherwise expressionless face. "Yes, there was a scullery maid named Margaret when I first arrived."

"What was her surname?"

Llewellyn exhaled loudly, as if at the end of his patience. "Simpson. Margaret Simpson."

"What became of her?"

"She married Leslie Dodson and went to work at Redmond Hall."

"Did the colonel ever fancy her?" Daniel asked, knowing the butler would never admit to it even if he had. His loyalty to the family was absolute.

"Why don't you ask her?" Lewellyn suggested. "She'll tell you everything you need to know. Loves a bit of gossip, that one. Always has."

"Thank you. I will."

Having exhausted that line of questioning, Daniel moved on to Alexander McDougal. "I believe Alexander McDougal, the man who's been murdered, came here on Tuesday."

"You believe wrong," Llewellyn answered rather quickly.

"Miss Chadwick saw him from the window. She mentioned it to Captain Redmond."

"She was mistaken. There was a tradesman who came to the house on Tuesday morning. I sent him round back."

"Surely a tradesman would know to go to the servants' entrance," Daniel remarked, hoping to catch the butler off-guard.

"Surely he would," Llewellyn agreed. "Impertinent fellow."

"What was his trade?"

"Clockmaker."

"Did he bring any samples with him?"

Llewellyn allowed himself a chuckle. "Do you honestly expect a man to go from house to house lugging clocks? He had sketches."

"Did you speak with him?"

"I did, but I told him we don't require any new clocks at the present."

"What was his name?"

The butler waved his hand in a gesture of dismissal. "I can't recall."

No, I don't suppose you can, Daniel thought angrily. Instead, he got to his feet. "Thank you for your time, Mr. Llewellyn. You've been most helpful."

The butler's smirk wasn't lost on Daniel as he left the pantry and made his way to the tradesman's entrance, from which he departed.

As he walked down the drive, Daniel considered his options. He could visit some of the other houses in the area and ask after the traveling clockmaker, and he would have had he for a moment believed such a person existed. Had Alexander McDougal come to the house, Llewelyn wouldn't want to admit the fact for several reasons. For one, no great house wanted to be associated with a murder, especially a house that had three children of marriageable age. Any trace of scandal would ruin their chances on the marriage market despite their considerable fortune. For another, Llewellyn, or his employer, probably had something to hide, a supposition of which Daniel had absolutely no proof other the fact that the butler had lied to him.

Or, Daniel thought sourly, Llewellyn had told the truth and Arabella had seen some other young man from the window. Perhaps claiming she'd seen the victim had given her a thrill. While working in London, he'd met plenty of people who came forward as witnesses or claimed an acquaintance with a victim just to get a bit of attention, or even get their name in the papers if their testimony was scandalous enough. More than one person had embellished their story to draw out their moment of glory, and a young woman who was stuck in the country and had just finished a year of deep mourning for her father was probably climbing the walls with boredom. She might take every opportunity to capture the attention of an eligible bachelor who could single-handedly spare her the anxiety of her first London season and offer her not only a very comfortable life and a title, but a home within a couple of miles of her family's estate, something a shy young woman like Arabella Chadwick might appreciate.

Perhaps it was worth checking the story of the clockmaker after all, Daniel thought as he passed through the gates. He'd go see Squire Talbot tomorrow. The squire would wish to know how the investigation was progressing and discuss the date for the inquest. Daniel let out a heavy sigh. He had nothing to tell the magistrate, and Alexander McDougal's death was hardly 'death by misadventure,' a verdict that was most frequently passed when there was a lack of evidence. It had been a misadventure, all right, but of the most malicious variety. Someone had clearly felt threatened by Alexander McDougal's presence and believed that he had something in his possession that could cause them harm. But what?

He had to speak to Mrs. Harris again. Now that she'd had some time to recover from the shock, perhaps she'd recall something the victim had said or done. Or maybe she'd even be able to tell him what Alexander McDougal had packed in his satchel. He didn't believe for a moment that Mrs. Harris, who was as curious as a magpie, would forego a discreet little rummage while her lodger was out. Having made the decision, Daniel quickened his steps, eager to get to the village.

Chapter 14

Daniel found Mrs. Harris at home. "I was just about to 'ave dinner," she said ungraciously.

"I'm sorry to have disturbed you. I only need a few moments of your time."

Mrs. Harris narrowed her eyes but didn't quibble. "Ye'd best come in, then."

She led Daniel into a small kitchen, where a pot of stew bubbled over the open flame of the hearth.

"Take a seat," Mrs. Harris said, and indicated one of the chairs. Daniel sat down, and she took the seat opposite him.

"Mrs. Harris, did you include any meals in your offer of a room?"

"'Course I did. Breakfast and dinner. The guests could go to the Stag for supper, if they 'ad a mind to do so."

"When you served Mr. McDougal his meals, did you two not speak?"

"We did. What of it?"

"He may have said something about why he'd come to Birch Hill or what he'd hoped to accomplish while here."

Mrs. Harris shook her head. "Tight-lipped, 'e were. Didn't say a thing."

"So, what did you talk about?"

"The weather, mostly. And nature. 'E said 'e enjoyed the fresh air and the country walks."

"Did he come here for his health?"

"Doubt it, although, 'e were a bit on the scrawny side and 'ad that city pallor to 'is skin."

"That he did," Daniel agreed. "Did he do a lot of walking?"

"'Ow should I know?" Mrs. Harris said with a shrug.

"Was he out for long periods of time?" Daniel asked, modifying the question.

"Not really."

"When did you clean his room?"

"In the morning, after breakfast. Why do ye ask?"

"Was Mr. McDougal there while you cleaned?" Daniel asked, striving for patience.

"'E weren't 'ere the first time. The second time, 'e sat in the parlor, reading the paper while I tidied up."

"And while you tidied up, did you notice what he'd brought with him?"

"I'm a good Christian woman. I don't snoop through other people's belongings."

"I wasn't implying that you did," Daniel replied, although he really was. "Perhaps he'd left something out. I noticed there's a small desk in the room. Did he write any letters or keep a journal?"

Mrs. Harris shrugged. "If 'e did, it's news to me."

"Surely he must have brought something other than a clean shirt and drawers," Daniel persisted.

Mrs. Harris's pale face suddenly brightened. "'E did. 'E had a photograph with 'im."

"Was it framed?"

"Yes. At first, I thought the frame might be silver, but it were pewter. Cheap."

"Who was in the photograph, Mrs. Harris?" Daniel asked, a spark of excitement igniting in his breast. Now he was getting somewhere.

"It were a man and a woman. The woman seated, the man standing behind 'er."

"Did you recognize anyone in the photograph?"

"My vision's not what it used to be, Constable. I suppose it were a photograph of 'is parents. It looked old."

"I see. Did you happen to find the photograph when you cleaned the room after the murder?" Daniel asked.

"No. Gone it were, like the rest of 'is things." Mrs. Harris gave him the gimlet eye. "If ye've no more questions, I'd like to eat now. I'm 'ungry."

"Of course. Thank you for your time."

Mrs. Harris was already ladling stew into a bowl by the time he stepped out of the kitchen and headed toward the Red Stag.

Chapter 15

Jason breathed a sigh of relief when the estate agent, Mr. Middleton, finally departed. After several hours of tedious discourse relating to accounts, investments, properties, and tangible assets Jason's head pounded like an Indian war drum. He retired to the drawing room, helped himself to a large medicinal brandy, and settled in a wingchair before the unlit hearth. Having drained the glass, he set it on a conveniently placed side table, leaned against the back of the chair, and closed his eyes, relishing the peace and quiet. The idyll didn't last long.

Micah burst into the room, looking happier than he had in a long time. "I'm back," he announced.

"I see that. How was your outing with Joe?" Jason asked.

Micah took the chair across from him and nodded happily. "Good. I met Tom. He's my age and he was very friendly. He asked lots of questions about America and the war. He couldn't believe I'd seen real battle and had spent time in prison. He was really impressed."

"I bet he was," Jason muttered. "So, what did you and Tom do?"

Micah settled more comfortably and eyed the empty glass. "Can I have some?"

"No. You can go to the kitchen and ask Mrs. Dodson for something to drink if you're thirsty."

"Maybe later. Tom and his parents live in a house in the woods," Micah began. "His father is the gamekeeper. I suppose he arranges games for when the Chadwicks have guests."

Jason chuckled with amusement. "He's not that kind of gamekeeper."

"Then what does he do?"

"He protects the wildlife on the estate."

"Oh. Well, that makes sense, I suppose. I didn't see anything that looked like it might be a game. When we first got there, Mrs. Marin, that's Tom's ma, gave us lunch, but she'd called it dinner. Cottage pie and cider. Delicious," Micah said "I like cottage pie. It tastes like something my own ma used to make. I miss her," he whispered.

"I know," Jason replied softly, wishing he could comfort Micah in some way.

Micah sighed loudly. "Mrs. Marin reminded me of my ma in other ways, as well."

"Really? How?" Jason asked. He could sense Micah's need to talk about his family and settled in to listen. It helped to talk.

"She was really mad at Mr. Marin," Micah said. "Didn't talk to him at all. Just slammed the plate in front of him. My ma used to do that when she was angry."

"Mr. Marin must have done something to upset her."

"She's upset about some woman. Tom told me when we went out after lunch. He said his ma says his pa is in this woman's thrall. What does that mean?"

"Means he's really taken with her," Jason said, going with the simplest explanation he could think of. He supposed Mr. Marin had a mistress and his wife had found out. He didn't ask any questions, not wanting to gossip about something that was none of his business, but Micah's mind was still fixed on the Marins.

"I thought it meant he was in her debt. She said he didn't owe her his soul and she should get someone else to do her dirty work for her."

Jason leaned back and studied Micah's flushed face. "What kind of dirty work?" he asked, keeping his tone casual. Perhaps Mr. Marin wasn't having an affair after all.

"Oh, I don't know. Tom didn't say. I guess she must need something done, around the house or the barn. I don't suppose she has a husband of her own to see to the man's work," Micah reasoned.

"No, I don't suppose she does. Did Mrs. Marin mention who this woman might be?" Jason asked. He had no wish to involve Micah in the investigation, but if Mrs. Marin's anger had something to do with the murder of Alexander McDougal, he couldn't pass up the chance to find out.

Micah shrugged. "No, she didn't."

"Where did you and Tom go?" Jason asked in an effort to redirect the conversation. Micah clearly didn't know anything else.

"Tom showed me his special place. It's this massive old tree with a hollow. It's near the lake. He keeps his treasures there."

"Oh? What sort of treasures?"

"You know, like interesting rocks, a rabbit's foot, and buttons he's found. The best thing was the cigarette holder. He found it only a few days ago when he was out walking by the lake."

Jason's curiosity was instantly piqued by this bit of information. "What did it look like, this cigarette holder?"

Micah scrunched his face in concentration as though trying to visualize the item. "Metal, with pretty etching on the top. It had initials engraved on it."

"What were they?"

"L.D.," Micah replied.

"Did Tom show the cigarette holder to his father when he found it?"

"No. His pa would have taken it away. Tom said it must belong to one of Mrs. Chadwick's guests. They lose things all the time, but he's never found anything as splendid as the holder. He means to hold on to it. There were even still cigarettes in it. It was almost full."

"Have you been smoking?" Jason asked, pinning Micah with his gaze.

Micah colored slightly. "We shared one cigarette. Don't be angry, Captain. Tom offered, and I didn't want him to think I was a sissy."

"You're the bravest boy I know," Jason replied warmly.

Micah nodded as tears sprang to his eyes. "I'm not brave. I was scared all the time, especially at the prison. At least during a battle there was no time to think, but at Andersonville, all I did was worry about what was going to happen and if I was going to die."

Had Micah been younger, Jason would have picked him up, settled him in his lap, and held him until the tears passed, but he couldn't treat Micah like a baby. He had to give him the respect he deserved.

"Being scared doesn't mean you're not brave. It takes courage to face your fears."

"You mean I should face that Mary's dead?" Micah asked, watching Jason for a reaction.

"That's really not what I meant."

Micah shook his head. "You didn't say no."

"I didn't say no because I don't know, but that doesn't mean I think Mary is dead. Mr. Hartley promised to write. You must have patience," Jason said, smiling at Micah's mutinous expression.

"The not knowing is worse than believing she's dead."

"No, it's not. If Mary were dead, there'd be no hope. Allow yourself to hope, Micah," Jason pleaded.

Micah shook his head. "I can't," he whispered. "I can't hope. It hurts too much when the hope dies."

"Yes, it does," Jason agreed, thinking frantically of how to cheer the boy up. "So, you liked this Tom?" he asked.

Micah nodded. "He asked if I could come again."

"Would you like to?"

"Yes, please," Micah said. "If you've no objection."

"You can invite him here, if you like," Jason said.

"Really? Can I?"

"For as long as we're here, this is your home, and you are welcome to invite your friends."

"Tom said he's never been to the big house at the Chadwick estate. I bet he'd love to see all the lovely things here. I'll show him the chess set first."

"Maybe you can even teach him to play," Jason suggested.

"Maybe," Micah replied. His eyelids were starting to droop.

"Why don't you go take a nap before supper? You look tired." Micah still tired easily, and he must have done a lot of walking with his new friend.

"All right. You should take a nap too. You look done in."

"I'll just sit here for a little while longer," Jason replied.

"You should have another brandy. It'll do you good," Micah said as he stood to leave.

"Go on with you," Jason said, chuckling at the boy's cheekiness.

After Micah had gone, Jason considered Tom's epic find as he stared at the empty hearth. The cigarette holder could have belonged to anyone who'd visited the house. Perhaps a guest had taken a walk by the lake and dropped it. The initials meant nothing. Or did they? The Chadwick estate was only a few miles from Redmond Hall, and Dodson's Christian name happened to be Leslie. L.D. for Leslie Dodson. Did he smoke? Even if he did, it proved nothing. Maybe he was friendly with someone on the staff of Chadwick Manor. He might have gone there and dropped his cigarette holder; that didn't make him a killer.

On the other hand, having been employed at a second-hand shop, Alexander McDougal might have purchased a cigarette holder someone had sold, which would explain the initials. This theory held very little merit except for the fact that Tom had found the holder only a few days ago. Given that his secret place was close to the lake, Tom probably spent a lot of time there. He'd have found the holder sooner had it been there longer. Perhaps Mrs. Chadwick had other guests to stay, but she had mentioned that she'd recently come out of mourning and was only just beginning to entertain again. Whoever had dropped the cigarette holder must have been at Chadwick Manor only a short while ago.

Having arrived at that conclusion, Jason decided to mention Tom's find to Constable Haze at the earliest opportunity. It might come to nothing, but one never knew. Jason glanced out the window. It was a beautiful day, and he had yet to set foot outside. He decided against pouring another tot of brandy and went for a walk instead.

He'd been walking for about a half hour when he spotted Miss Talbot walking along the lane, a wicker basket slung over her arm. Her bonnet shadowed her eyes, but he could clearly make out the delicate curve of her lips. She seemed to be deep in thought, but her face broke into a smile when she saw him.

"Good afternoon, Captain," she said a little shyly.

"Good afternoon, Miss Talbot. Are you out for a walk?"

"I went to visit one of my father's parishioners who had a baby yesterday," she explained. "I baked some muffins for her."

"That's very kind of you," Jason replied as he fell into step with Miss Talbot.

"More selfish than kind," she replied, surprising him with her candor.

"How is visiting a parishioner selfish?" he asked.

Miss Talbot looked up at him, her gaze wistful. "I've run my father's household since my mother died when I was eleven. I missed her dreadfully, but so long as I had my sister, I was content, for I had a companion who loved and understood me. When Jane died, a part of me died with her," she explained. "I have many tasks to occupy my time, Captain, but few that bring me joy, and almost no one to talk to aside from a father who thinks my only worth lies in darning his socks or preparing his favorite dinner.

Visiting the parishioners not only gives me an opportunity to escape the soul-crushing silence of the vicarage but allows me to feel useful and needed. I have no power to change anyone's life, but if I can help a mother by looking after her children for a few hours, or read to an elderly woman who's taken ill, I feel my day wasn't completely devoid of purpose. So, you see, I do good works to make myself feel better. Is that not selfish?"

"Not at all," Jason replied, but didn't think she believed him. He wasn't sure if it was a desire to reassure her or the long-suppressed need to talk to someone about his experiences, but suddenly he found himself sharing things he hadn't told another living soul. "I was taken prisoner toward the end of the American Civil War and sent to a military prison in Georgia. It was a hellish place, a death trap. More than half the inmates were either ill or wounded. Some of the injuries were superficial, but the unsanitary conditions in the prison made them just as dangerous as the more serious wounds. I had no medical supplies to hand, not even clean water, but I spent my days ministering to the men. I couldn't save them. Though most of them died, it made me feel better to know I was doing something and to be there for a man who otherwise would have died alone. Perhaps I was being selfish as well because it allowed me to forget my own pain and fear for a few hours at a time," Jason said sadly.

"I'm glad you survived," Miss Talbot said, looking up at him earnestly, her dark eyes full of sympathy.

"Just barely. Another few weeks and I probably would have died of starvation. I was one of the lucky ones. I lived long enough to be liberated."

"And then you returned home to find that your parents had died," she said softly.

"Yes."

"I'm sorry. That must have been awful for you," she said, her sorrow for him etched into her pale face.

"The war was awful for everyone, not just me. Everyone lost someone, directly or indirectly. The woman I was engaged to married someone else while I was in prison. She believed I was dead, but she certainly didn't mourn me for long." Jason heard the bitterness in his voice, and it made him ashamed. What right did he have to feel sorry for himself when so many had lost so much more?

Miss Talbot smiled, her face transforming instantly. "I'm glad she didn't wait for you," she said.

"Why is that?"

"Because then you would never have come to Birch Hill. Your arrival has reenergized this sleepy old village."

"I should think it's the murder that's done that."

Miss Talbot shook her head. "No one wants to dwell on the murder. It's frightening, so people rationalize it by choosing to believe that the young man had done something to bring it on himself. Since he was an outsider, they think it has nothing to do with them and want only to see him buried, so they can forget it ever happened."

"I don't know what Alexander McDougal did, but no one deserves to be murdered."

"Especially in a church," Miss Talbot agreed. "A church has traditionally been a place of sanctuary. Murdering a man in a church compounds the sin somehow. Don't you think?"

"I don't think it matters where you do it. Taking a life destroys a piece of your soul, even if you're never held accountable for your actions."

"Have you killed anyone, Captain? In the war, I mean?" Miss Talbot asked.

"Yes, I have."

"So, you speak from experience."

"Yes."

"You must have saved many men as well," Miss Talbot said, her expression hopeful.

"I've saved numerous men, but that doesn't wash away the stain of killing. I realize killing in battle is not the same as killing a man in cold blood, but the result is still the same."

"At least your sacrifice wasn't in vain," Miss Talbot said. "You have fought to make the world a better place. Because of you, a new generation of people will be born free."

"That's what I tell myself when I wake up in the middle of the night, the faces of those I've killed swimming before my eyes, their mouths open in a silent scream."

"But do you believe it, deep inside?" Miss Talbot asked.

Jason considered her question. "Yes. Yes, I do," he finally said. "If I had to do it all over again, I'd do nothing differently. I felt morally obligated to fight and to save as many men as I could using my surgical skills."

"Then your soul is on the mend," Miss Talbot pronounced.

Jason smiled down at her. "If my soul is ever in torment, will you come visit me and bring me muffins?" he asked playfully.

"I'll even bring some honey to sweeten the deal."

Jason hadn't realized they'd stopped walking. He stood in the lane, looking at her, content in the knowledge that he'd found a friend.

"Miss Talbot, may I call on you sometime?" he asked.

"Only when father is there. I can't receive you without a chaperone," Miss Talbot replied bitterly. "But if we happened to meet by accident, as we did today…"

"When can I accidentally bump into you next?" Jason asked.

"I usually visit the parishioners on Tuesday and Thursday afternoons. You'll also find me doing the flowers at the church every Saturday before Evensong. Father doesn't arrive until the service is about to start."

"Then perhaps I'll see you then," he said, and was rewarded with a shy smile.

Chapter 16

Daniel entered the tavern and headed straight for the polished counter, behind which Davy Brody was wiping pewter mugs. He flexed his thick shoulders and fixed Daniel with a narrow stare.

"What are ye doing here?"

"My duty," Daniel replied.

"Well, don't let me stop ye," Davy replied sourly.

"I know you turned the murdered man away when he came asking for a room," Daniel said.

"What of it? I had other customers."

"And I wager you charged them double the price since they were in dire need of a room and in no condition to look elsewhere."

Davy shrugged. "Business is business. Ye going to charge me with something, Constable?"

"I'm not here to charge you, only to ask a couple of questions."

"Get on with it, then. I'm a busy man," Davy said, clearly relishing Daniel's discomfiture. They'd been friends once, when they were boys, but things were different now with them being on opposite sides of the law.

"Did the murdered man come in here to sup?" Daniel asked. He tried to sound authoritative, but knew his questions were less than brilliant. He was on a fishing expedition, and Davy knew it.

"He did. Twice."

"Did he meet with anyone?" Daniel asked. Davy missed little of what went on in his establishment, so he'd know, and if he didn't, he'd ask Moll, who was the ears to his eyes.

"Not that I noticed."

"Did he speak to anyone?" Daniel asked.

"Not at first, but once he had a few pints in him, he became more friendly," Davy replied, smiling crookedly.

"Whom did he speak to?"

"Archie Wells and Roddy Styles, mostly."

Daniel knew both men. They spent more time at the Stag than at home, which probably made their wives very happy, given their penchant for strong drink and love of brawling.

"Did they argue?"

"Nah. They got on like a house on fire, those three, especially once the young buck treated them to a round."

"Throwing around his money, was he?"

"Not throwing, exactly, but he didn't come off as some tight-fisted sod. Understood the value of making friends," Davy replied acidly.

"Let me know if you think of anything else that might help the investigation," Daniel said.

"I will make it my first priority," Davy replied solemnly, making Daniel want to wipe the smirk off his face.

Daniel ordered a half-pint of cider and made his way to a table in the corner, where Archie Wells and Roddy Styles were nursing their pints. "Good day to you, gents," he said, using the term loosely.

"Good day yerself, Constable," Archie replied. "We 'ear ye've been 'ard at work trying to catch a killer. Must make ye miss the old days when ye was a peeler."

"It does, actually," Daniel replied. "Brings back some memories."

"Good thing we've got the benefit of yer vast experience," Roddy Styles remarked sarcastically.

Daniel allowed the comment to slide. "Can I buy you a drink?" he asked instead. He wouldn't get anything out of these two without offering an incentive.

"Well, what d'ye say, Roddy?" Archie asked. "A body can't be ungracious and turn down such a fine offer."

"Right ye are, Archie. Ungracious we ain't."

Daniel signaled to Moll, who was on the other side of the room, and asked her to bring two more pints of bitter.

"Well, thank ye kindly, sir. Much appreciated," Archie said as he took a sip and then licked the foam off his lips. "And 'ow can we 'elp ye today?"

"Tell me about Alexander McDougal," Daniel invited, taking a sip of his cider.

"Nice lad. Generous with 'is money," Roddy said. He drank deeply, as if he had a mighty thirst on him despite having been drinking at the Red Stag since it opened, as he did every day.

"Bought you a round, did he?"

"That 'e did," Archie said. "Curious too."

"What was it he was curious about?"

"Oh, this and that," Roddy said. He'd finished his pint, and his eyes were now following Moll, who was near enough to summon.

"You're not getting another one till you answer my questions," Daniel said. "And I better like the answers."

"Wanted to know about the local gentry. Innit right, Roddy?" Archie said. "The Chadwicks, in particular. Seemed to 'ave a grievance against them."

Daniel leaned forward in his eagerness. "What sort of grievance?"

"'E didn't rightly say," Roddy said, and scratched his graying hair, his gaze still on Moll.

"Did he mean them harm?" Daniel asked.

"Not so far as I could tell," Archie said. "Just seemed resentful like. Asked a lot of questions."

"What did he want to know?" Daniel tried again.

"Asked 'bout young Master Harry and Mrs. Chadwick. What type of people they was. If they was kind to folk. Fair like."

"And what did you tell him?" Daniel asked.

"Told 'im the truth, didn't we, Roddy? Don't 'ave too close a knowledge of them. Don't see them much about the village. Mr. Chadwick, he were a good cove."

Roddy scoffed. "The man was weak. Easily led."

"And how would you know that?" Daniel asked, intrigued.

"My da was 'ead groom at Chadwick Hall for over twenty years. Said Master Robert lived in fear of 'is father. Did as 'e were told."

"Don't know that yer da was a reliable source," Archie said, rolling his eyes. "Wasn't 'e dismissed for drunkenness?" Roddy colored hotly but didn't deny the charge.

"And what about when his father wasn't around?" Daniel asked. Colonel Chadwick was gone from Birch Hill for long periods of time, especially after Robert had married Caroline.

"Lived in fear of 'is wife." Archie guffawed, his chest rumbling with phlegm. He spit into the corner and took another long sip of his beer. "'Tis the missus as wore the britches in that family."

"Did Alexander McDougal ever tell you the purpose of his visit?" Daniel asked.

Both men shrugged.

"Wanted to see the sights?" Archie quipped.

"Beautiful part of the country, this," Roddy agreed. "Now 'ow 'bout another round?"

"I think not," Daniel said. "The load of codswallop you've handed me isn't worth more than one pint."

"Well, that'll teach us to 'elp folk," Archie said without heat. He lifted his pint and saluted Daniel. "I still appreciates it, if some don't." We winked at Roddy and gulped the rest of his beer.

"Thank you for your time, gentlemen," Daniel said, and stood to leave.

"Ye gonna finish that?" Roddy asked, eyeing Daniel's leftover cider.

"Go on."

Roddy snatched the glass and drained it, then slammed it down on the table and belched loudly.

"I think our business is done," Daniel said, and strode toward the door.

Frustrated with the lack of progress, Daniel dreaded the prospect of facing Squire Talbot, but he had little choice in the matter, so he might as well get it out of the way, he decided, as he left the Red Stag and hailed a passing wagon.

"Where're you headed?" he asked the man.

"To the Home Farm. Need a lift?"

"Please," Daniel said, and climbed onto the bench. He found himself surprisingly tired.

Chapter 17

Having spent a less than pleasant hour with Squire Talbot, who'd quizzed him endlessly on his progress and set an unrealistic date for the inquest, Daniel finally returned home. He found Sarah in the garden, sitting on her favorite bench with an open book on her lap. But she wasn't reading. Her gaze was fixed on something just beyond the horizon, her face a mask of sadness. Daniel didn't need to ask what she was thinking about. He approached quietly, so as not to startle her, but she heard his footsteps and instantly rearranged her features into an expression of polite welcome.

"Daniel, I didn't see you there," she said.

"May I?" Daniel asked, indicating the other side of the bench.

"Of course."

Daniel sat down heavily. He was tired and disheartened by the progress of the investigation but coming home to Sarah didn't lift his spirits. There'd been a time when she would have run to him, wrapped her arms about his neck, and kissed him. She would have taken his hand and led him to the bench and listened attentively as he told her about his day and would have smiled at him and told him she was proud of him. She'd have told him about her day and shared any funny or concerning behaviors Felix might be exhibiting, her face glowing with love when she spoke of their son. But not now. They kept up a pretense of politeness and spoke of everything but the gulf between them, or the future that looked so bleak.

Even now, on a lovely summer afternoon, with the sun shimmering in a cloudless blue sky and birds singing in the oak tree behind them, there was a deep chill between them, and a silence that couldn't breach the chasm that seemed to widen with every passing day. Sarah sat with her hands clasped in her lap, lest Daniel dare to reach for them, and her gaze, although not as cloudy with memory as before, was on the hollyhocks she'd planted in the spring. They had yet to bloom, but Sarah stared at them as if they were the only thing she saw in the world.

"What are you reading?" Daniel asked to fill the silence.

"Oh, nothing," she replied airily, and moved the book to the other side of the bench. "It's really not very good."

The silence settled again, broken only by the rustling of leaves overhead. "Are you any closer to finding out who did it?" Sarah finally asked.

"No."

"But you will figure it out," she persisted. She finally looked at him, and Daniel wondered if she saw the pain in his eyes or could hear the words that were trapped in his throat, words of entreaty, of love, of sorrow. She hadn't allowed him to share her grief, nor had she permitted herself to move on. Sarah was trapped in a recurring nightmare of loss and pain, and there was nothing he could do to wake her.

"I'm out of my depth," Daniel said instead. "I don't have the experience or the training to deal with a murder investigation."

"But surely you must have learned something," Sarah said.

"Not enough to show me a way forward."

"What about the new Lord Redmond? Is he still willing to help?"

"Yes, he's eager to help me, but I'm not sure why," Daniel confessed. He wanted so desperately to engage her in conversation, to feel that she cared about what he was going through, rather than just making small talk to fill the silence.

Sarah looked puzzled. "I don't understand."

"It was kind of him to examine the body and determine the cause of death, but he has no obligation toward me. He needn't concern himself with the progress of the investigation. I'm sure he has more important things to do than assist me in my inquiry."

Sarah frowned as if some thought had just occurred to her. "Perhaps he doesn't. Time may weigh heavily on him in this place he's not familiar with, surrounded by people he doesn't know."

Does time weigh heavily on you? Daniel wanted to ask, studying her lovely profile. *Do you feel like this place is no longer familiar and you're surrounded by people who no longer know you?*

"I think there are things he wishes to forget," Daniel said.

"Or maybe after witnessing so much injustice, he wants to right at least one wrong," Sarah suggested, rather astutely.

"I think you might be right. Not every man is cut out to be a soldier. Some never recover from the horrors they've been forced to witness."

"And participate in," Sarah said.

Daniel smiled at her. This was the closest they'd come to a meaningful conversation in months. She wasn't just listening and offering polite responses; she was contributing. "Shall we dine together?" he asked, feeling hopeful, but Sarah instantly pulled back, as if she'd realized they were at risk of getting comfortable in each other's presence.

"I'm not very hungry. You can dine with Mama. She'll keep you company." She picked up her book and stood, turning to face him for just a moment. "I have no doubt you'll figure it out, with help or without. Goodnight."

"Goodnight," he said, and watched her walk away. It was too early to retire, so Sarah would return to her room and spend several hours alone, reading or looking out the window and thinking of Felix, imagining what he'd be like had he lived. She'd rather nurse her grief than spend an hour with him. The thought stung, but it was nothing new. A few more years of this, and it'd no longer matter, Daniel decided bitterly as he left the bench and went inside to change for dinner. The day Felix had died, Daniel had not only lost a son he'd adored, but he'd also lost his wife and any hope he'd had for the future. He'd been surrounded by people all day long, but he'd never felt so alone.

Chapter 18

Thursday, June 7

Jason was roused from deep sleep by a gentle hand on his shoulder. For just a moment, he thought it was Cecilia, but then recalled where he was and allowed himself to drift back to sleep, eager for a few more minutes of oblivion.

"I'm sorry to disturb ye, yer lordship," the quiet voice repeated. "Ye must wake up now."

Your lordship, his mind repeated groggily. Cecilia would find that really funny, some part of his brain thought. Or maybe she wouldn't. Maybe she'd have waited had she known she'd become Lady Redmond had she married him instead of Mark, who was just plain Mr. Baxter. Lady Redmond had a nice ring to it, Jason thought blearily.

"Sir," the voice pleaded.

This time he actually woke up. Opening his eyes, Jason was faced with Fanny, the newly hired servant girl. As soon as she saw that he'd woken, she snatched her hand away, as if he might punish her for touching him.

"I'm sorry, my lord," she whispered. "There's an urgent message for ye. From Constable Haze. He requires yer assistance."

"What time is it?" Jason asked, his gaze sliding toward the window. The rain was coming down in sheets, the light in the room leached by the threatening clouds. It might have been dawn, or it may have been close to noon, for all he knew.

"Just gone nine, sir," Fanny replied.

"What's happened?" Jason asked as he swung his legs out of bed.

Fanny looked scandalized and averted her gaze from his bare chest. Jason grabbed for his dressing gown and hastily put it on to save Fanny embarrassment. He supposed he should sleep in a nightshirt, but he was always too warm and preferred to sleep in his drawers.

"I don't rightly know, sir. It were Dodson as told me to wake ye, sir."

"Where's Henley?" Jason asked, wondering why Fanny had been dispatched to wake him up.

Fanny blushed furiously. "Down with stomach gripes since last night, sir. I'm sorry for the intrusion," she mumbled, still not making eye contact.

"Don't worry, I'm not angry with you," Jason said gently. "Can you ask Mrs. Dodson to brew some coffee while I dress?"

"'Course, sir."

Fanny made her escape, leaving Jason to wash and dress in peace. He decided not to shave, then came downstairs to speak to Dodson.

"What's happened?" he asked.

Dodson looked nearly as uncomfortable as Fanny had but drew himself up and replied with all the dignity he could muster. "Constable Haze sent a message with a boy from the village. Asked you to meet him at Mrs. Harris's cottage posthaste and to bring your medical bag. Shall I have Joe bring around the brougham?"

"Yes, I think you'd better," Jason replied, watching rivulets of rainwater course down the window. "I need coffee before I go."

"Almost ready, sir."

"I'll go fetch my bag," Jason said.

"No need, sir. Fanny has already brought it down."

"Shall I examine Henley before I leave?" Jason asked, feeling sorry for the man. Dysentery had been rampant at the prison, so he knew all about stomach gripes and the misery they could cause. He couldn't do much to stop the cramps, but he could make sure Henley took enough fluids to keep from becoming dehydrated as his body purged itself.

"No need, sir," Dodson replied, his gaze sliding away guiltily. "He's sure to be better by this afternoon."

"He's hung over, isn't he?" Jason asked. The answer was obvious in Dodson's eyes. Jason wasn't sure why the old butler was protecting the man, but it didn't matter. "If it happens again, he's to be dismissed on the spot without a character reference."

"Yes, sir. I'm sorry, sir," Dodson muttered. "I was meant to keep an eye on him."

"Why?" Jason asked. "Has this happened before?"

"Roger is my nephew, you see. My sister's boy. He's a good lad but has a taste for the spirits. This is the first time he's slipped up in a long while."

"That you know of," Jason said irritably. Everyone in this godforsaken village seemed to be related to everyone else. "I'll take the coffee in the drawing room," he said. He'd have a word with Henley later, but was in no doubt that Dodson would put the fear of the devil into him as soon as the man sobered up.

"As you wish, sir."

"And please tell Micah not to worry," Jason added. Micah wouldn't like to wake up and find him gone.

"Of course, sir."

Jason gulped down two cups of coffee, then accepted his hat and an umbrella from Dodson and stepped outside. The rain had let up somewhat, but it was dreary and damp, and he was grateful for the dry comfort of the carriage. The ride to the village didn't take long, and he was at Mrs. Harris's door a few minutes later. He walked up the path and knocked.

"Who is it?" Constable Haze called from within.

"Jason Redmond."

"Come in, Captain."

Jason closed his umbrella and pushed open the door. He found Constable Haze and Mrs. Harris in the parlor, the latter stretched out on the settee with a pillow beneath her head and a

131

compress on her forehead. She looked even paler than the last time he'd seen her, and there was a bluish tinge to her lips. The constable, who'd been perched on the side of the settee, stood in order to allow Jason to examine the woman.

"Mrs. Harris, can you hear me?" Jason asked gently.

"I'm not deaf," came the barely audible reply.

"Can you tell me what happened?"

"I 'eard a noise in the night and went to investigate. There was someone in the spare bedroom. 'E coshed me and fled," Mrs. Harris replied tersely, her hand going to her head.

Jason lifted the compress and saw that the graying hair at Mrs. Harris's temple was crusted with dried blood, and a nasty bruise was already forming just above the temple. Had the assailant hit Mrs. Harris a little lower, he most likely would have killed her. Jason examined her thoroughly before announcing the diagnosis.

"A bump on the head," he said in his most soothing tone.

"I 'ave one of them cushions," she argued, seeming disappointed. "I just know it."

"I don't believe you have a concussion, Mrs. Harris."

"And 'ow can ye tell?" she asked indignantly.

"For one thing, you're far too alert for someone who's suffered a concussion. I recommend cold compresses to bring down the swelling, and rest."

"I don't need a tonic?" she asked hopefully.

"No. You'll be right as rain in a day or two."

"Hmm," was all Mrs. Harris said in response.

"Why don't I help you to your bed," Jason suggested. "You'll be more comfortable there."

"Might as well," Mrs. Harris replied. "But have the constable do it."

"Of course," Constable Haze replied, and came forward to assist her.

Jason didn't question her wishes. He assumed her bed was unmade, since she'd got up in the middle of the night, and perhaps the chamber pot beneath the bed was full. Mrs. Harris might be too proud to allow someone of his station to see the room. Jason sat down on the settee she had vacated to await the constable's return. They had much to discuss.

When Constable Haze came back into the room, he beckoned to Jason to join him in the spare bedroom, which was the room Alexander McDougal had stayed in. The room was in disarray, the mattress tossed carelessly to the floor and the bedding nearly stripped. The drawers hung open, and the chest of drawers had been pushed away from the wall, as if someone had searched behind it.

"How did you know Mrs. Harris had been attacked?" Jason asked as he surveyed the chaos.

"I came by to ask her if she'd remembered anything else Alexander McDougal might have said or had in his possession. The front door was unlocked, and Mrs. Harris was lying on the floor, her head bleeding."

"What are your thoughts?" Jason asked.

"I reckon whoever killed Alexander McDougal did so to obtain whatever it was he had in his possession. It wasn't money; it was something much more valuable. Since McDougal didn't have it on him at the time of the murder, the killer returned to steal his things in the hope that the item would be among them, but whatever he was looking for wasn't there, so he returned to search the room one more time. Mrs. Harris disturbed him, and he hit her and fled through the front door, but I don't believe he got what he came for."

Jason nodded. "I agree. I think Alexander McDougal might have been blackmailing someone at Chadwick Manor."

"That's a strong possibility, since everything I've learned thus far points to the fact that he had some sort of grudge against the Chadwicks."

"Have you spoken to Caroline Chadwick or the colonel?" Jason asked.

"Not yet, but I'll have to now."

"There's something I need to tell you. Micah spent the afternoon with John Marin's son yesterday."

"The Chadwicks' gamekeeper?" Daniel asked, clearly surprised by this bit of news.

"Marin is our groom's brother, and Joe thought Micah might benefit from the company of someone his own age."

"Very wise of him," Haze replied. "Has this some bearing on the investigation?"

"Tom Marin has a secret hiding place near a lake located on the Chadwick estate. He showed Micah a cigarette holder he'd found by the lake a few days ago. The initials L.D. were engraved on the lid."

"How does that help?" Constable Haze asked. "The Chadwicks have always liked to entertain. The cigarette holder might have been dropped by one of their guests, someone whose initials are L.D. It might have been there for a long time before the boy came across it."

"It might have been, but Tom claimed that it wasn't there before, and given the timing, I think it's worth pursuing. Is there anyone in the village whose initials are L.D. besides my butler?"

Constable Haze chuckled. "You think good old Dodson arranged a clandestine meeting at the church, then knifed a young man between the ribs? To what end?"

"Dodson's wife, Margaret Dodson, worked as a scullery maid at Chadwick Manor before they were married. I'm not saying Dodson is our killer, but there is a Chadwick connection."

Constable Haze shook his head. "Captain, everyone around here has some connection to everyone else. It's to be expected in a place like this. When I questioned the Dodsons, they said they had not left the house after you and Micah arrived on Sunday afternoon. They could have been lying, of course, but I've found nothing to connect them to the murder thus far."

"Is there anyone else who bears the same initials?" Jason asked.

"Yes. There's Lawrence Davies. He's a farmer whose family has lived in these parts since the Conquest."

"Will you question him?" Jason asked.

"Lawrence Davies is eighty, if he's a day, and blind to boot. Nor is he the type of man to own such a luxury item."

"Who looks after him?"

"His daughter and son-in-law, whose initials are R.S. Given that Alexander McDougal worked in a second-hand shop, it's much more likely that he'd purchased the cigarette holder for himself or had taken it without the owner's knowledge."

"That was my next theory," Jason agreed. "We need to find out if McDougal had a cigarette holder."

"Wait here," Constable Haze said, and left the room. He returned a few moments later, looking thoughtful. "Mrs. Harris says that she did see Alexander McDougal taking out a cigarette from a silver-colored holder, but she can't say if it was made of real silver or metal, or if there was any engraving on the lid."

"Still, knowing he owned a cigarette holder makes it quite possible that the one Tom Marin found had belonged to McDougal," Jason reasoned.

"And if it had, that means Alexander McDougal visited Chadwick Manor."

"Perhaps he trespassed," Jason suggested.

"Or perhaps Arabella Chadwick was correct about the identity of the man she'd seen through the window. In any case, I think it's time I called on Mrs. Chadwick."

"Can I give you a ride? It's still raining."

"I'd be most grateful," the constable replied. "It's quite a walk to Chadwick Manor."

"If you've no objection, I'll wait for you. I'm curious to hear what the lady has to say for herself."

"I have no objection. In fact, I'd be most grateful, both for the ride and for the opportunity to discuss Mrs. Chadwick's testimony. I'm afraid I'm rather stumped," Constable Haze admitted as they walked out of Mrs. Harris's cottage toward the waiting carriage.

"Chadwick Manor, Joe," Jason said before climbing inside. "Stop at the gates." He waited for Constable Haze to get in and sit down before using his umbrella to knock on the roof to let Joe know they were ready.

"Once you discover what it was Alexander McDougal had that was worth killing for, everything else will fall into place," Jason said as the carriage started to move.

"But how do I find out?" Constable Haze asked, pinching the bridge of his nose in frustration. "The unrelated scraps of information I've been able to gather don't add up to even the flimsiest of theories. I know for a fact that Alexander McDougal was murdered and that his body was disposed of by someone who had some basic knowledge of anatomy and was strong enough to lift him into the tomb. McDougal had in his possession something that posed a threat to someone in or around Birch Hill, something that's still out there."

"You also know that whatever it was had something to do with the Chadwicks," Jason supplied.

"I don't know that," Constable Haze argued. "Mrs. McDougal had kept several clippings pertaining to the Chadwick family and had underlined verses in her Bible that alluded to forgiveness and unwavering faith, but there's nothing to indicate that those passages had anything whatsoever to do with the Chadwicks or some injustice she might have suffered at their hands. I examined the Bible very carefully but found nothing that might offer a clue. The clippings prove only that she'd heard of the family in some capacity. As far as we know, she wasn't employed by them or married to anyone who'd come from Birch Hill. If McDougal was her married name, which it must have been, then it stands to reason that she'd married a Scot despite what she'd told Mrs. Glynn about her husband being English, and no one can recall anyone like that living around here in the past few decades."

"Perhaps she never married, and McDougal was her maiden name," Jason suggested.

"Even if that's true, someone like her, who had a Scottish name and accent, would be easy to recall in a place like this."

"Valid point," Jason agreed. They had arrived at the wrought-iron gates to Chadwick Manor. "I'll wait here."

"Thank you."

Constable Haze got out, unfurled his umbrella, and walked down the gravel drive toward the manor house, which was just visible in the distance.

Chapter 19

Daniel walked directly toward the front door and rang the bell. He had no intention of using the tradesman's entrance. A young footman opened the door and inquired after his business, looking at Daniel with the pained expression of someone who thought Daniel was highly deluded in thinking he'd be received.

"Constable Haze to see Colonel Chadwick," Daniel said, giving the colonel his due as the head of the household and asking for him first.

"The colonel is indisposed, sir," the footman replied smugly.

"Then I wish to see Mrs. Chadwick," Daniel said, already expecting a negative reply.

"Mrs. Chadwick is at breakfast."

"Then I will wait until she's finished. Kindly inform her that I'm here."

"Very good, sir," the footman said, his smirk warning Daniel that it may be a long wait indeed.

He took Daniel's hat and umbrella and directed him to a small parlor to wait, leaving him without another word. Daniel hoped Caroline Chadwick wouldn't keep him waiting too long. She didn't. She appeared less than ten minutes later, dressed in a morning gown of pale lavender. She looked lovely as ever, her eyes bright with curiosity and her skin as dewy as that of a woman half her age.

"Good morning, Constable. May I offer you some refreshment?"

"Thank you, no," Daniel replied. "I would like to ask you a few questions, if that's all right."

Caroline Chadwick smiled at him indulgently. "If you must."

Daniel didn't converse with Mrs. Chadwick often, but the few times he had, she had struck him as a woman of wit, intelligence, and grace. If Robert Chadwick had been the head of their family, Caroline Chadwick had been the neck that decided which way it turned. She was no simpering female, and he had no intention of treating her as such.

"Mrs. Chadwick, I'll come straight to the point," Daniel began. "A young man by the name of Alexander McDougal was found murdered in the crypt of St. Catherine's Church. I'm investigating his murder."

"And you think I might know something about it?" Mrs. Chadwick asked, arching one shapely brow in mock horror.

"I think you might have information that might help me with my inquiry."

"I doubt that, but I will do what I can."

"The victim's mother had some clippings relating to your family. Announcements from the paper. Do you have any idea why Margaret McDougal would single you out in that way?"

Caroline Chadwick shrugged. "How should I know?"

"Could she have had some connection to your family?" Daniel asked.

"Absolutely not. Do you honestly believe we have dealings with such riff-raff?" she asked, bristling with indignation.

"Why do you assume Mrs. McDougal was of the lower classes?"

"Wasn't she?"

"Well, yes, but how could you know that?"

Mrs. Chadwick looked momentarily taken aback. "I suppose I just made that assumption," she admitted. "Given that her son was murdered in such a gruesome way. Must have brought it on himself. Those people always do."

"What people are those?"

Mrs. Chadwick didn't reply, but her earlier forbearance had gone, leaving impatience in its wake.

"Did Mr. McDougal come here on Tuesday?"

"Where would you get such an idea?" Daniel noted that Mrs. Chadwick never actually denied that the young man had called at Chadwick Manor.

"From your daughter. Arabella had seen him through the window," Daniel said, and instantly regretted his choice of words when Mrs. Chadwick's eyes flashed angrily.

"You have questioned my daughter? How dare you?" she sputtered.

Daniel found himself at a loss. Telling Mrs. Chadwick that the new Lord Redmond had passed on comments Arabella had made to him at the dinner party wouldn't reflect well on the captain and might make Mrs. Chadwick even angrier. He chose not to reply and persisted in his questioning, but knew the interview was effectively over.

"Can you think of any reason Mr. McDougal might have wished to speak to you?" Daniel tried again.

"I do not."

"May I speak with your son?" he asked.

"You many not."

"Harry is of age. Surely, he can decide for himself," Daniel argued.

Caroline leveled a look of pure disdain at Daniel but refused to engage in a debate about Harry's ability to decide for himself. "Now, if you're quite finished…"

Daniel rose to leave. "I thank you for your time, Mrs. Chadwick."

She gave him a brief nod and swept from the room without a backward glance. The footman was already waiting by the door when Daniel came out. He handed Daniel his hat and umbrella and walked him to the door, closing it firmly behind him.

The rain had stopped while he was inside, and a watery sunshine bathed the dripping park. Daniel's boots crunched on the gravel as he walked briskly toward the gates. He wasn't surprised in the least by Mrs. Chadwick's answers, but he was still annoyed. She knew more than she was saying; he was sure of that.

Captain Redmond looked at him expectantly when Daniel climbed into the waiting carriage. "Well? Did she tell you anything of interest?"

"Not a thing, but she didn't deny that Alexander McDougal came to the house."

"Did she confirm it?"

"Not exactly," Daniel muttered, shaking his head.

"Tell you what. You've made me miss breakfast again, so how about we go back to the house and talk over an early lunch?"

"I thank you for the invitation, Captain, but I must decline. The squire has set the inquest for Sunday morning at eight. I don't have much time left to solve this murder."

Captain Redmond stared at him in astonishment. "But that's only two days away, and you haven't got a case to present. Doesn't the squire in his role as magistrate wish to see whoever has done this brought to justice?"

"The squire wants a speedy resolution. Scheduling the inquest before the Sunday service insures that it will not drag on. We'll have two hours, at best. Once the inquest is over, Alexander McDougal will be buried, and everyone will go back to doing what they normally do instead of speculating about the murder."

"Are people not fearful of letting a murderer roam free among them?"

"They are, but the squire will skillfully put their fears to rest," Daniel replied, sighing with resignation. "He will make a case for some London lunatic following Alexander McDougal to Birch Hill and killing him over a matter that has nothing to do with anyone here. They will be invited to believe that the perpetrator has returned to the den of depravity from which he'd come and go on with their lives, thanking the good Lord for allowing them to live in such a peaceful, bucolic spot and for being ruled over by such a wise and practical man."

"But that theory can't possibly be true," Jason argued. "What about the clippings, the break-ins at Mrs. Harris's house, the cigarette holder Tom Marin found?"

Daniel shook his head. "The clippings will be explained away as a strange coincidence because they're not enough to build a case on. We have no motive, no murder weapon, and no suspects. Perhaps the notion that someone had followed him here from London is not so far-fetched."

"Are you giving up?" Captain Redmond asked, his mouth settling into a grim line of disapproval.

"Not yet," Daniel said. "I wonder if I might ask a favor of you. Can Joe drive me to the train station in Brentwood?"

"Of course. What do you mean to do?"

Daniel cocked his head to the side as he considered his next step. "Had I been allowed more time, I'd have questioned everyone Alexander McDougal came in contact with upon arriving in Birch Hill, but the time constraint imposed on me by Squire Talbot makes that impossible, and frankly, unnecessary, since McDougal seems to have kept largely to himself and revealed nothing of significance. The fact that he owned a cigarette holder doesn't prove that the one Tom found belonged to him or that it had belonged to Leslie Dodson, whose only connection to Chadwick Manor comes in the form of his wife's employment as a scullery maid nearly thirty years ago. I need something more concrete, something that ties Alexander McDougal to this place."

"And how do you plan on going about discovering that connection?" Captain Redmond asked.

"I need to speak to someone who knew Alexander McDougal well and who might shed some light on what might have motivated him to come to Birch Hill, so I will seek out his employer. If he's unable to tell me anything useful, I will call on Mrs. Glynn one more time and ask her if Alexander had any close friends. Perhaps if I knew more about the man and his plans for the future, I could establish if anyone had reason to kill him."

"That's a sound plan," Captain Redmond replied. "In the meantime, I will see what I can find out here."

"And how will you do that?"

"By becoming better acquainted with the locals."

"I wish you luck with that," Daniel replied, smiling for the first time since returning to the carriage. "They're a rum bunch."

"So I hear," Jason replied, returning the smile.

Chapter 20

Once back at home, Jason retired to the library to consider his course of action. He thought of inviting Caroline Chadwick and her children to tea, but other than fending off Mrs. Chadwick's subtle matchmaking attempts, he didn't think he'd accomplish anything of value, and her children weren't likely to reveal anything of interest in front of their mother. He had no reason to suspect that Squire Talbot or his kin had anything to do with the murder, despite the squire's eagerness to have the matter put to rest. Their names had not come up at all during the investigation. But someone had to know something, and someone had to have driven a dagger between Alexander McDougal's ribs, someone who knew how to kill a man quickly and efficiently.

Jason abandoned the comfort of the chair and went out, crossing the yard and walking toward the stables, where Joe, who had just returned from Brentwood, was brushing down the chestnuts and speaking to them in gentle tones.

"Something I can help ye with, my lord?" Joe asked solicitously.

"Is there any way I can speak with your brother, Joe?" Jason asked.

Joe blanched. "Did he do something to offend Master Micah?"

"No. Not at all," Jason was quick to reassure the man. "Micah very much enjoyed his outing and the time he spent with Tom."

Joe smiled, his relief obvious. "I thought they'd get on. Tom couldn't stop talking about it."

Jason leaned against the side of the stall, doing his best to look like a clueless American. "I only wanted to ask for some advice," he explained. "I have some wealthy American friends who might come to visit me this summer, see my new abode, as it were. They would expect to go shooting or stalking, or whatever it is the English do on an estate such as this one."

144

He didn't have to feign ignorance, since he really had no idea how the wealthy and idle amused themselves. His father had rarely spoken of his life in England, and Jason had never felt the slightest interest in hunting or shooting helpless birds for sport. He'd been too busy with his studies and then his work at the hospital to have much spare time, and when he did, he'd spent it with Cecilia. "I thought your brother, being a gamekeeper, might offer some insight," Jason continued, smiling at Joe innocently.

"I've no doubt he'd be happy to talk to ye, my lord."

"Splendid. Can you arrange it?"

"I'll see him tonight and ask him to call on ye on his afternoon off," Joe offered.

"I would much prefer to visit him," Jason replied. "No need for him to waste his precious free time on me."

Joe looked taken aback but didn't quibble. "As ye wish, my lord. When did ye intend to go?"

"Tomorrow morning would suit."

"I'll tell John to expect ye then. He'll meet ye by the gates to the park. Say 'round ten?"

"Perfect. Thank you for your assistance, Joe."

"Don't mention it, my lord."

Jason retreated to the house, where he was surprised to find that Micah had a guest. The two boys were in the library, heads bent over a chessboard. They weren't really playing, just studying the beautifully carved pieces. Micah was explaining the purpose of each piece to a dark-haired boy who sprang to his feet as soon as he saw Jason, his eyes wide with apprehension.

"Hello," Jason said. "I'm Captain Redmond. And you must be Tom."

The boy nodded vigorously.

"It's a pleasure to meet you, Tom."

"Th-thank ye, my lord.".

"Tom's pa has an extra fishing pole," Micah announced. "He said I can have it. May I go fishing tomorrow?"

"Of course, you may," Jason said.

"You won't be upset?" Micah asked, his blue eyes anxiously searching Jason's face. "I know we said we'd go together, but…" His voice trailed off as his gaze fell on Tom.

"Not at all. You go fishing with your friend. And ask Mrs. Dodson to pack you a picnic lunch."

Micah's face lit up at the prospect of having a picnic by the river. "I will. Great idea, Captain."

"Well, you two are busy, so I'll leave you to it," Jason said, gratified to see Micah's beatific smile. He was happy, and Jason's heart turned over with tenderness for the boy. He hoped he'd found a friend in Tom Marin.

Jason retreated to the drawing room and sat down in his favorite chair by the window, but the silence oppressed him, making him long for company. He missed his friends and the carefree days before the war, when they'd gathered in each other's rooms after their classes at the university or trooped to nearby bars for a pint and a sandwich. Their conversations and debates had usually run into the small hours, and they'd arrived at their morning classes looking bleary-eyed, tired, and desperate for a mug of coffee. And after university, there'd been the camaraderie of the hospital, young doctors working long hours and arguing endlessly about radical new treatments and surgical techniques. Those had been happy times, made even better by his blossoming relationship with Cecilia, the daughter of one of his university professors.

Jason closed his eyes and recalled the gay ball his future father-in-law had thrown to celebrate their engagement. Cecilia had been radiant in a gown of apple green silk, bouncy curls framing her flushed face, her eyes bright with merriment as she danced without stopping to rest, asking Mark to stand in for Jason when he excused himself to dance with his mother and future mother-in-law. She'd been happy and in love, or so he'd thought. He couldn't wait to be married, and to finally touch her in the way he'd dreamed of doing since the first time they'd met. They'd spoken of the children they would have and the life they would create once they were man and wife. Life had been full of promise and hope, and then he'd joined up and the glittering dream had become a horrifying reality that stripped him of all he'd held dear. Cecilia was lost to him forever, and most of his friends had been killed during the war. Those who had survived were irrevocably damaged by their experiences and desperate to forget, some going as far as California to begin anew.

He suddenly wished he could speak to Daniel Haze. He liked the man, and despite knowing him for such a short time, he trusted him. Having spent years surrounded by other men, Jason had learned much about what people did when frightened, threatened, or, worst of all, suddenly found themselves in a position of power. He'd seen the worst of humanity and realized that before he'd joined up, he'd trusted people much too easily and had believed the best of everyone, certain that people were basically good. Life had shown him different, but he'd also met some genuine heroes and learned that it was what was inside a man that counted. Wealth and breeding couldn't vanquish cowardice, treachery, or jealousy. And no amount of money could buy honor or sincerity.

Jason stood and looked out the window at the green expanse of lawn that ran down to the woodland, the trees standing shoulder to shoulder like a line of soldiers ready to advance. There wasn't a person in sight, only acres of land that now belonged to him. He was a wealthy man, but except for Micah, he was alone in the world. Until today, he'd been certain he wanted to return to New York after disposing of his grandfather's estate, but what was the rush? What did he have to go back to?

Chapter 21

This time, Daniel didn't enjoy the train ride. He felt anxious and upset, unable to accept that he may never get to the bottom of what had happened and allow Alexander McDougal to go to his grave without seeing justice done. Had he still been with the Metropolitan police, he would have had resources at his disposal and other trained officers to consult with, but he was on his own, and he was floundering. He was grateful to Captain Redmond for his help, but it wouldn't be right to impose on him further. Once the inquest was over, Daniel doubted they'd have much to do with each other.

He disembarked at Paddington Station and took a hansom to Fletcher's Thrift Shop. The storefront was far grander than he'd expected of a second-hand shop, with a green-painted front door and a bow window offering the passersby a glimpse of the merchandise inside. Two dressmaker's dummies stood in the center, one wearing a fashionable gown, the other dressed as a well-to-do gentleman, complete with a walking stick affixed to the sleeve of the coat and a pocket watch. It was clear from the display that the shop sold high-quality hand-me-downs.

Daniel opened the door and stepped inside. The interior was no less impressive. Along one side of the shop ran a long mahogany counter flanked by numerous drawers and display cases glittering with jewelry. Across from the counter, behind a low railing, were several racks of clothes, the back wall fitted with built-in shelves used to display hats and shoes. A tall, angular man stood behind the counter, his intelligent dark eyes fixed on Daniel, no doubt assessing him to determine if he was there to sell or buy.

"Good day to you, sir. How may I be of assistance?"

"Are you Mr. Fletcher?"

"Guy Fletcher, at your service. And you are?"

"My name is Daniel Haze. I'm investigating the murder of Alexander McDougal."

Daniel was purposely vague in the hope that Mr. Fletcher would assume he was with the Metropolitan police. A London merchant was under no obligation to answer the questions of a parish constable, but Daniel was desperate for answers, so was willing to bend the rules in his favor.

"A terrible business. Terrible," Mr. Fletcher said, shaking his head. "I was shocked to the core when I heard. Alex was such a fine young man."

"How did you know what happened?" Daniel asked, surprised that Fletcher already knew of Alexander's death.

"Mrs. Glynn, Alex's landlady, sent word. Very kind of her it was too."

"Did you know Alexander McDougal well?" Daniel asked.

"I did. Had known him since he was a boy. His mother worked as a seamstress in a shop not far from here. She was a marvel with a needle, so I availed myself of her services, since she was eager to supplement her wages, and I needed the clothes I acquired to be mended before putting them on display. The arrangement suited us both."

"You have a fine establishment here. Some very nice things," Daniel commented, hoping to get Fletcher talking.

"Thank you, sir."

"You must get many wealthy clients."

"Sometimes even those who are blessed with large fortunes have need of ready cash, being land rich and cash poor, particularly gentlemen who find themselves saddled with crippling gambling debts. A filthy habit, gambling," Mr. Fletcher said. "Ruined many a family."

"You must benefit handsomely from gentlemen who suddenly find themselves forced to sell family heirlooms or their wives' jewelry."

"I offer but a humble service, Mr. Haze. I help them in their hour of need, and they help me make a comfortable living."

"How did Alexander come to work here?"

"I took him on as a favor to his mother. After years of working as a seamstress, she suffered from chronic pain in her fingers and shoulders, and her eyesight wasn't what it used to be. She charred for two families but didn't earn enough to support herself and Alex. Once Alex turned sixteen, she asked me if I might help him find employment in one of the shops. I decided to hire him myself."

"Had you ever met Alexander's father? Bartholomew McDougal, was it?" Daniel asked, watching Mr. Fletcher closely.

The man shook his head. "By the time I met Margaret, she was already widowed."

"And when was that?"

"When Alex was around five. She worked at a different establishment before that."

"Was he a Scotsman?" Daniel asked, still unclear on that point, given the disparity between Mrs. Glynn's account and the obviously Scottish surname.

"I always assumed he was," Fletcher said.

Daniel nodded. There wasn't much to be learned from pursuing that line of questioning, so he moved on. "Was Alexander a good employee?"

"Very."

"Trustworthy?"

"Absolutely."

"Is there anything else you can tell me about him? Frankly, I'm at a loss as to why someone would wish to kill him."

Mr. Fletcher sighed. "I don't know. He was a kind and considerate young man, but he changed after his mother died. There was a bitterness in him, an anger I hadn't noticed before. He became more reckless with his wages as well."

"In what way? Gambling? Women?" Daniel asked, hoping to learn something disparaging about Alexander McDougal that would explain the manner of his death.

"Not that I know of. Alex was always modest in his needs, but after Margaret died, he began to take an interest in the merchandise we sold here and bought several luxury items. I gave him a discount, of course, but some of the purchases he made were rather extravagant."

"Such as?"

"Such as an ebony walking stick with a silver-plated handle in the shape of a falcon. He was very taken with it. He also bought an evening suit and top hat. Said he needed suitable attire for the theater."

"Did he buy a cigarette holder with the initials L.D. engraved on the lid?"

"Yes, he did. He meant to have the initials altered."

Daniel breathed a sigh of relief. At least the holder hadn't belonged to anyone in Birch Hill, confirming his earlier assumption and supporting Captain Redmond's theory that Alexander McDougal had visited Chadwick Manor and dropped the cigarette holder while there.

"Mr. Fletcher, did Alexander ever mention Robert or Caroline Chadwick?"

"Not that I can recall."

"What about his mother? Did she have any interest in the Chadwicks?"

Fletcher shook his head. "Margaret was a private woman. We never spoke of personal things."

"Since you've known Alexander since he was a young boy, would you know of any friends he might have been particularly close with? Or a woman he might have been interested in?"

Fletcher looked thoughtful. "I normally discouraged idle chatter during work hours, but Alex did mention a Charles Boyd several times. His father owns the Pale Horse tavern in Seven Dials. Alex and Charles had known each other since boyhood."

"Anyone else?"

"Sorry, no."

Daniel was about to ask if Alexander had ever shown an interest in any of the female customers when a woman, whose face was difficult to make out behind a veil she'd clearly worn for that very purpose, came into the shop. She stopped just inside the door, her hesitation obvious when she realized Fletcher wasn't alone. She carried a bulging reticule that probably contained whatever she'd come to sell.

"Good afternoon, madame." Fletcher beamed. "I will be with you presently. Are we done here?" he asked Daniel quietly.

"Yes. Thank you for your assistance, Mr. Fletcher."

"Good day, sir," Fletcher said louder, behaving as if Daniel were just another customer and not someone investigating a murder. Murder was never good for business.

Daniel left the shop and walked down New Bond Street, admiring shop displays and studying the people who passed him. Most looked affluent and strolled down the street in a leisurely fashion, chatting and carrying wrapped parcels. Several gleaming carriages rolled by, two of them disgorging beautifully dressed ladies who'd obviously come to shop.

Daniel turned the corner and found himself in a narrower street with slightly less glamorous shop fronts. A street vendor stood near the corner, a tray of pies suspended by a leather strap around his neck. Daniel bought an eel pie and wolfed it down, wishing he could have another. But he couldn't afford to be wasteful. It was either another pie or hansom fare, and he opted for the hansom since he was eager to get to Seven Dials.

Chapter 22

The hansom deposited Daniel in front of the Pale Horse, one of the taverns he'd visited before while searching for Alexander McDougal's address. The place had gone to pot since it was built, like most businesses in the area, and had a disreputable air that probably appealed to the lower orders.

Daniel pulled opened the door and walked inside. After the brightness of the afternoon, his eyes took a moment to adjust to the gloom. The taproom reeked of spilled ale, unwashed bodies, and despair. Some patrons were sitting by themselves, others in small groups, their shoulders hunched, and their hats pulled low over their eyes as if they were afraid to be recognized, even by their friends. No one addressed Daniel, but he had a sense of being watched.

He walked toward the bar and ordered a half-pint of cider. The man behind the bar was the one who'd directed Daniel to Mrs. Glynn's lodging house. His eyes narrowed in recognition as he slid the glass across the bar and splayed his hands on the bar-top, his fingers thick as sausages, his skin a mottled red.

"Ye again," he said, his tone a curious combination of surprise and menace.

"I'm looking for Charles Boyd."

"And what d'ye want with 'im?"

"I'm investigating the murder of Alexander McDougal. I was told Charles and Alexander were friends. I just wanted to get a sense of the man, find out something about his life."

"'E were a good lad, Alex," the man said, smiling sadly. The tension had gone out of his body, as if he no longer had anything to fear. "Didn't deserve what 'appened to 'im."

"No, he didn't."

The man opened a grimy door behind the bar and called down to what had to be the cellar. "Charlie, come up 'ere. Some bobby wants a word."

Daniel didn't bother to correct the publican. Having Charles believe he was a local policeman aided his cause, especially in a place like Seven Dials, where no one would tell him anything willingly if they could help it.

A young man who greatly resembled the publican came up the stairs. He had a shaggy mane of fair hair, blue eyes, surprisingly good teeth, and the body of a boxer, his upper arms thick with muscle and his head pulled into his shoulders as if he were expecting a blow.

"What can I do ye for, guv?" he asked as he wiped his hands on a dirty apron, all the while eyeing Daniel with suspicion. "Ye don't look like no bluebottle," he said, referring to Daniel's lack of the blue uniform that would identify him as a policeman. "Are ye an inspector, then?"

"My name is Daniel Haze, and I'm the parish constable from the village of Birch Hill, where Alexander McDougal was murdered. I believe you two were friends."

"Aye, we was mates. Alex were a good bloke. I can't imagine who'd done for 'im."

"Can we talk somewhere more private?" Daniel asked.

"Sure. I'll take me break now, Da."

"Go on with ye," the publican replied good-naturedly.

Charles helped himself to a half-pint of bitter and invited Daniel to follow him to a table in the corner. The wood was sticky and scarred, the floor beneath blackened with grime. Daniel inwardly cringed at the squalid conditions of the tavern, but sat down nonetheless, resolving not to drink his cider for fear of ingesting something he'd surely regret. Lord only knew what pestilence he could contract from the dirty glass or the drink itself.

"So, what ye want to know, guv?" Charles asked as he took a long pull of his beer.

"Tell me about Alex."

Charles shrugged. "Not much to tell."

"Did he have any enemies?"

"Nah. Alex were a saint." Daniel thought Charles was being sarcastic, but he seemed to mean what he said.

"How did he take the death of his mother?" Daniel asked, recalling what Mr. Fletcher had said about Alex becoming more reckless with his wages.

"'E took it bad," Charles said. "'E were angry summat awful."

"With God?"

"With 'is ma."

"Why was that?"

"She lied to 'im, that's why," Charles said, nodding as if he understood Alex's anger and couldn't blame him for the way he'd felt.

"What did she lie about?"

"Everything. Told 'im 'is da passed afore 'e was born. Turns out 'e were alive and kickin' all this time."

"Who was he?" Daniel asked, keeping his tone nonchalant. Charles seemed willing to talk, and Daniel had no wish to spook him and force him to retreat behind a wall of silence, as witnesses often did when they realized they had valuable information.

"Some rich cove as tumbled 'er and left 'er. Didn't give 'er a farthing for Alex's upkeep."

"Did his father know about Alex?"

"His ma wrote to 'im. Begged 'im for 'elp, 'specially once her eyes started to go and she couldn't earn as much from 'er needlework. That's when she moved them to this shithole. Afore that, they lived in Clerkenwell, I think."

"Was that why Alex traveled to Birch Hill? To confront his father?" Daniel asked, his body thrumming with excitement. He was finally getting somewhere.

"'E would 'a, but 'is ma told 'im 'is da 'ad popped 'is clogs a few months back. Seen it in a newspaper."

"Did Alex come up with another plan?" Daniel asked.

"'E must of. 'E said 'e 'ad summat as would make them all stand up and take notice. Summat that'd bring 'em to their knees."

"Like what?"

"Like a marriage certificate," Charles said triumphantly. "Alex showed it to me. They was married, Margaret and the rich cove, so Alex was 'is legitimate heir."

"What was the man's name?" Daniel asked. He found he was holding his breath.

"Robert Chadwick."

Daniel let out a low whistle. He'd entertained the possibility that Robert Chadwick had been Alexander McDougal's natural father, but the existence of a marriage certificate came as a shock. "Are you sure, Charles?"

"'Course I'm sure. Saw it meself, didn't I? They was married in Scotland nine months afore Alex were born."

"So why did Alex's father abandon his wife?" This didn't make sense. If the certificate Charles had seen was legitimate, then Robert Chadwick had married Margaret before he'd married Caroline. Unless he'd had the marriage annulled or obtained a divorce, Margaret had been his lawful wife and Alexander his heir.

"Cause 'e were a lily-livered coward, that's why," Charles spat out. "When 'e told 'is own da 'e'd married the daughter of the mine captain, 'is da told 'im to end it. She weren't good enough for the likes of 'im, and 'is father wouldn't sanction the marriage. Said 'e'd cut 'im off without a farthing."

"But if they were married in a church, the marriage was legal and binding," Daniel argued.

"They married in a Popish church on account of 'is mother being Catholic, and the Chadwicks are C of E. The marriage weren't binding for them, not 'aving taken place 'afore their

Protestant God," Charles said with disgust. "Chadwick married what's-'er-name within the year, despite already being wed to Alex's ma."

"Did Alex change once he'd found out the truth?" Daniel asked. He could understand Alexander McDougal's rage. All his life he'd known nothing but poverty and isolation, and all the while, he'd been the son of one of the richest men in the land, an heir to a great estate. And what had Margaret's life been like, knowing that she was bound to Robert Chadwick before God, unable to move on with her life because all that time she had been married to a man who wanted nothing to do with her?

"Oh, aye, 'e changed," Charles spat out. "Started puttin' on airs. Got a fancy suit, took 'imself to the theater. Even got a walking stick and a cigarette holder—thought it made 'im posh. Fancied 'e'd be living the good life real soon."

"So, he went to Birch Hill to blackmail the family?" Daniel asked, hoping Charles would confirm his suspicions.

Charles shook his head vehemently. "'Aven't ye been listening, guv? Alex were not the blackmailing kind. 'E went to claim what was rightfully 'is. It were that simple."

"And he was killed for his pains."

"Aye, 'e was."

"Charles, do you know where the marriage certificate is?" Daniel asked.

"I reckon 'e took it with 'im to show 'is father's other wife. It were 'is only proof."

"Thank you, Charles. You've been most helpful," Daniel said, suddenly weary. If what Charles had told him was true, Alex had stirred up a hornet's nest, and now Daniel had to do the same if he meant to flush out the killer.

"Promise me ye'll see 'em 'ang. Promise me," Charles growled.

"I promise," Daniel said, but the words felt hollow.

157

Daniel left the tavern and headed toward the train station on foot. He needed time to think. He had no proof that what Charles had told him was the truth, but the information fit the facts. Alex, who'd believed that his father had died years before, had discovered that his father had been very much alive for most of his life, and a wealthy man to boot. Daniel wasn't sure what had driven Margaret to tell Alexander the truth at last. Perhaps it was the fear of approaching death, or perhaps it was a desire to see Alexander get what was rightfully his. He'd been a man of twenty with his whole life ahead of him, and he'd had the proof he needed to support his claim.

Daniel took a sharp right to avoid a pile of refuse and nearly stepped out in front of a dray wagon in his distracted state. He cursed under his breath and jumped back onto the filthy sidewalk. Quickening his steps in agitation, he pondered whether Alexander might have tried to stake his claim legally. He didn't think so. Having grown up in Seven Dials, where the law was synonymous with imprisonment and execution, Alexander might have distrusted the system and thought he wouldn't get anywhere through legal channels. But had he really thought the Chadwicks would welcome him with open arms? Had he really believed they'd simply hand over the estate that would pass to Harry once the colonel *popped his clogs*, as Charles had so crudely put it?

And what of Robert Chadwick? Had he really been a polygamist? Charles had mentioned that Margaret had been the daughter of a mine captain. Daniel didn't know the particulars, but everyone in Birch Hill had heard that the Chadwicks had made their fortune mining coal. It was entirely possible that they owned coal pits in Scotland and that Robert Chadwick had met Margaret while visiting the site. Perhaps he'd even fallen in love with her, but his feelings hadn't been deep enough to risk his future. Faced with the threat of being disinherited, he'd left Margaret and kept the marriage a secret from his family.

Daniel entered the train station and purchased a ticket, ignoring the plucky young lad who was selling penny bloods by the door. On any other day, he would have purchased the periodical to read on the train ride, but his mind was completely focused on the case. Why hadn't Margaret confronted Robert? Why had she kept quiet when she knew full well that his marriage to Caroline wasn't valid and she had leverage that could destroy him?

Had Robert Chadwick threatened her? Had he paid her off? Was that how Margaret had been able to afford to live in Clerkenwell for years before running out of money and being forced to relocate to Seven Dials? Or had the marriage not been legal? Daniel had heard of wealthy men staging fake weddings to bed women they desired, then leaving them without so much as a word of farewell once they'd satisfied their lust. Could Robert Chadwick have tricked Margaret into such a marriage, then left her once he tired of her? Was that why he'd ignored her letters and refused to send money for his son's upkeep, because he'd believed Margaret had no recourse? Had Robert Chadwick really been that callous?

Daniel found an empty carriage and boarded the train, shutting the door behind him with a bang. He'd known Robert Chadwick. Not well, but well enough to take the man's measure. He'd been soft-spoken and polite, devoted to his wife and children, but many a man wore a mask in public. Robert Chadwick had been a liar and a fraud, and Alexander McDougal had been the only living person who'd known that. He'd paid for that knowledge with his life.

Daniel realized he was tapping his foot on the floor of the train carriage in his excitement. It was all coming together now. Having finally learned the truth of his parentage, Alex had been angry and desperate to act. He'd been naively hopeful that his father's wife would step aside once she discovered the truth and allow him to claim what was rightfully his, but Caroline Chadwick was not a woman to be trifled with. She would not allow some upstart from Seven Dials to steal her son's inheritance and humiliate her and her children before the world. If the truth had been allowed to come out, it would have revealed that her marriage to Robert Chadwick had never been legal and her children were illegitimate, ruining any chance they had of a promising future.

Feeling cornered, Caroline had had Alexander McDougal disposed of, but the marriage certificate hadn't been on his person at the time of the murder, so she'd sent someone to find it, which explained the break-ins at Mrs. Harris's house. Daniel still didn't know why Alexander had been killed in the church, but the motive was now crystal clear. Caroline Chadwick had to be behind it, but she wouldn't have been the one to do the killing, he thought bitterly. People like her got others to do their dirty work for them—but who? It would be someone Caroline Chadwick thought of as disposable, someone who'd face the full extent of the law should they be caught. She would be an accessory to murder, but only if anyone could prove that she'd arranged for Alexander McDougal to be killed, and a clever woman like her would never leave evidence lying around that would lead back to her.

Daniel stared out the window morosely as he considered this theory. It was plausible, but there could be other equally reasonable possibilities. Harry Chadwick had the most to lose if his older brother made the marriage certificate public. Harry was only a year and a half younger than Alexander, but he was taller and broader, having enjoyed a plentiful diet, fresh air, and sporting activities, unlike Alexander, who'd lived in abject poverty. Harry was often seen tearing through the countryside on his stallion and was fond of fencing. A fencing instructor came to Chadwick Manor three times a week from Brentwood and had been employed by the Chadwick family for at least two years. Daniel had met the man at last year's church fete, and they'd spent a few minutes chatting while they waited in line for tea and sponge. Harry was strong enough to drag Alexander's body down to the crypt and lift him into the tomb, and he was young and careless enough to leave a trail of bloodstains before fleeing the scene. Harry was also agile enough to scale the wall behind Mrs. Harris's house and then climb in through the window or sneak in through the back door.

Daniel considered the rest of the family. Colonel Chadwick was seriously ill and had rarely been seen in public since the death of his son. One didn't have to be a medical man to notice his jaundiced appearance or the way he leaned on his stick as he progressed up the nave toward the Chadwick family pew at St. Catherine's. Charles Boyd believed the colonel had known about the marriage, so it was reasonable to assume that he'd also known about Alexander. He'd taken no steps toward preventing Margaret from going to the authorities, so it didn't seem likely that he'd felt threatened by his son's secret marriage, perhaps because he either knew it to be fraudulent or was secure in the knowledge that it was no longer valid. It was entirely possible that Robert Chadwick had never formally informed Margaret that the marriage had been annulled or that he'd divorced her and married Caroline openly and legally. And if he'd assumed that Margaret had remained in Scotland after he absconded, he'd have no reason to suspect that she ever knew about his marriage to Caroline.

There were also Arabella and Lucinda, but Daniel dismissed them from his mind. Not only were they too young and sheltered, but they didn't have the physical strength to pull off such a feat. Besides, whoever had killed Alexander had known something of anatomy. The man had been killed with one thrust of the blade, delivered directly to the heart. Daniel knew of one person on the Chadwick estate who was not only strong enough, but knowledgeable enough to carry out such a clean kill. John Marin. Would John kill on his mistress's orders? In truth, Daniel had no idea. John was a good man, by all accounts, but he was also a man whose livelihood depended entirely on the Chadwicks. He'd been a gamekeeper on the Chadwick estate for at least fifteen years, as had been his father before him. Birch Hill was not a place where John could easily find other employment if sacked. He'd have to apply to other estates and move his family to God-knew-where in pursuit of a new position.

Daniel leaned back against the seat and closed his eyes, his shoulders sagging in defeat. He now had a motive and several possible suspects, but he didn't have a shred of physical evidence, and no one would take the word of a tavernkeeper's son. Charles Boyd was the only person to have seen the phantom marriage certificate with his own eyes, but his evidence would be seen as nothing more than hearsay in a court of law and easily dismissed. Caroline Chadwick was a pillar of the community, a woman who devoted much of her time to charitable works, and Harry Chadwick was a nineteen-year-old boy who'd be given an alibi by his mother should his movements the night of the murder come into question. Daniel also strongly doubted that Caroline Chadwick would give up her gamekeeper, since he might point the finger at her under the threat of the noose. Without the marriage certificate, the murder weapon, or a confession, Daniel had nothing to build his case on. The Chadwicks would get off scot-free, especially since Squire Talbot was a longtime friend of the family and wouldn't care to be tainted by association.

The train finally chugged into Brentwood station and screeched to a stop, the billowing smoke from the stack momentarily enveloping the platform in a thick haze. Daniel shoved his hat onto his head, picked up his umbrella, and headed out into the late afternoon, his mind teeming with questions and his heart heavy with a sense of failure.

Chapter 23

Friday, June 8

Jason presented himself at the gates to Chadwick Manor at 10:00 a.m., as instructed, eager to meet with John Marin. He briefly wondered if he might be violating some unspoken rule of British etiquette by consulting Mrs. Chadwick's gamekeeper without her express permission but didn't allow the thought to deter him. He was an ignorant American come to ask for advice, and that was the story he'd stick with if challenged. Being a foreigner had its advantages, since people saw him as a curiosity.

As John Marin approached the gate, Jason took the opportunity to assess the man. He appeared to be a few years older than Joe and was tall and broad, his skin weathered to a deep bronze from all the time he must spend outdoors. Jason tipped his hat to the man, and John Marin took off his own as a sign of respect, revealing black hair liberally sprinkled with gray and shapely eyebrows furrowed over deep-set blue eyes that studied Jason warily. He didn't smile or offer a greeting, waiting for Jason to speak.

"Good morning, Mr. Marin. I had the pleasure of meeting Tom yesterday. You have a fine boy," Jason said, finally eliciting something resembling a reaction from the man.

He nodded his thanks. "Aye, he's a good lad. How may I be of service, your lordship?"

"Would you be so kind as to show me something of the parkland, Mr. Marin? I can ask my questions while we walk."

The man looked a bit dubious, so Jason rushed to reassure him. "Don't worry. I will clear any awkwardness with your mistress, should the need arise."

"Very well, then. Come."

They walked along the drive for a few minutes before turning right. The parkland beyond was thick and lush, the sun-dappled leaves forming a green canopy above their heads as they left the lawn and entered the woodland, the trilling of birds the only sound. Jason took a deep breath, enjoying the scents of pine and resin that filled the air. It'd been a long time since he'd walked in the woods, not since he'd gone riding with Cecilia in Newport. Jason pushed the memory aside and turned to his companion.

"As you probably know, my grandfather hadn't employed a gamekeeper in some years. He became something of a recluse, I'm told, and limited his entertaining to a few intimate soirees for close friends. I know precious little of hunting parties, so thought I'd consult an expert before making any decisions on how to proceed. I might have friends visiting from America later this summer, and I'd like to introduce them to some honored British pastimes," he added lamely.

John Marin listened to Jason's blathering with silent respect, nodding his head in agreement when Jason admitted to knowing nothing of 'honored British pastimes.'

"What would you suggest?" Jason asked, wishing the man would abandon his reserve and speak.

"Well, my lord, with all due respect, before you plan any parties, I'd suggest you find a competent man. One does not simply take guests hunting without making the necessary preparations."

"Such as?" Jason asked, genuinely curious.

"Pheasant and partridge shooting usually take place 'round October, and the birds need to be bred in advance, so I don't think you'll be in a position to oblige your friends this year."

"Well, that's disappointing," Jason said, frowning as if not having enough birds to shoot were his biggest problem.

"If you're so inclined, you can invite your friends to do some grouse shooting in Scotland. There are estates that cater to gentlemen like yourself, who like to come up for a week or two for some sport. If that idea is not to your liking, you can always stalk deer."

"Deer are such lovely creatures," Jason said. "It's a shame to kill them."

"Deer breed like rabbits if you don't keep them in check," John said, shaking his head at Jason's ignorance. "You don't want your estate overrun. Besides, your friends are sure to enjoy the venison, most specially if they don't eat it much where you come from."

"No, venison is not a dinner staple in New York," Jason replied. "And what about fishing? I quite like fishing."

By this time, they'd approached the lake. The placid surface shimmered in the sun, the clouds floating overhead reflecting in the water as if the lake were a mirror. A narrow path encircled the lake, and a wooden jetty stuck out at the far end, with a rowboat tied to a post.

"Is this lake stocked with fish?" Jason inquired.

"No, your lordship. Mr. Robert did not enjoy fishing, as such. Mrs. Chadwick and the young ladies like to walk by the lake, and Mr. Harry occasionally takes out the skiff, but he doesn't fish either."

"And the colonel?" Jason asked.

John Marin looked surprised by the question. "The colonel has been spending more time at the manor recently, on account of his health, but he's a city man through and through. Likes to stay in London, where he can visit his club and meet up with his army friends to talk over old times."

Jason was surprised John Marin knew so much of the colonel's activities but was grateful for the information, nonetheless. "I see. Do the Chadwicks bring their guests here? It's such a peaceful spot."

"No, they don't," John Marin replied.

"Is the lake deep?"

"Deep enough."

"Do you ever go swimming?" Jason asked, smiling at the gamekeeper. "I had a friend whose family owned a summer house in upstate New York. There was a lake nearby. We went swimming nearly every day when I visited him."

"That must have been nice for you, my lord."

Jason could tell the man was beginning to lose his patience. He'd answered Jason's questions to the best of his ability and was eager to be rid of him.

"I've no doubt you have duties to be getting on with," Jason said. "I appreciate you taking the time to instruct me. I'll give what you said some thought and perhaps place an advertisement in the paper seeking the kind of individual you've recommended."

"Glad to be of service, my lord." John Marin looked relieved to be set free.

"Would it be all right if I took a walk by the lake?" Jason asked. "It brings back such wonderful memories. I'm sure Mrs. Chadwick won't mind."

An expression of extreme annoyance crossed the gamekeeper's face, but it was so fleeting, Jason had to ask himself if he'd really seen it. He was putting the man in an awkward position by forcing him to either agree—something he had no right to do without his mistress's permission—or be rude to someone who was socially his superior and had the power to do John Marin and his family potential harm by complaining to Mrs. Chadwick about his insolence. Choosing the lesser of two evils, John Marin inclined his head.

"Of course, your lordship. Enjoy your walk. Do you remember how to get back to the gates?"

"I do. Again, thank you for your help, Mr. Marin." Jason extracted a half crown from his pocket and held it out to the gamekeeper. "For your trouble."

John Marin looked surprised but accepted the coin and pocketed it quickly. "Thank you, my lord. Much obliged."

Jason gazed at the lake until John Marin took his leave, then started to walk, his eyes glued to the path and the growth beyond. If Mrs. Chadwick didn't bring guests to this spot, then what had Alexander McDougal been doing here? Perhaps he had trespassed on Chadwick land and dropped his cigarette holder while walking by the lake. Or maybe he'd stopped to enjoy a cheroot, heard someone coming, and lost the case in his haste to get away unseen. Or had he been there at all? Could the person who'd ransacked his room have dropped the cigarette holder in his hurry to dispose of Alexander's possessions? And if that were the case, where would he have stashed them? He might have hidden them in the woods or tossed them into a lake that no one fished.

It took Jason nearly an hour to walk all around the lake, but to his chagrin, he found nothing. Even if he could prove that Alexander McDougal had been there, it gave him no insight into who'd wanted him dead.

Retracing his steps, Jason headed back toward the gates. He saw John Marin as he passed the gamekeeper's cottage. The man was in his shirtsleeves, sawing wooden planks in half. He appeared to be building something. Jason gave a friendly wave, and the gamekeeper nodded in acknowledgement, the rhythmic motion of his arm never slowing as he continued to saw. Jason left the shadow of the wood and stepped onto the gravel drive, the gates in his sights, when he heard a voice behind him.

"Good morning, Captain."

Jason pivoted on his heel to find Colonel Chadwick behind him. He'd been walking on the verge lining the drive, the sound of his steps muffled by the grass.

"Good morning, Colonel," Jason replied. "How do you do?"

"Very well. Just out for my morning constitutional. Never miss a day."

"Today is a fine day for it," Jason remarked, wondering if the old man had seen him emerging from the woods.

"Indeed, it is. My favorite kind of weather. Summers in England are so unpredictable; must take advantage of every lovely day. Were you coming to call on my daughter-in-law?" the colonel asked as he fell into step with Jason, slightly out of breath. Jason slowed his steps so as not to embarrass the older man, who was clearly fighting with every ounce of will he had against the disease that was sure to kill him soon.

The colonel returned the kindness by not commenting on the fact that it was too early to be paying morning calls, which were actually paid in the afternoon, and embarrassing Jason, which Jason thought he might have greatly enjoyed under different circumstances. This was another strange British tradition he chose not to question but was grateful that Dodson was there to guide him through the myriad pitfalls that awaited him in his ignorance.

"I actually came by to consult Mr. Marin. I was thinking of engaging a gamekeeper and needed some advice. I'm afraid I didn't ask Mrs. Chadwick for her permission."

"Cheeky of you," the colonel replied with an amused smile. "Don't worry, Captain, your secret is safe with me. If there's anything you'd like to ask, you can always come to me. Unlike my son, I've always enjoyed a bit of sport." He smiled suggestively, reminding Jason that some Brits saw wenching as a sport. It was perfectly acceptable to go to a brothel with one's friends for an evening of drinking and fornication and then spend a pleasant half hour comparing the charms of the women they'd enjoyed.

"Thank you, Colonel. I will."

"Come November, we'll introduce you to riding to hounds," the colonel said. "Squire Talbot hosts an annual fox hunt. You should practice your equestrian skills. It's not easy to keep your seat when you're not accustomed to the terrain. In fact, since you've already made the acquaintance of John Marin," the colonel said tartly, "you should ask for his advice when buying yourself a horse. He's quite the expert on horseflesh."

"We have horses," Jason replied.

The colonel let out a guffaw. "You are unenlightened, aren't you? You don't use the same horses for pulling a carriage as you do for hunting, my boy. Your grandfather would have been horrified by your ignorance."

"Then perhaps it's a good thing he's not here to see it," Jason replied, failing to keep the annoyance out of his voice.

"You need a field hunter," the colonel continued, as if Jason hadn't spoken. "Perhaps the squire will lend you one of his," he added, shaking his head as if there were no hope for Jason.

"That would be most kind of him," Jason replied. He had no intention of going fox hunting, even if he still found himself in England come November.

"Well, since you're not coming up to the house, I think I'll leave you here. Nothing like a hearty breakfast after a brisk walk. Lucinda will be waiting for me to join her. She is a dear girl. Spirited, not like her sister, whose sensibilities are so delicate, she swoons several times a day. That ninny," the colonel added under his breath.

Perhaps it's not her sensibilities that are the problem, Jason thought, recalling Arabella's plumpness. If he were a betting man, he'd say that her corset was laced so tightly, the poor girl could scarcely draw breath.

"Enjoy your breakfast, sir," Jason said politely. "My regards to Miss Lucinda."

The colonel tipped his hat and headed toward the house, leaving Jason to his own thoughts.

When Jason returned home, he found Micah watching for him from the drawing room window.

"Where've you been?" Micah demanded. "You weren't at breakfast."

"I went to Chadwick Manor to speak to Tom's father," Jason explained.

"Why? What'd you want with him?"

"I just had some questions about organizing a hunting party."

Micah looked astonished. "You hate hunting."

"I know. It was just a ruse. I simply wanted to question him regarding the case," Jason explained.

"What's with you and this case?" Micah asked petulantly. "Why can't you leave well enough alone and let the constable do his job?"

Jason considered the question for a moment. He had to word his response carefully, so as not to upset Micah, but he felt the need to explain what was driving him to help Daniel Haze in his inquiry. "Micah, no one deserves to be murdered and stuffed into someone else's coffin. Even in death, people deserve respect and a sense of closure. Alexander McDougal has no one left to mourn him, but he might have, and they would be entitled to know what happened to him and why, just as you need to know what happened to Mary."

Micah's eyes filled with tears, and he hung his head in misery, clasping his hands in his lap to keep them from shaking.

"I'm not saying Mary is dead," Jason quickly corrected himself. "I only meant that unless someone finds her, you'll never know what became of her."

"So, you're that someone? You need to find out what happened to this Alexander McDougal?"

"Someone must. He deserves justice."

"Few people get justice in this world," Micah said quietly. "You know that as well as I do."

"Dying in a time of war is different than being murdered in cold blood," Jason argued, even though he agreed with Micah wholeheartedly.

"Dying is dying," Micah said. "Pa and Patrick don't even have a proper grave."

"I know," Jason said softly. "I know. What do you say we go for a ride? The chestnuts need exercising, don't they?"

Micah looked up. "Yeah. I suppose."

"Come on. It'll be fun. We can ask Mrs. Dodson to pack us a picnic lunch. Would you like that?"

"I guess. Can I still have a picnic with Tom, though?" Micah asked, as though suddenly worried that Jason would change his mind.

"Of course, you can. Have you set a date?"

"Saturday," Micah replied. He still looked sad, but Jason though he saw a hint of a smile.

"Saturday it is, then. Come on."

Chapter 24

Daniel slept badly. He kept dreaming of being trapped in the tomb with Alexander McDougal, the dead man's mouth set in a scowl of despair, his eyes accusing. When Daniel woke, his nightshirt was damp with sweat and his head pounded, the pain originating behind the eyes and reverberating into his temples. He reached for his watch and flipped open the lid, swearing under his breath when he saw the time. It'd gone ten and he had yet to get out of bed. Daniel tore off the soiled shirt, washed and dressed, and hurried downstairs. It was Friday, the last day before the inquest, and he still had no case.

"Good morning, Harriet," Daniel said to his mother-in-law, whom he'd found in the morning room, nursing a cup of tea. He still felt awkward calling her by her Christian name, but she'd insisted, claiming that it was needlessly formal for him to refer to her as Mrs. Elderman in her own home.

"Good morning, Daniel. Are you all right?" she asked.

Daniel had never expected Harriet to become an ally, but since Felix's death, she'd been extra careful with him, cognizant of the pain caused by Sarah's aloofness toward him and sympathetic to his frustration with the situation. She'd loved Felix as much as any of them, but she'd lost a child in infancy, Sarah's older sister, and understood like no one else the necessity of allowing yourself to grieve and move on. "Man proposes and God disposes," she'd said when Sarah had raged at the unfairness of Felix's death. "It's not for you to question his will. You still have a husband to care for." But the words had fallen on deaf ears.

"I'm well. Thank you," Daniel replied. He sat down at the table and reached for the still-hot teapot, pouring himself a cup of tea. He added milk and sugar and asked Tilda, their maid, to bring him a fried egg and toast. The steam from the tea fogged up his glasses, making Harriet appear a bit hazy around the edges.

"Have you made any progress on the case?" Harriet asked once Tilda had departed.

"Yes and no. I have a fairly good idea of what got Alexander McDougal killed, but I still don't know who did it. There are several suspects, but, at this stage, it's all supposition."

"Why was he killed?" Harriet asked. "What you share with me will never leave this room," she said, smiling at him gently.

"I know. It's just that this information has the power to destroy several lives, some of them innocent."

"Now I'm really curious," Harriet replied.

Daniel glanced toward the door to make sure Tilda wasn't skulking around outside. She was a notorious gossip, and he wouldn't care for her to overhear what he was about to say. Tilda was likely still in the kitchen, waiting for Cook to finish cooking his breakfast, but he lowered his voice, nonetheless.

"According to a close friend of the victim, Alexander McDougal was in possession of a marriage certificate that proved beyond a shadow of a doubt that Margaret McDougal and Robert Chadwick were his parents and had been legally married. The marriage predated his marriage to Caroline Chadwick. If it were made public, the consequences to the Chadwicks would be catastrophic, since not only would it show that Caroline Chadwick wasn't Robert Chadwick's lawful wife, but that his children were born out of wedlock and Alexander was his lawful heir."

"But all you have is this person's word for it?" Harriet asked.

"Yes. The only way to prove the validity of the marriage would be to travel to Scotland, but I haven't got the time, nor do I know where in Scotland the Chadwick concerns are located."

"Rutherglen," Harriet replied without missing a beat.

"How do you know that?"

"Caroline Chadwick mentioned it only a few weeks ago when we were having a chat after the Sunday service. She said that Harry would have to make the journey north to visit the coal pits, since Colonel Chadwick is not up to the task. She said it was time he familiarized himself with the business. I don't think she expects her father-in-law to be around much longer. He has been looking rather ill these last few months. So, you think this boy, Alexander McDougal, tried to blackmail the Chadwicks?"

Daniel shook his head. "I don't believe he tried to blackmail them. I think he tried to claim what was rightfully his. He wanted the lot."

"And got himself killed for his pains."

"Exactly."

Daniel smiled in anticipation as Tilda entered the room and placed a plate heaped with fried eggs, mushrooms, sausages, and a grilled tomato before him. She set a rack of toast on the table and looked at him for approval, which he was more than ready to give.

"Thank you, Tilda. That will be all." She departed, leaving the door open behind her.

"She forgot the butter," Daniel grumbled, but made no move to summon her back.

"So, who do you think killed him?" Harriet asked, her eyes sparkling with curiosity.

"I still don't know. My money would be on Caroline, but I can't imagine she'd do the killing herself. Nor would she endanger her son."

"Who, then?"

Daniel shrugged. "Your guess is as good as mine."

Harriet took a sip of her tea, her gaze piercing over the rim of the cup. "John Marin," she said as soon as she set down the cup.

"What?"

"John Marin."

"I have considered the possibility, but why do you think it was him?" Daniel asked, astounded by how quickly his mother-in-law had put forth a name.

Harried tilted her head to the side, as if debating whether to tell him, but, in the end, her desire to help won out. "John Marin came out of St. Catherine's with his wife and son just as Caroline and I were speaking. He tipped his hat to her, and she blushed in a way no grieving widow blushes when faced with an employee."

"She blushed?" Daniel echoed. "You accuse a man of murder based on a blush? Maybe she grew too warm."

"Oh, she grew warm, all right," Harriet said with relish. "Look, Daniel, you might think me a dried-up old crone, a woman widowed these twenty years, but I know a look of desire when I see one. And it wasn't one-sided either. He looked at her like a man who knows a thing or two about the woman hiding beneath that prim mourning gown."

"So, you think that Caroline Chadwick and John Marin are lovers, and that he killed Alexander McDougal at her behest?"

"I think it's very possible. I mean, who else would do it?"

"Harry?" Daniel suggested lamely.

Harriet shook her head. "Not a chance. Harry is as squeamish as a girl. The colonel wanted to purchase him a commission in the army for his eighteenth birthday. Harry flat out refused, just as his own father had. To the colonel's endless disappointment, Harry takes after his father, whose greatest pleasure was tinkering with his stamp collection and spending a peaceful evening at his club in London."

Daniel gave Harriet a questioning look.

"I was on friendly terms with Imelda Chadwick, Robert's mother. God rest her soul. She was a quiet, self-contained woman who preferred to remain at her country estate while the colonel was stationed in India. Of course, he wasn't a colonel then. I think she was happiest when he was away. She invited me for tea often and spoke to me of her children."

"There's a sister, isn't there?" Daniel asked as he reached for a second piece of toast.

"Yes, Robert Chadwick had a sister. She lives up north. Newcastle, I believe. She and the colonel are not on the best of terms. She hasn't been seen in Birch Hill since before her wedding."

"I see," Daniel said.

"What do you see?" Harriet asked playfully.

"I see that I must question Caroline Chadwick again."

Harriet nodded. "Well, don't rush your breakfast. Caroline won't see you before one o'clock."

"No, but John Marin will." Daniel mopped up the last of his egg with a leftover piece of crust and wiped his mouth. "Thank you, Harriet. You've been a great help."

"You're welcome. I only wish I could be a help to you in other areas of your life." She sighed as she rose from the table. "I would dearly love to have another grandchild," she said wistfully.

And I would dearly love to make love to my wife. And if wishes were horses, beggars would ride, he thought ruefully, recalling the old proverb.

Chapter 25

Normally, Daniel would have walked, but time was short, so he took the dogcart and made his way to the Chadwick estate. It had been overcast when he'd woken, but now the sun was peeking from behind wispy clouds, the clear blue sky heralding another fine day.

As the horse trotted down the lane, Daniel considered his upcoming interview with John Marin and felt his heart sink with the futility of the task. John Marin was not a man who could be easily intimidated, nor would he ever betray a confidence. Even if Harriet was correct in her supposition that Caroline Chadwick and John Marin were having an affair, if that was what a liaison between the lady of the house and her gamekeeper could be described as, he'd never admit to it, even if Daniel asked him straight out. To ask such a question of Caroline Chadwick would amount to professional suicide. One word to Squire Talbot and he'd be immediately dismissed.

Daniel shook his head in frustration as he continued his internal argument. No, speaking to Caroline Chadwick would get him nowhere, and putting John Marin's guard up would yield no results. But there was one person who'd talk, Daniel thought suddenly. Arlene Marin. He sat up straighter and urged the horse to go faster. If he were lucky, he'd find Mrs. Marin alone and would have a chance to question her without John's hulking presence forcing her to mind her p's and q's.

Having decided on this course of action, Daniel drove the dogcart to the village. Arriving at the Chadwick estate and leaving his horse and cart with a groom would be paramount to showing his hand, so he drove directly to the Red Stag. Matty Locke was in the stables, mucking out a stall.

"Hey, Matty. I need a small favor," Daniel said, sizing up the lad. At fifteen, Matty was tall and slim, his face covered with spots. His hair was a bit greasy and his shirt was none too clean, but he'd do the trick.

"I can't, Mr. Haze; I'm working."

"Don't worry. I'll clear it with Brody. It'll take no more than an hour of your time, and you will be well compensated."

Matty shrugged. "If Mr. Brody will let me go, I'm all yers, Constable."

Daniel turned on his heel and marched into the Red Stag. He had no intention of clearing his plan with Davy Brody, since he knew the publican wouldn't be there. It was Friday, and Davy went into Brentwood on Friday mornings to purchase stock for the bar. Since he could no longer smuggle in French brandy and avoid the crippling taxes and visits from the excise men, he had to find legal alternatives for a reasonable price. Daniel had no doubt that what Davy was buying in Brentwood had shady origins, but, just now, Davy's clandestine dealings were working in Daniel's favor, since he needed Matty's help and Davy would have refused on principle. Moll was a different matter, though.

Moll smiled sweetly when she spotted Daniel. "Good morning, Constable. Nice to see ye again so soon. Were ye passing by and found ye 'ad a mighty 'unger on ye that couldn't be denied?" Moll asked coyly, her gaze sliding to Daniel's crotch, a maneuver that he found crass and off-putting in a young woman, even in jest. "I'm afraid it's too early for luncheon, but I'm sure I could think of something if you're in dire need."

Daniel matched Moll's sly grin. "As it happens, I am in need, but not of sustenance. I came to ask you if I might borrow Matty for an hour."

"What d'ye need 'im for?" Moll asked, clearly disappointed. Had she really expected him to fall for her antics?

Daniel tapped the side of his nose. "Police business," he said, lowering his voice. "Highly confidential."

"Oh, go on, then. Uncle Davy would never stand in the way of justice," Moll said with a giggle. She knew all about her uncle's run-ins with the law. "Just have 'im back 'ere by noon, ye 'ear?"

"You have my word."

Daniel thanked Moll and returned to the stables. "Come on, Matty. You're with me."

"What d'ye want me to do, then?" Matty asked as he climbed into the dogcart.

"I need you to drive me to Chadwick Manor, drop me off at the gate, then bide somewhere—out of sight, mind you—until I've finished. Can you do that?"

"Oh, aye," Matty replied, no doubt thrilled to have an hour to himself.

Daniel was pleased to find Arlene Marin alone. She was in the yard, hanging laundry, when he approached the cottage. She looked surprised but tried to hide her dismay behind a welcoming smile. "Good day, Constable. John is not here."

"Oh, that's a shame," Daniel said, feigning disappointment. "I was hoping to have a word."

"He'll come back in time for dinner," she said, hanging up the last shirt and picking up the empty basket. "Would you care to wait?"

Daniel made a show of pulling out his pocket watch and flipping it open. It was a quarter past eleven, and he only needed a few moments of Arlene's time. Perfect. He could leave well before John came back for dinner.

"Yes, if I may."

He followed Arlene into the house. It was immaculately clean and very tidy. The smell of stewed meat filled the small living area, and a jug of wildflowers stood on the scrubbed table. Arlene pointed to a chair and Daniel took a seat, his gaze straying to the mantel of the stone fireplace, where a photograph of John and Arlene stood in pride of place.

"That was taken on our wedding day. Thirteen years ago, now," Arlene said sadly. "We were happy then."

Daniel made no comment, partially because his gaze had settled on a musket that hung on the wall above the portrait, the bayonet gleaming in the light streaming through the window.

"Is that John's?" Daniel asked, tilting his head to get a better look.

"Oh, no. That there belonged to John's granddad," Arlene said, following Daniel's gaze. "He fought Napoleon in Spain, and in Portugal, I think."

"That's quite something," Daniel said. The bayonet looked sharp and lethal and appeared to have been recently cleaned. "John keeps it in good order, I see. Does it still work?"

"Oh, yes, but he never uses it. It's just there for show. A bit of family history, you might say. He does clean it from time to time. I'm not allowed to touch it," Arlene said, shaking her head. "He thinks I'll do myself an injury. Can I offer you a cup of ale?"

"Thank you. That would be nice." Daniel accepted the cup and took a sip. "Wonderful. Do you make it yourself?"

"Lord, no. I've enough to be getting on with. John buys a cask from Davy Brody once a week. He likes his ale, John."

"Won't you join me?" Daniel asked.

Arlene hesitated for a moment, then poured herself a cup and sat down at the table across from him. "How's the investigation going?" she asked.

Daniel shook his head. "Not well, which is why I'm asking every man in the village to account for his movements on Saturday night—to rule them out, you understand," he added.

"Oh, I see. Well, John was here with me."

"All evening?" Arlene nodded. "He went down for a kip when he came home 'round four. He finished early on Saturday. He woke 'bout an hour later and he and Tom sat outside for a time while I got supper ready. We ate, then went to bed around ten."

"He never left the house?"

Arlene shook her head. "No."

"So, he didn't receive a summons from the big house?" Daniel asked nonchalantly.

Arlene's expression instantly changed, her lips pursing in annoyance. "No. Why would he?"

"I don't know. I heard Mrs. Chadwick can be a demanding employer."

"Oh, she's demanding, all right. You'd think she wouldn't be interested in what John does, but she pokes her nose into everything."

"Does John resent being called to the house so frequently?" Daniel asked.

"Not as much as he should. He runs to her like a dog to its master," Arlene exclaimed angrily.

"Did Mrs. Chadwick take an interest in estate business before her husband passed?"

"No. It's just these last few months. Wants to know everything all of a sudden. Won't leave John alone. She's a viper, that one," Arlene said, then instantly looked contrite. Speaking of her husband's employer in such scathing terms could lead to John losing his job. She wasn't doing her family any favors by allowing her bitterness to show. "Sorry. I shouldn't have said that. It's just that she…" Arlene's eyes filled with tears. She was still a good-looking woman, but years of hard work had left her looking tired and worn. "He's been different of late, that's all," she whispered, her shoulders sagging in defeat. "He hardly sees me." A tear slid down her cheek, and she wiped it away with the back of her hand. "Sorry," she said again, her head dipping to hide her distress.

Daniel fumbled in his pocket and drew out his watch, as if to check the time, giving Arlene Marin a moment to compose herself. He wished he could comfort her somehow, tell her that he understood what the loss of love did to a heart, to a life, and pour out his heart to her, knowing she'd understand. Daniel pulled out his handkerchief and held it out to her, but she shook her head and used her sleeve to wipe her tears instead. Daniel used the handkerchief to clean his glasses, wondering all the while if it was possible to get love back once it had gone. He didn't think so. Once something was broken, it could never be properly mended. It might still be serviceable, useful even, but it'd never be the same; it would never be perfect.

Arlene finally looked up. "I'm sorry, Constable. I don't know what's come over me."

"It's quite all right," Daniel said. He hadn't meant to, but he reached out and patted her hand. She seemed startled by the gesture but didn't yank her hand away. Instead, she lifted her eyes, gazing at him with sympathy, as if she could see straight into his heart.

"I have just one more question for you," Daniel said as he removed his hand and smiled awkwardly. "Tom found a cigarette holder by the lake. Has he shown it to you?"

Arlene Marin looked thoughtful for a moment. "I haven't seen it. Tom likes to hide his treasures in a tree by the lake. We never go there. It's his special place." She faced the window, her gaze thoughtful. "I suppose the holder might belong to the colonel. He walks there sometimes. Or Mr. Harry."

"The initials on the holder were L.D.'"

Arlene shrugged. "Sorry, can't think of anyone with those initials 'cept Leslie Dodson."

"Does he smoke?"

"I wouldn't know, Constable."

"Does he ever come to Chadwick Manor?" Daniel tried again.

Arlene shook her head. "Why would he?"

Daniel sighed and pushed away his empty mug. "Since you've already accounted for John's movements on Saturday night, there's no reason for me to wait for him. Thank you, Mrs. Marin, and thank you for the ale."

"Oh, you're welcome, Constable. Are you sure you won't wait for John?"

"There's no need. I'll see myself out."

Daniel left the cottage and walked back in the direction he had come, his mind teeming with questions and possibilities. Arlene Marin's reaction to questions about Caroline Chadwick wasn't proof in itself, but it had confirmed Daniel's suspicions that something was going on between Caroline Chadwick and John Marin. It was very much within the realm of possibility that Caroline Chadwick had instructed John Marin to kill Alexander McDougal upon finding out about Robert's first marriage and the threat to her family.

However, Arlene Marin had seemed sincere when she'd said that John had been at home all Saturday evening. Could he have left after she'd fallen asleep and gone to the church to meet Alexander? He could have, Daniel decided. If the Marins had gone to bed around ten o'clock, John Marin could have easily left the cottage once Arlene and Tom were asleep. He could have walked to the village, killed Alexander, and been back in his own bed less than an hour later. John Marin had a motive—Caroline Chadwick's plea or threat. He had the means to carry out a murder—the blade of the bayonet was the right width and would probably match the entry wound on Alexander McDougal's back, and it had recently been cleaned, which couldn't be mere coincidence. And he had opportunity.

If Alexander McDougal had agreed to meet someone at the church, possibly Caroline Chadwick herself, John would have found him alone and unarmed. John Marin was a powerfully built man who'd have no difficulty dragging the victim to the crypt, even if he were unconscious. He was certainly strong enough to push aside the lid and lift the man into the tomb. And, since the cigarette holder had been found by the lake, it stood to reason that John had broken into Mrs. Harris's house, collected Alexander McDougal's possessions, and tossed them into the lake. The holder may have fallen out of the satchel without his knowledge, and Tom could have found it the next time he'd gone to his secret hiding place.

Daniel exhaled loudly. The facts fit into this new theory very neatly, and although he still had no physical proof, he now had a main suspect. Now all he had to do was find a way to prove that John Marin had been the one to stab Alexander McDougal through the heart at the behest of Caroline Chadwick.

"Hello, Constable."

Daniel started. "Eh, good afternoon, miss," he said, tipping his hat.

Lucinda sat astride a dappled gray mare, clad in men's riding britches and a white shirt. Her hair was scraped back from her face and twisted into a low knot, and her eyes blazed with defiance. Arabella was behind her, riding sidesaddle in a riding habit of blue velvet. With her reddish curls and wide blue eyes, she looked regal and beautiful, unlike her sister, who might have been mistaken for a boy.

"What are you doing here?" Arabella asked as she brought her horse to a stop.

"I came to have a word with the gamekeeper, but he wasn't at home," Daniel replied. "It's a fine day for a ride."

"Yes, it is," Lucinda agreed. "Harry was supposed to come with us, but he's been moping for the past few days. He's been as sour as a lemon."

"Has something happened to upset him?" Daniel asked.

"You could say that," Arabella replied, her gaze anxious in her flushed face.

"Arabella, be quiet," Lucinda hissed. "Mama will be cross if you tell anyone."

"I wouldn't tell," Arabella replied, her tone defensive. "Not that it matters. The deed is done, and soon everyone will know."

Lucinda's lip curled. "So what? We must all do our duty to further the interests of the family. Mustn't we, Constable?" she asked playfully. "Well, good luck with your investigation. Are you any closer to finding out who killed that chap?"

"I think I am, actually," Daniel replied. He tipped his hat to the girls and set off toward the gate.

"Where to now, guv?" Matty asked Daniel once he climbed into the dogcart.

"Back to the village. Thanks, Matty."

"Did ye find what ye were looking for?" Matty asked as he skillfully maneuvered the conveyance.

"I think so." Although, since the Chadwick girls had seen him, his attempt at secrecy had failed miserably. They'd no doubt tell their mother they'd seen him as soon as they returned from their ride. "Secrecy be damned," Daniel muttered under his breath. He was on parish business, and he had every right to question whomever he pleased.

"What was that?" Matty asked, his mouth turning up at the corners.

"Nothing. Never mind."

"Whatever ye say, guv."

Having returned Matty to the Red Stag, Daniel headed home. He had no more leads to follow, and he'd hardly seen Sarah all week. It'd be nice to have supper together. It was Friday, and he hoped Cook was making chops and mash—his favorite.

Daniel's gaze fell on the church as he set off. It stood proud and silent, its tower rising against the cobalt blue of the summer sky, as it had for centuries. There wouldn't be anyone there now, but perhaps he could speak to the vicar again. Now that he had a suspect in mind, maybe the reverend would recall something that would support Daniel's theory. He drove to the vicarage and reined in his horse, tying it before walking up the path to knock on the door.

It was opened by Katherine Talbot. She seemed surprised to see him but invited him to come inside. "Are you here to see Father?" she asked as she led him into the shabby parlor and offered him a seat.

"Yes. I thought I might ask him a few more questions about the morning he found the body."

"He's not here at the moment," Katherine said, her voice dipping with sadness. "He was called out to Dr. Miller's house about an hour since. I'm afraid Dr. Miller's taken a turn for the worse."

"Oh dear," Daniel said. "I am sorry to hear that." Mrs. Miller wouldn't have summoned the vicar unless she thought her husband was dying, so the situation had to be dire. "Well, I do hope it's a false alarm," Daniel said lamely.

"As do I. Can I offer you a glass of cider, Constable? It's a warm day out there," Katherine said.

"Thank you. I'm parched, to tell you the truth."

Katherine left and returned with two glasses of cider, one of which she set on a low table in front of Daniel. He took a sip and nodded in appreciation. The cider was cool and delicious. Daniel set the glass back down and leaned against the back of the settee, surveying Katherine's lovely face. She was an intelligent young woman, and very observant. It was worth it to get her impressions, since he was already here.

"Miss Talbot, does your father ever lock the church?" he asked.

"No. Traditionally, a church is a place of sanctuary, so it's always open, should someone need a place of safety."

"Surely not too many people claim sanctuary these days," Daniel remarked. He associated such practices with the Middle Ages, not nineteenth-century England.

"No, they don't, but that doesn't change the fact that the church is still, and always will be, a place where someone can seek refuge."

"I see," Daniel said. "So, anyone can enter at any time."

"Yes."

"Who cleans the church?"

"Janet Dowd. She comes in every Saturday."

"What does she do, exactly?"

"She sweeps the floor, polishes the pews and the pulpit, collects the wilted flowers, and replaces the candles," Katherine explained. She took a dainty sip of her own cider, but her bespectacled gaze never left his face.

"But she hasn't been there since last Saturday, the day before the murder?"

"That's correct."

"Miss Talbot, did you come in contact with Alexander McDougal at all?" Daniel asked. He expected her to say no, just as everyone else had, but she took him by surprise.

"Yes, I did. I met him last Saturday when I was doing the flowers before Evensong."

Daniel sat up straighter, now alert. "Did you speak to him?"

"Yes."

"What about?"

"Nothing of significance. He seemed a pleasant young man and he had lovely manners. He complimented me on the flowers and said he liked old churches. 'They keep all kinds of secrets,' he said."

"Did you know what he meant by that?"

Katherine shrugged. "I suppose he meant that people tell God their troubles and confess their sins," Katherine replied. "It's the one place where people feel they're safe."

"Did he say anything else?"

"Not really. He asked if he may have a look around. He was still there when I finished doing the flowers and left."

Daniel felt a sudden flutter of excitement. He drained the last of his cider and got to his feet. "Thank you, Miss Talbot. You've been very helpful."

"Have I?" she asked, clearly surprised by the compliment.

"More than you know."

Daniel left the vicarage and headed toward the church on foot. The church was a place of sanctuary, a place where people were meant to feel safe and protected. St. Catherine's had weathered nearly eight centuries. It'd seen wars, famine, and plagues, and had survived Henry VIII's Dissolution of the Monasteries. It was not just a building; it was an institution that had withstood the test of time. Was that why Alexander McDougal had chosen to meet his killer there? Did he erroneously assume that no harm would come to him in the house of God? Or did he think the church might be the perfect place to hide his own secret?

Pushing open the heavy oak door, Daniel entered the church and stopped at the end of the nave, his gaze traveling over the wooden pews that were darkened with age, the ornate rood screen, and the stone steps that led up to the altar. The stained-glass windows above depicted the life of St. Catherine of Alexandria, and the round window set into the wall behind the altar was also known as the wheel-window to commemorate the wheel St. Catherine was supposed to have been tortured on for her devotion to Christ and her piety.

Alexander McDougal had probably been raised in the Church of Rome, given that Margaret McDougal had been Catholic, so this church would have been nothing more to him than just another Protestant church converted from a Roman Catholic one after the Dissolution. He likely would not have thought of it as a holy site; still, it was as good a place as any to hide something.

Daniel dismissed the rows of pews, since they were made of wood and didn't have any pockets or crevices where one might hide something of value. Instead, he walked to the front of the church, faced the altar, and stood still, wondering what might have caught Alexander's eye. He lifted the cross and pulled back the altar cloth, but there was nothing there. The cross had been cleaned and the blood washed out of the fine cloth. Had Alexander hidden something beneath, it would have come to light by now. Daniel assumed that since Janet Dowd hadn't been in to clean since Saturday, the cloth would have been attended to by Katherine Talbot, and she hadn't mentioned finding anything. Daniel checked every possible nook but found nothing but evidence of Janet

Dowd's thoroughness. Every surface gleamed with polish, even after nearly a week, and there was very little dust.

Sighing with frustration, Daniel sat down in the first pew and gazed up at the round window. It was lovely. He could recall staring at it as a young boy, mesmerized by the colors and desperate to find something to distract him from the bottom-numbing boredom of sitting through the Sunday service. He'd often snuck peeks at Sarah, who sat across from his family, bracketed by her parents, her little face solemn as she listened to the sermon, taking every word to heart.

Daniel tore his gaze away from the window. He'd been so sure that Alexander McDougal had hidden the marriage certificate inside the church, but he'd been wrong, as he'd been wrong about so many things in his life. Daniel stood and was about to leave, when a sudden memory stopped him in his tracks. He remembered a day, many years ago now, when he was barely in his teens and had worked up the nerve to speak to Sarah. She'd dropped her Book of Common Prayer and had gone back inside after the service to retrieve it. Daniel had seen his chance and had followed her inside, only to find the church empty. He'd looked around, wondering where Sarah had gone, then saw the top of her head, the sun shining on her and forming a halo. She'd been standing beneath the wheel window, her slight form obscured by the altar and the massive cross.

Daniel's breath had caught in his throat as he watched her, then he'd cursed himself for a fool and strode down the nave, too scared to miss his chance. He'd found Sarah standing in front of an alcove beneath the window. The alcove was small and narrow, and not visible from the pews. It contained a statue of St. Catherine, her hair modestly covered, and her body shrouded in a flowing robe etched of stone. She was gazing heavenward, her hands clasped in prayer.

"Isn't she beautiful?" Sarah said, never looking away from the martyr's face.

"Yes, I suppose she is," Daniel replied. "I never knew she was here." He hadn't known it then, but Anglican churches frowned on openly displaying statues of saints, believing the practice smacked too much of Catholicism.

"Sir Percival brought the statue from the Holy Land when he returned from his last crusade," Sarah explained. "He wished to keep it here, so a niche was made especially for her."

"I see," Daniel said, thrilled that they were having an actual conversation. "She must be quite old, then."

"Yes. Vicar said she must be close to one thousand years old."

"Where did Sir Percival get it?" Daniel asked.

Sarah's face fell as she considered the question. "I suppose he took it from a church."

"You mean he stole it?"

"He was a man of honor. He wouldn't have stolen a holy relic," Sarah replied hotly.

"No, of course not," Daniel rushed to reassure.

Sarah reached out and carefully touched the statue, her face glowing with reverence. "I wish I could be as brave as she was."

"Why? So you could get your head chopped off, or worse?" Daniel asked.

"You wouldn't understand," Sarah snapped. She turned on her heel and stormed out, leaving him to think that he had much to learn about girls.

Daniel pushed up his glasses, which had slid down his nose in the stagnant heat of the June afternoon, and ran up the steps leading to the altar. He made his way to the back wall, relieved to see that the statue was still there. He'd completely forgotten about its existence. Daniel reached out and felt around with careful fingers, mindful of the ancient statue's fragility. There was nothing behind her, so he carefully lifted the statue. It was heavier than he'd expected, and he wondered how Sir Percival had lugged the thing all the way from the Holy Land, but then, he'd probably had his squire see to the statue's transport.

Daniel reached beneath the base of the statue. His breath caught as his fingers touched what he was sure was paper. He slid the square out and replaced the statue in its niche. With shaking fingers, he unfolded the paper. It was the marriage certificate issued to Robert Chadwick and Margaret McDougal on August 17, 1845.

Daniel stuffed the document into his pocket. "Thank you," he said. He wasn't sure if he was thanking God, St. Catherine, or Sarah, for unwittingly guiding him to Alexander's hiding place. Daniel crossed the dais, skipped down the steps, then hurried down the nave toward the door. The afternoon had become overcast while he'd been inside the church, and ominous-looking clouds had rolled in, hanging low and threatening rain. He tipped his hat to Colonel Chadwick and Harry, who were making their way toward the lychgate.

"Good afternoon, Constable," the colonel said. "Come to pray?"

Daniel didn't answer. "Looks like it might rain," he said instead.

"Yes. We'd better hurry. Harry has been kind enough to bring me. I wished to visit my wife's grave. Today would have been the anniversary of our marriage," Colonel Chadwick said. "And I thought Harry might like to visit his father's grave."

Harry looked like he'd rather be anyplace else, but he remained quiet, waiting for his grandfather.

"Have you stumbled on a clue?" Colonel Chadwick asked, his eyes twinkling with mischief.

"No, I simply wished to see the crypt again," Daniel lied. "In case I'd missed something the first time."

"Really? Did you find anything?" Harry asked. He suddenly grew animated, his eyes sparkling with excitement. "What pluck to murder someone in a church," Harry said. "I almost hope the bugger gets away with it."

"Harry, mind your tongue," Colonel Chadwick snapped. "It's a mortal sin to take a man's life, probably doubly so in the house of our Lord. *Did* you find anything that might help you solve this crime, Constable?" he asked.

"No, I haven't," Daniel said.

Harry's face seemed to relax. "Come on, Granddad. It's starting to rain," he said.

Colonel Chadwick leaned heavily on his stick as he ambled through the lychgate, heading for the carriage waiting on the other side.

"Good day to you, Constable," Harry said as he prepared to follow. "I suppose the murderer was too clever for the likes of you," he added, smiling insolently.

"I suppose so," Daniel agreed.

He returned to the vicarage and retrieved his dogcart. Several fat drops of rain splattered on the seat next to him as he took hold of the reins. He pulled his hat lower and hunched his shoulders as the rain came down in earnest. Daniel took the marriage certificate out of his pocket and slid it inside his coat, positioning it between his shirt and the waistcoat to keep it dry. It was the only piece of physical evidence he had, and he meant to protect it.

Chapter 26

By the time Daniel arrived at home, he was soaking wet. The rain was coming down in sheets, the sky dark and forbidding. Having seen to the horse and cart, Daniel ran toward the house and kicked off his squelching boots before taking the steps two at a time in his stockinged feet. He rang for Tilda and asked for hot water to be brought up. He was shivering in his wet clothes and needed a bath.

Daniel put the marriage certificate in a safe place, then stripped off his wet clothes and pulled on his woolen dressing gown. Half an hour later, his bath was ready, and he sank into the hot water, sighing with pleasure as the chill inside him was replaced with a glowing warmth. He luxuriated in the tub until the water grew tepid, then dressed and presented himself downstairs in time for supper.

Harriet preferred to eat early, so supper was always served precisely at six o'clock. This evening it was consommé, steamed fish served with carrots and peas, and stewed fruit with a dollop of custard cream for dessert, instead of the chops and mash he'd hoped for. Daniel's sense of well-being quickly evaporated at the prospect of this unsatisfying meal. Harriet suffered with her digestion and opted for light, under-spiced food, and Sarah didn't seem to care what she ate, picking at whatever was put in front of her. Daniel tried to hide his displeasure as he finished the thin consommé and started on the fish. He was still hungry by the end of the meal and wished he could slip out to the Red Stag and gorge himself on good, rich stew or a steak and ale pie.

"Goodnight, Daniel," Sarah said as she rose from the table.

Daniel glanced at the carriage clock on the mantel. It was half past seven. "Are you unwell?"

Sarah smiled wanly. "No, but I feel awfully tired today. I'll just read for a while and go to sleep."

"Goodnight, then," Daniel said, and watched as Sarah and Harriet left the dining room and headed for the stairs. He felt frustrated and restless, and the prospect of spending the evening alone didn't appeal.

Having come to a decision, Daniel returned to his bedroom, retrieved the marriage certificate, and asked Tilda for his coat and hat. He armed himself with an umbrella, even though the rain had stopped and the evening outside was clear and fresh, and set off for Redmond Hall. He regretted his decision to walk as soon as his feet slipped and slid on the muddy path, but persevered, not wishing to return home.

Mud notwithstanding, he enjoyed the walk. This close to midsummer, the daylight lingered, the lavender haze of twilight just beginning to cast lengthening shadows on the world around him. Pink streaks left over from the setting sun blazed across the sky, and the first stars twinkled faintly in the purpling heavens as a mere hint of a three-quarter moon hovered above the tree line, its outline translucent against the still-light sky.

The evening was filled with the chirping of crickets and the secretive rustle of leaves in the gentle wind. Daniel turned his face into the breeze and took a deep, cleansing breath, his mood improving with every step. When he reached Redmond Hall, he carefully wiped his boots on the grass to get the mud off, then marched up the gravel drive toward the house, hoping Captain Redmond wouldn't resent the intrusion. Daniel needed to discuss his findings, and the captain was the only person whose opinion he respected. He'd help Daniel make sense of the facts and possibly poke holes in the theory he intended to present at the inquest.

Dodson's eyebrows lifted theatrically when Daniel presented himself at the door, but the butler made no comment, taking Daniel's hat and umbrella with all the dignity of a well-trained servant.

"I'll tell his lordship you're here," Dodson said, stressing Captain Redmond's title, the only hint of criticism he'd permitted himself in the face of an uninvited guest.

A moment later, Dodson led Daniel into the drawing room, where Captain Redmond was nursing a brandy in front of a roaring fire.

"Come in, Constable," Captain Redmond said with genuine warmth. "Would you care for a brandy? It's so damp in here after that rain. Please, have a seat."

Daniel settled in the wingchair across from the captain, who sprang to his feet, poured another brandy, and held it out to Daniel as if he were a servant and not the lord of the manor. Daniel accepted the glass gratefully.

"Where's Micah?" Daniel asked. It was too early for the boy to be in bed, and he hoped Micah wouldn't come bounding into the drawing room and interrupt the conversation.

"He's in the kitchen with Mrs. Dodson. He seems to like spending time there," the captain replied sadly.

Daniel nodded, taking his meaning. "He must miss his mother," he said.

"He does. I suppose it's natural for him to seek someone who makes him feel coddled, and Mrs. Dodson has taken to him like a duck to water."

"There are some things you can't give him," Daniel said gently.

"I know, but I'll give him whatever is in my power to give."

Daniel took a sip of his brandy. It burned its way down his gullet, igniting a warm glow in his belly. It was nice not to drink alone. Sarah never took a drop, and Harriet allowed herself a small sherry on Sunday afternoons. Daniel missed the company of men, and the camaraderie that went hand in hand with working in an environment where strong bonds were forged. When he'd agreed to return to Birch Hill, he had given up more than a promising career. He'd given up the friends he'd made while on the force and the sense of belonging he'd so valued. Captain Redmond was the first person he'd bonded with since leaving London, and the realization took him by surprise, more so because he'd never have expected to like the American this much.

His thoughts were interrupted by the arrival of Dodson. "Shall I hold back dinner, sir?"

"Have you eaten?" the captain asked, turning to Daniel.

Daniel was about to assure the captain that he'd dined at home, but common sense prevailed. He was still hungry, and he really did want to speak to the captain about the case. Whether they spoke in the drawing room or the dining room made little difference, but it was always more pleasant to converse over food.

"Please, join me," Captain Redmond said, correctly interpreting Daniel's awkward silence.

"Thank you, Captain," Daniel said, his cheeks heating with embarrassment. He felt like a poor relation.

"Will Micah be joining us?" the captain asked Dodson, who smiled guiltily.

"No, sir. Master Micah got stuffed on jam tarts and has fallen asleep at the table."

Captain Redmond laughed, his normally serious face transforming instantly and making him look years younger. "Perhaps you can help Master Micah to bed before he falls off his chair."

"Yes, sir."

"Have you discovered anything useful?" Captain Redmond asked Daniel once they took their places in the dining room and were served the first course, which was salmon mousse on toast points.

"Do you always eat like this?" Daniel asked as he took the first bite and rolled his eyes in silent ecstasy.

Captain Redmond grinned. "Mrs. Dodson had a piece of salmon left over from last night's dinner, so she put it to good use. She's a wonderful cook, isn't she?"

Daniel nodded enthusiastically, his mouth full of the creamy mousse. He finally swallowed and went on to answer the captain's question.

"I've learned quite a lot since our last conversation," Daniel said, leaning forward in his eagerness to share his findings.

"According to Mr. Fletcher, Alexander McDougal's employer, Alexander had been a mild-mannered young man, content with his lot, until his mother's death three months ago, at which time he began to spend his money carelessly and seemed angry and upset."

"Was it grief that prompted the change in his behavior?"

"Yes, but it was also anger and the sense of injustice he must have felt upon learning that his mother had lied to him for nigh on twenty years. The husband, whom she'd claimed had died before Alexander's birth, had, in fact, been very much alive until quite recently, living right here in Birch Hill and married to another."

Captain Redmond's eyes widened in surprise. "Robert Chadwick?"

"The very same."

"Did Fletcher tell you that?" Captain Redmond asked.

"No, but he directed me to someone who did. Charles Boyd was Alexander's closest friend and heard the story from him."

"And what is the story?"

Daniel was about to reply when a maidservant entered the room, ready to clear the plates from the first course. She was closely followed by Dodson, who set a platter of roast beef in the middle of the table, the mouthwatering meat surrounded by roast potatoes and grilled vegetables. Dodson offered to serve the men, but Captain Redmond waved him away. He did the honors, refilled Daniel's glass, then invited him to continue.

"From what I could piece together," Daniel said after taking his first bite of the succulent roast, "Margaret McDougal met Robert Chadwick when he went to Rutherglen to inspect the coal pits owned by his family. Margaret's father was the mine captain, so they must have come into contact regularly. Robert fell in love with Margaret and married her in a Catholic church, then left her in Scotland to go home and break the news to his father. When Margaret failed to hear from him, she wrote, but her letters went unanswered. Already pregnant with Alexander, she departed for England, most likely making it only as far as London before seeing the announcement of Robert Chadwick's marriage to Caroline Browning in the paper. Feeling duped, she couldn't very well return to her father and tell him the truth, so she remained in England and tried to make a life for herself and her son, all the while following Robert Chadwick's life from afar. Before she died, Margaret gave Alexander the marriage certificate she'd held on to all those years."

"So, that's what the killer must have been searching for," Captain Redmond said.

"It must have been, since that one document has the power destroy the lives of Caroline Chadwick and her children. Having learned the truth, Alexander became angry and bitter, probably as much with his mother for keeping this from him as with the father who'd wanted nothing to do with him. He spent money on frivolous things, carrying on as if he truly was the son of a wealthy man. My guess is that Alexander would have confronted his father had he not died, robbing Alexander of the chance to say his piece."

Captain Redmond nodded, his expression thoughtful, his food growing cold on his plate. "So, Alexander McDougal must have come to Birch Hill to confront his father's widow instead, and demand what? That being Robert Chadwick's eldest son, he was the true heir to the estate and should be handed the keys to the kingdom? Ask for a substantial amount of money to make Caroline Chadwick's problem go away? Or seek retribution for his mother's humiliation and suffering?" the captain theorized.

"Any of those would give Caroline Chadwick a motive for murder," Daniel replied.

"But the murder was not committed by a woman," Captain Redmond countered. "Caroline Chadwick would not have had the strength to open the tomb and lift Alexander's body into it, nor do I think she'd know exactly where to strike to stab him in the heart from behind."

"I agree," Daniel said, his excitement mounting. "I believe she compelled someone else to do it for her."

"Who? Her son? Harry Chadwick would have the most to lose should the truth come out," Captain Redmond remarked.

Daniel shook his head. "Caroline Chadwick would never allow her son to risk his neck, nor do I think that Harry Chadwick has the physical strength or the know-how to kill a man in cold blood. I believe it was John Marin, with whom Caroline Chadwick may be having an illicit affair and whose very livelihood depends on her goodwill. John Marin also happens to have a musket with a bayonet, the blade of which is approximately the same width as a dagger. My theory is that she ordered Marin to kill Alexander and steal his possessions from Mrs. Harris's house. Marin might have dropped the cigarette holder when he brought Alexander's valise from the village. My guess is he threw the valise in the lake."

"But he didn't find the marriage certificate, so Caroline Chadwick sent him back to search Mrs. Harris's house again," the captain said, nodding.

"Exactly. But Alexander McDougal hid the marriage certificate in a safe place, knowing full well that it was his only real leverage against the Chadwicks," Daniel said.

"Without the document, this is all supposition."

Daniel triumphantly whipped the folded document from his coat pocket and passed it to Captain Redmond, who let out a low whistle.

"Where on earth did you find that?"

"I found it at St. Catherine's, stashed beneath the statue of the martyr herself. The statue must have appealed to Alexander McDougal because it's not readily visible to parishioners."

"Why's that?" Captain Redmond asked.

"Displaying statues of saints is seen as a Popish practice," Daniel replied. "This particular statue had been brought from the Holy Land by Sir Percival Talbot, who would have been Catholic, given that Protestantism hadn't even been invented yet. No one dared to remove it for fear of offending the Talbots, so it was relegated to a location that's easily overlooked by any visiting bishops."

"Clever," Captain Redmond said. "Does anyone know you have this?" he asked, tapping his finger on the folded document.

"No, but Harry Chadwick was outside when I left the church. He'd brought the colonel to visit his wife's grave."

"And you think Harry Chadwick would make the connection between you coming out of St. Catherine's and the missing marriage certificate?"

"I don't see how he could," Daniel replied. "But given that Alexander McDougal must have agreed to meet whoever he was meeting at St. Catherine's and that's where he was killed, I can't afford to dismiss the possibility. The killer knows the document is still at large and will probably do whatever it takes to obtain it."

Captain Redmond took a sip of wine, set the glass down, and steepled his fingers as he considered what he'd learned. "I don't understand how Robert Chadwick could have married two women without any legal repercussions. Is it possible that his marriage to Margaret McDougal was staged and this marriage certificate is not valid?"

"I don't believe so," Daniel replied. "I think Robert Chadwick really did marry Margaret McDougal. Having returned home, he must have thought better of marrying the mine captain's daughter and became engaged to the beautiful and wealthy Caroline Browning, who was his family's choice of bride. Since he'd married Margaret in a Catholic church, he probably assumed that no one would be the wiser if he chose to disregard it, and since he didn't recognize the authority of the Catholic Church, he simply pretended the marriage had never taken place."

"Why did Margaret McDougal not go to the authorities? Surely as his lawfully wedded wife she had a case against him. At the very least, she could have made life very uncomfortable for him," the captain said, his brow furrowing in confusion.

"I can only assume that Margaret McDougal genuinely loved Robert Chadwick and didn't want to hurt him. She was either very proud or very foolish," Daniel said.

"Or a little of both," Captain Redmond agreed. "Perhaps she didn't understand that under the law, she couldn't simply be discarded in favor of another wife."

"Or maybe she was led to believe that the marriage had been annulled. He might have had a document to that effect forged and forwarded to her, so she'd think she had no claim on him," Daniel suggested.

"And how do we know it wasn't annulled?" the captain replied, playing devil's advocate.

"Had the marriage been legally annulled, whoever killed Alexander would have had no cause to commit murder. Alexander would be nothing more than a bastard, one of thousands of bastards born in this country every year. He'd be no threat to the status quo."

"But he could have caused Caroline Chadwick and her children great embarrassment had he made his claims public, and this on the eve of her daughters entering society with a view to a good marriage," the captain pointed out.

"When faced with a dowry the size of the Chadwick girls', I think most prospective suitors would choose to overlook the youthful indiscretion of their deceased father," Daniel replied wryly.

"So, we are back to Harry Chadwick? Might he not have done it?"

"Harry Chadwick lacks the physical strength to carry out such a feat, and frankly, I don't think he has the stomach for it," Daniel said.

"He might have had help," the captain replied. "As Robert Chadwick's heir, he'd have the most to lose."

"Yes, he would," Daniel agreed. "My mother-in-law, who has her ear to the ground when it comes to local gossip, believes that an engagement between Harry and Imogen Talbot is imminent. A whiff of scandal might put Squire Talbot off the match, since Imogen won't be short of suitors once she comes out into society this Season. Had Harry been involved in the murder, the only person who might have helped him would have been John Marin, recruited by Caroline Chadwick to do the family's dirty work."

"So, we are back to square one," Captain Redmond said with annoyance. "We have a motive for the murder, but we still don't know who killed poor Alexander."

"No, we don't," Daniel agreed. "Without physical proof to substantiate my theory, this murder will remain unsolved, and the culprit will be allowed to get away. Have you any ideas?" he asked, feeling desperate.

Captain Redmond shook his head. "The marriage certificate will go a long way to showing why Alexander McDougal was killed, but not by whom."

Daniel sighed loudly and stood. He felt tired and defeated, and angry. Someone had killed that young man in cold blood, and they would almost certainly get away with it unless he found tangible proof of their crime. "Captain, I wonder if I might ask a favor of you. Would you mind holding on to the document until the inquest?"

"I will keep it safe," Captain Redmond said. "I'll have Joe drive you home."

"Thank you, but there's no need. I'll walk. I do my best thinking while I'm walking."

"Goodnight, then. I'll let you know if I think of something," Captain Redmond promised.

"Do. Goodnight, Captain, and thank you for your hospitality."

Daniel left the house and strode down the drive, stomping like a frustrated child who'd been sent to his room, his mind arranging and rearranging the facts without much success. He'd calmed down somewhat by the time he passed through the gates. It was clear and cool, the moon lighting his way and the stars twinkling playfully in the endless expanse of the nighttime sky.

Daniel stopped walking, his senses attuned to the sounds of the night. He thought he'd heard something, but it must have been a fox or a badger going about its nocturnal business. All was eerily quiet.

A blinding pain bloomed in Daniel's head as the world exploded into a million fragments of brilliant color. He swayed on his feet and attempted to turn around to see who'd hit him, but a second blow prevented him from catching a glimpse of his assailant. Daniel sank to his knees, then collapsed onto the dirt road, his cheek pressing against the scraggly grass on the verge as the world went dark.

Chapter 27

Saturday, June 9

Jason woke early, his head throbbing dully after a restless night. He'd hovered on the verge of wakefulness as strange dreams drew him into a world where darkness and pain had left him paralyzed with terror. It was still dark, but he didn't think he'd be able to get back to sleep and wasn't sure he wanted to since he had no desire to return to his dreamscape. Annoyed, he got dressed and went downstairs, hoping to find Mrs. Dodson in the kitchen. She was there, kneading dough for bread, her plump hands and forearms covered in flour, her face pink in the glow of the gas lamps.

"Good morning, Captain. Did you not sleep well?" she asked, referring to his disheveled appearance and bloodshot eyes.

"I'm afraid not. Can I trouble you for some coffee?" Jason asked, taking a seat at the table.

Mrs. Dodson shook her head in disapproval. *Lords of the manor do not take coffee in the kitchen*, her gaze seemed to say, but she was becoming accustomed to Jason's strange ways and uttered no word of complaint.

"Of course. There are some jam tarts left over from yesterday if you'd like a little something before breakfast."

Jason nodded. "Jam tarts sound grand."

Mrs. Dodson wiped her hands on a towel, fetched the coffee tin, and spooned the fragrant grinds into a saucepan, which she set to simmer. She placed a bowl of sugar, a jug of milk, and a plate of jam tarts in front of Jason before fetching a cup and saucer, a silver spoon, and a serviette, setting the table as if he were in the formal dining room. The heavenly smell of coffee filled the kitchen, instantly lifting Jason's spirits. Once it was ready, Mrs. Dodson poured the coffee into a silver pot and set it on the table before him.

"Shall I pour?" she asked.

"No need. Thank you."

Jason helped himself, then added milk and sugar and took the first restorative sip. He reached for a jam tart and took a bite, savoring the sweet-tart flavor that filled his mouth. "Really good," he said as soon as he swallowed.

"Master Micah helped me make these. He's quite the cook."

"I think he enjoys eating a lot more than he enjoys cooking," Jason said, finishing off the tart in two bites.

"Who doesn't?" Mrs. Dodson asked with a smile and returned to her task.

Jason took another sip of coffee, then decided to pursue his advantage. He was alone in the kitchen with Mrs. Dodson, who, like most women, enjoyed a bit of a chat. She'd lived in Birch Hill all her life. Perhaps she could shed some light on the Chadwick family. But Jason had to tread gently. She wouldn't want to be caught gossiping about her 'betters,' as she called them.

"Mrs. Dodson, you previously mentioned that you worked for the Chadwick family when you were a young woman. Robert Chadwick—what was he like?" Jason asked innocently.

Mrs. Dodson shrugged her ample shoulders. "He was handsome in his own way, I suppose, and well mannered."

"But what type of man was he?"

"Inconsequential," Mrs. Dodson said, surprising Jason with her choice of adjective.

"How so?"

"There are men who give orders and there are men who take them. Robert Chadwick was the latter. Now, Colonel Chadwick—he was a force to be reckoned with. Terrified everyone, from his wife to the lowliest servant. He was quick to anger and wont to punish the offender for the slightest transgression. It was his army training, I suppose. Couldn't deal with insubordination."

"Was he a violent man, the colonel?" Jason asked as he refilled his cup.

"Not violent, but hard. Unforgiving. He's mellowed with age, or so I hear."

"In what way?" Jason asked.

"Dotes on his grandchildren in a way he never did on his own children. Miss Lucinda, in particular."

"Is she so different from Harry and Arabella?"

"I think Harry reminds the colonel too much of Master Robert. Meek and unambitious, is Harry, except when it comes to his pursuit of sport or pleasure. Arabella is sweet and pliant, but Miss Lucinda, oh, that one is a card. Likes to ride astride, decked out in britches, and I hear she's taken up fencing. Demanded Mrs. Chadwick engage an instructor. I think the poor lady almost had the vapors, but the colonel seemed to find it amusing and saw to finding the right man. This is not common knowledge, of course. It wouldn't do for her to be seen as mannish, not when there's a husband to catch, and Mrs. Chadwick will have nothing less than a baronet for either of her girls. He might be impoverished, but there's enough money in the Chadwick coffers to buy a title for the girls. Noble status is the only thing that family lacks."

Jason was about to reply when an erratic banging reverberated through the ground floor, startling Mrs. Dodson and bringing Jason to his feet. It was too early for anyone to come calling. Something was wrong. Jason sprinted toward the door, where he nearly collided with Dodson, who was pulling on his coat over his nightshirt as he hurried across the foyer. When he finally opened the door, someone who looked like a wild animal practically fell into his arms, causing Dodson to jump back in alarm.

"Help," the man whispered hoarsely.

"Dear God, Constable, is that you?" Dodson cried.

206

"Daniel, what happened?" Jason cried, using the constable's Christian name without having been invited to.

Constable Haze swayed on his feet and would have fallen had Jason not caught him and pressed him against the wall to steady him. He was covered in mud, his clothes damp. The hair on the back of his head was matted and thick with dried blood, and his face looked ashen, his gaze unfocused as he tried to get his bearings.

"Lord preserve us," Mrs. Dodson said as she stared at the constable in horror.

"Mrs. Dodson, get me some warm water. Dodson, help me bring him into the drawing room," Jason instructed.

Between them, they managed to carry the constable into the drawing room and settle him on the butter-yellow settee. Dodson sucked in his breath in alarm as the silk became streaked with mud and clumps of dirt fell onto the carpet, but wisely said nothing.

"I'll need my medical bag. And some brandy," Jason said as he lifted the constable's drooping lids and peered into his mud-crusted eyes.

While Dodson went to fetch the bag, Jason took the man's pulse. It was faint but steady. He then carefully rolled him onto his side to examine the wound. Daniel gasped when Jason's fingers touched the tender area where he'd been struck. The blow must have knocked him senseless, but thankfully, his skull didn't appear fractured, as far as Jason could tell. His attacker hadn't been strong enough to kill him with one well-aimed blow, so he'd hit him again, but not in exactly the same spot.

When Mrs. Dodson bustled into the room with a basin of water, Jason slid a towel beneath Daniel's head and carefully washed the dirt from his face. The warm water seemed to revive Daniel somewhat, and his eyes fluttered open, his pupils dilated as he stared up at Jason.

"Daniel, who attacked you?" Jason asked gently.

"I don't know," Daniel muttered. "Sarah…"

"What about Sarah?"

"She'll be frantic. Please, let her know…"

"Mrs. Dodson, please wake Joe and ask him to get a message to Mrs. Haze. Perhaps Joe should bring her here, since Constable Haze isn't ready to be moved."

"Yes, sir," Mrs. Dodson replied, and hurried from the room.

When Dodson returned to the room with Jason's medical bag, Jason extracted a bottle of alcohol and a handful of cotton. "This will sting," he warned as he moved Daniel's head to the side and dabbed at the wound.

Constable Haze sucked in his breath but made no other sound. Having thoroughly cleaned the wound, Jason set aside the soiled cotton and reached for another piece, soaking this one with camphor.

"This will help with the pain and swelling," he explained.

Daniel exhaled and seemed to sink deeper into the settee, as if about to lose consciousness.

"Daniel, stay with me and tell me what you're experiencing," Jason urged as he held a tumbler of brandy to Daniel's lips.

Daniel took a healthy gulp, which seemed to rouse him somewhat. "Aside from a splitting headache?" he asked, his lips curling into a sarcastic half-smile.

"Yes, aside from that."

"I feel nauseated, my vision is blurry, and the room is spinning in a most disconcerting manner."

"You've suffered a concussion, but with bedrest and proper care, you should feel better in a few days."

"I don't have a few days," Daniel muttered, his speech slurred. "The inquest is tomorrow."

"Leave it with me," Jason said, using his most authoritative tone.

Daniel screwed up his face as he peered at Jason. "What are you going to do?"

"I'm not sure yet, but I think I know who killed Alexander McDougal."

Daniel smiled hazily and sank even deeper into the settee. "I'm tired," he whispered. "So tired."

"Daniel, try to stay awake," Jason urged, but Daniel was already asleep, his breathing shallow and even.

Jason covered Daniel with a blanket Mrs. Dodson had left and sat on the edge of the settee, studying his patient intently, wishing he could see into his head. If the blow had been severe enough, it might have caused a brain bleed, which would result in the constable slipping into a coma, but if the brain was intact, sleep would probably help rather than harm. There was no way for Jason to verify the severity of the trauma. He'd have to keep an eye on Daniel throughout the day and pray he didn't begin to display signs of a hematoma.

"What do you mean to do, Captain?" Dodson asked. Jason had almost forgotten he was still in the room and was startled by the sound of his voice.

"I mean to confront the killer," Jason said as he stood.

"Are you sure that's wise, sir?"

"It's the only way to see justice done, Dodson," Jason replied. "There isn't enough evidence to make a case at the inquest. The killer will go free."

"And you mean to administer justice, Captain?" Dodson asked, his gaze fearful.

"Not directly."

"I don't understand, sir," Dodson replied. "Can you be more specific?"

"I'm afraid not, since I haven't quite figured it out yet."

"I see," Dodson said, clearly not seeing at all. "Shall you require a weapon, sir?"

Jason's eyebrows lifted in surprise. He hadn't considered the possibility of being attacked, but it'd be foolish to blunder unarmed into a situation that had every possibility of escalating. Jason kept his pistol in the bedside table in his bedroom and there were several guns in the gun cabinet that his grandfather must have used for hunting.

"Please bring me my revolver. It's in the top drawer of the bedside table."

"Yes, sir."

"And make sure to keep Micah indoors. He's not to leave the house."

"Yes, Captain."

Jason glanced at the carriage clock on the mantel. It was only seven o'clock. He had at least two hours in which to tend to Daniel, see to his affairs should his plan go horribly wrong, and clean and oil his Colt before heading out. Plenty of time.

Chapter 28

The sun was warm on his shoulders, the dew sparkled on the grass, and the scent of wildflowers and sun-warmed earth was fragrant and sweet. The animal beneath him was beautiful and strong, its chestnut mane moving in the breeze as it trotted at a steady pace. Jason wished he could ride forever, just keep going until all the ills of the world were behind him and he was in a place that held no painful memories or constant reminders of the family history he was sadly unfamiliar with. But he had a murder to solve, and Daniel Haze to protect. Daniel had obviously been asking the right questions, since the murderer had felt threatened enough to attack him and leave him for dead. It was time to crack this case wide open, but there would be no justice meted out at the inquest, not if Jason's hunch proved correct.

He passed through the gates of Chadwick Manor, cantered down the drive until he reached the stables, then dismounted and tossed the reins to the surprised groom who'd stepped out to meet him. He checked that his pistol was securely stowed in the waistband of his riding britches before presenting himself at the front door.

Jason was almost amused by the comical expression on Llewelyn's face. He doubted the man had ever seen a visitor arrive at this hour, but he wouldn't be turned away, not today.

"I wish to see Colonel Chadwick," Jason said in a tone that brooked no argument, but the butler remained unmoved, his body blocking the door.

"M-my lord, it's rather early," Llewelyn said, his face turning pink with discomfort. His mistress wouldn't wish for a member of the nobility, especially an unmarried one, to feel insulted or unwelcome, not when she had two daughters of marriageable age, but propriety had to be observed. The poor man was caught in quite a conundrum.

"I know what time it is, and I know the colonel is awake. Does he not usually set off for his morning walk at this time?"

Llewelyn seemed taken aback by Jason's familiarity with the colonel's routine but made no mention of it.

"Kindly let me in and inform the colonel that I'm here," Jason said, taking a step forward.

Llewelyn relented and stepped back, allowing Jason into the foyer. "Yes, my lord."

He didn't invite Jason to wait in the parlor or offer him any refreshment. Instead, he left him standing in the middle of the foyer, where he was gawked at by several female servants who used the quiet hours of the morning to see to their chores in the ground floor rooms and hadn't expected to come face to face with an impatient nobleman.

It was a good ten minutes before the colonel finally appeared. He was dressed for walking, in a fawn-colored suit of the finest broadcloth, paired with a crisp white shirt and puff necktie in shades of brown and burgundy. Jason noted that his color was better than it had been the night of the dinner party, probably because he was well rested, but there was no mistaking the jaundiced hue of his skin or the yellow tinge to the whites of his eyes.

"Have you no manners, man?" Colonel Chadwick demanded. "It's grossly impolite to call on someone at such an early hour."

"This is not a social call," Jason replied. "I would like to speak with you. Privately."

"Then join me for a walk. This house isn't the place for a private conversation."

Llewelyn, who'd been hovering in the background, instantly sprang into action and handed the colonel his hat and walking stick before opening the door. Jason followed the colonel as he descended the steps and walked down the drive and away from the house.

"I've a mind to walk by the lake this morning," the colonel said.

"As you wish, Colonel," Jason replied, not in the least surprised that the old man had decided to deviate from his usual route.

They walked in silence until they left the expanse of the freshly cut lawn and entered the green sanctuary of the wood. Birdsong filled the air and the sun-dappled path wound toward the lake that shimmered invitingly in the distance. In a different time and place, Jason might have considered going for a swim, but he hadn't done anything even remotely fun since he'd returned from Georgia nearly a year ago. He was long overdue.

"What it is you want of me, Captain?" Colonel Chadwick asked. "Or was this just another excuse for snooping around the estate?"

"Constable Haze is alive," Jason announced, watching the colonel's face.

There was just the merest flicker of surprise in his bright blue eyes. "I should hope so."

"He was set upon last night and beaten severely about the head."

"You'd think a constable would be able to defend himself from ruffians," the colonel said. "But he doesn't have the wits or the ambition to succeed. Didn't have it in London and doesn't have it in this country backwater we like to call home."

"On the contrary. Constable Haze is a very intelligent man. Seems to me he got uncomfortably close to the truth and nearly paid with his life."

"Do tell," Colonel Chadwick said nastily. His pace was slowing, and he was growing short of breath, either because of the exertion or because he didn't care for the direction the conversation was taking.

Jason stopped walking and faced the man. "I have in my possession a marriage certificate for your son Robert and his bride Margaret McDougal. It predates his marriage to Caroline Browning. That's what you were after when you killed Alexander, wasn't it?"

"You're even more deluded that I first thought," the colonel replied calmly. "I'm very ill. And that's not the diagnosis of that fool, Dr. Miller. I've seen the best medical men in Harley Street. I have six months to live at the outside. I can barely walk to the gates and back. You think I have the physical strength to kill a strong young man, drag him down to the crypt, and put him to bed in a tomb? Your lack of common sense is astounding," he said, chuckling mirthlessly. "And you, a medical man yourself."

Jason smiled back pleasantly. "I know you're ill, Colonel. Cirrhosis of the liver, is it? Was it the trauma from an old injury or fondness for drink that destroyed your liver? No, don't answer that," Jason said, holding up his hand. "It really doesn't matter. And no, I don't believe you could have pulled off this caper by yourself. You had help."

"And who do you think helped me, you dolt?"

"Lucinda."

For the first time, Jason saw a flicker of alarm in the colonel's eyes and knew he was on the right track. "Don't talk rubbish, man. Lucinda is but a slip of a girl."

"No, she isn't. Lucinda is strong and fit, and not afraid to flout convention. I hear she tears around the countryside in britches and takes fencing lessons with an instructor engaged for her by you. Neither you nor Lucinda could have disposed of Alexander McDougal on your own, but together, you just about managed it."

"And what, precisely, are you basing this theory on?" the colonel demanded, his breath now coming in shallow gasps. "It might have been Caroline," he suggested slyly, displaying his willingness to sacrifice his daughter-in-law in order to protect Lucinda.

"I'm a fairly good judge of character, Colonel, and I don't think your daughter-in-law is capable of murder, even by proxy. I don't believe Caroline ever knew about your son's first marriage. In fact, I'm not sure you knew about it either, not until this week at any rate. Alexander McDougal came to the house, but he was turned away, which is not to say that he didn't speak to someone, most likely you, his grandfather, who just happened to be taking his morning walk. He would have gladly told you the truth of the matter and appealed to your sense of family, but you're not a sentimental man. You are a soldier, trained to deal with the enemy using whatever method is deemed most effective.

And Alexander was the enemy, wasn't he? He had the power to destroy your family. Harry would lose his inheritance, and your granddaughters would be turned away at the door at any polite gathering, being illegitimate and disgraced. Alexander had to be dealt with before he had a chance to make the marriage certificate public, and you were just the man to do it, but you needed help from someone who loves you enough to do anything you ask, someone who might even admire your ruthlessness. Tell me, Colonel, how did it feel to kill your own grandson?" Jason asked savagely, pressing his advantage.

The colonel's level gaze met Jason's as his hands tightened on the knob of his walking stick. "He was no grandson of mine. Had I known my fool of a son had married that Scotch harlot, I'd have made him a widower within the week, but he was wise enough to keep the marriage from me and try to correct his mistake on his own. Of course, being the cretin that he was, he never dissolved the marriage legally, just went on to marry Caroline and thought no one would be the wiser. Well, I'll give him his due; he got away with it for twenty years and went to his grave thinking he'd outwitted us all, but then fate came calling to present her bill."

"Tell me what happened," Jason invited softly. He needed to learn the details of the crime, and like most men who felt no remorse for their actions, the colonel seemed eager to talk about his role in Alexander's death.

"The boy came to Birch Hill and tried to see Caroline. I'm not sure what he thought he'd accomplish by ambushing her that way, but thankfully, Llewelyn turned him away. He tried the servants' entrance, thinking he could gain access to her that way, even lied about being a clockmaker or some such, but of course, he was asked to leave. He spotted me coming out of the stables and correctly assumed I was one of the family. Said he must speak to me urgently, so we went for a walk," the colonel said. A small smile played about his lips, as if he were recalling some particularly clever subterfuge on his part.

"Go on," Jason prompted when the colonel stopped speaking and fixed his gaze on the shivering canopy of leaves above his head. The wind was picking up.

"He introduced himself and told me he was Robert's son. He had the proof and wouldn't hesitate to use it if we failed to meet his demands."

"What was it he asked for?" Jason asked.

"What do you think?" the colonel snapped. "He wanted to be recognized as the heir to the estate, the daft fool, and thought I'd help him claim his birthright, now that I'd been made aware of his existence. Grandfather, he called me." Colonel Chadwick laughed, a cruel and brittle sound. "I told him his revelation would destroy Caroline and her children. Her marriage to my son would be declared invalid and her children would be called bastards. That gave him pause. He wasn't a cruel lad, just not an overly bright one."

"What did you propose?"

"I implored him to reconsider his position. Told him I'd give him a substantial amount of money, enough to live on comfortably for the rest of his days, so long as he didn't destroy my family. I pleaded with him," the colonel added smugly, his lip curling in distaste. "He thought me a sentimental old man, especially when I held him to my breast and called him grandson."

"And then?"

"I told him I'd need several days to secure the funds. We agreed to meet at the church on Saturday evening, and he would hand over the certificate in exchange for the cash. He agreed. I couldn't very well get to the church on my own, so I enlisted Lucinda's help. She saw to the horses."

"And would you have given him the money?" Jason asked. "Would you have allowed him to walk away?"

"Truth?" the colonel asked, his eyes crinkling at the corners.

"Truth," Jason replied.

"I would have. Without the marriage certificate, he'd have no proof, so his accusations would fall on deaf ears even if he'd chosen to make them public."

"But he wouldn't hand it over, would he?" Jason asked.

"No. He accepted the money and thanked me, but then refused to surrender the certificate. He said he wouldn't make the document public. I had his word, as a gentleman." The colonel laughed out loud, as if genuinely amused. "Evidently, he was a chip off the old block after all."

"So, you became angry and struck him with the cross."

The colonel nodded, but only after a moment's hesitation. "It was clumsy of me. I should have thought it through, but my temper got the better of me. Once he was unconscious, I searched through his pockets, but he didn't have the document on him."

"He was still alive after you struck him," Jason said, watching the man closely. He strongly suspected it had been Lucinda who'd wielded the cross, but the blow hadn't been fatal, so who'd administered it didn't matter in the long run.

"Yes, he was still alive, but I could hardly let him walk out of that church, knowing what he knew and ready to use it against us. Which he would have. Again, and again. This would have been the first payment of many. He might not have inherited the estate, but by the time he was through with us, we'd wish he had done, the faithless parasite. Lucinda and I dragged him down to the crypt and shoved him into Sir Percival's tomb. That little maneuver nearly killed me; I'll gladly tell you that."

"Was the bruise I saw on your wrist caused by your efforts?"

"That one and many more. I bruise easily these days," the colonel replied sadly. "This useless body is failing me."

"And then you stabbed him through the heart," Jason said, failing to hide his disgust. "And left him to rot."

Colonel Chadwick scoffed. "It was kinder to kill him outright than let him come to in that tomb and suffocate slowly."

"Except he wouldn't have suffocated, since you never closed the lid properly."

"We should have been more careful, I'll grant you that, but I could barely keep upright by that point, and Lucinda was too frightened for me to worry overmuch about what we might have left behind. The poor girl thought I'd drop dead then and there. So, she helped me to my horse and saw us safely home."

"And it was Lucinda who broke into Mrs. Harris's house and removed Alexander McDougal's possessions."

"Yes. She dressed in Harry's cast-offs, walked to the village, and got into the house by the back door. She said it was almost too easy, since the old bat had left the door unlocked."

"And what of the attack on Constable Haze? I'm inclined to think that was you, but I can't imagine you'd be able to sneak up on him, not in your condition," Jason said, taunting the old man.

"The man's got no one to blame but his own nosey self," Colonel Chadwick said, his voice dripping with derision. "He as good as told Arabella and Lucinda that he knew who'd done it, and then I saw him coming out of the church. He had no business there in the middle of the afternoon, unless he'd come looking for something, and judging by his swagger, I'd say he'd found it."

"It was no coincidence you were in that graveyard, was it?" Jason asked, fascinated by the old man's cunning.

"Of course not. As soon as Lucinda told me what Haze had said, I asked Harry to take me into the village. Told him I had an overwhelming desire to visit my late wife's grave. Harry practically ran to the stables to order the curricle to be made ready, sentimental boy that he is," the colonel said with a chuckle. "I haven't visited my wife's grave since the day of her funeral, which was a good day in my books. I was glad to be shot of her."

"And the attack on Constable Haze?" Jason prompted.

The colonel shrugged. "Had to happen. He left us little choice. Certificate or not, he was getting too close. I had Lucinda keep an eye on his house while I told Caroline that she was unwell and wouldn't be joining us for dinner. I knew Caroline wouldn't bother to check on her. She's not overly maternal, my beloved daughter-in-law," he said sarcastically. "So, Lucinda followed Haze to your house and lay in wait. She knew what had to be done, and she did it. No hesitation, no remorse. Should have been born a man, that one. Much smarter and braver than her ninny of a brother. She's the only one in that family who takes after me."

Jason heard the note of admiration in the old man's voice and saw something in his startling blue eyes that gave him pause. Colonel Chadwick truly loved the girl, that was easy to see, but there was something else there in his gaze, something akin to paternal pride. And then a sickening realization dawned.

"She's yours, isn't she?" Jason asked, awestruck by the magnitude of the man's depravity.

The colonel's eyes widened in surprise, then a slow, sly smile spread across his face. "She is. My son preferred Scotch whisky to his wife, so I stood in for him from time to time. Caroline didn't object too strenuously, not after the first time anyway. She needed a real man in her bed, not a quivering lump of insecurity. I can't be sure about the other two, since Robert was still attempting to do his husbandly duty in those days, but when she became pregnant with Lucinda, he hadn't been near her in months. There was never any doubt whose child Lucinda was. And she's my girl through and through. She's the best part of me, the only person I've ever truly loved."

Jason shook his head, astounded by the man's arrogance. What had it done to his son to know that his own father was sharing his wife's bed and had fathered at least one of her children? No wonder Robert had preferred whisky to his wife's company. And what of Lucinda? Did she know who her real father was? Had she been a willing participant in Alexander's murder, or had the colonel forced her to help him?

"And yet you've involved her in a murder and instructed her to attack Daniel Haze," Jason said, failing to hide his disgust. "Have you ever considered what that might do to her, especially if Constable Haze were to die of his injuries?"

"I have, but whatever damage she might have sustained, the damage to her future would have been far worse had the truth come out. Lucinda is strong; she will move on, certain in the knowledge that she did what had to be done to protect her family."

"You don't feel an ounce of remorse, do you?" Jason said, studying the old man's set expression. "Did you even intend to give Alexander McDougal the money, as you claim, or did you plan to kill him all along?" Jason had a difficult time believing that Colonel Chadwick had ever intended to let his grandson leave Birch Hill unmolested. The money had to have been an excuse to get Alexander to a place that'd be deserted at that time of night, so that the colonel could murder him and dispose of his corpse. The colonel must have brought the dagger with him, knowing he'd have need of it.

Colonel Chadwick shrugged as if his grandson's death made little difference to him. "I'd have given him the money had he kept his word. I said so, didn't I? It wasn't his fault his father was a spineless nincompoop who left him to his fate, not that I think it's a man's responsibility to support his bastards. Lord knows I have one or two out there, and that's not counting the ones I sired in India. Those half-breeds should thank me for the English blood I pumped into their veins. Gave them a chance at rising above their limitations. But I digress. I feel no remorse over his death; he brought it on himself. The only thing I regret is shattering Lucinda's innocence. I would have liked to spare her that, and I will go to my grave knowing that I hurt my precious girl," the colonel said, his voice quivering with emotion.

He hunched over his walking stick, as if all his remaining strength had flowed out of his body, his energy drained by the intense conversation he'd been forced to participate in, but Jason wasn't fooled. Colonel Chadwick was not a man who'd allow himself to be hauled before a magistrate and accused of murder, an accusation that would undo everything he'd worked to prevent. He might be old and frail, but he was still a soldier, a man who saw killing as a means to an end. Jason casually slid his arm behind his back, making sure the pistol was within easy reach.

"I need a moment," Colonel Chadwick said wheezily. "I tire so easily these days."

He leaned against the trunk of a tree and closed his eyes, breathing deeply, his hands still clutching the walking stick for support. Jason watched and waited, his gaze never leaving the man's ashen face.

When the colonel finally struck, he was as quick as lightening. He yanked the knob out of his walking stick, revealing a wicked-looking blade, and lunged at Jason with a shrill shriek. Jason had to give the old boy credit. Despite his illness, his years of military training and self-discipline were still his greatest assets, and he seemed to have mustered the last of his strength to mount an attack. Despite anticipating the assault, Jason was still taken by surprise, fumbling for the gun as the colonel charged him, the blade raised to strike downward, into the heart.

Momentary panic was instantly replaced with dead calm, his surroundings falling away as he focused on the blade that seemed to be moving in slow motion, when in fact it was slicing through the air, the tip mere inches from Jason's chest. His own soldier's instinct kicked in, and he grabbed the colonel's wrist with his left hand, stopping the blade midair. With his right hand, he yanked the Colt out of his waistband and aimed it at the old man, but the colonel wasn't deterred. He was stronger than Jason had anticipated, desperation sending adrenaline through his wasted arm. He bore down hard, his eyes glowing ferociously as the tip sank into the fabric of Jason's coat.

Jason felt a sharp pain as the blade bit into his skin about two inches above his nipple. A familiar wetness alerted him to the blood that was now trickling from the wound and down his chest, soaking his shirt. Jason gritted his teeth and tightened his grip, his fingers mercilessly squeezing the old man's brittle wrist. Colonel Chadwick cried out in anguish as the blade slid from his hand, dropping to the ground and glinting in the sun. Jason did not release the colonel's wrist, but continued to squeeze, wanting to crush the old man's bones.

"Did you really think you could overpower me?" Jason growled, his breath coming hard and fast. He was both furious and scared, knowing how close he'd just come to death. Again.

The colonel was wheezing, his face a grayish green beneath the tan. Jason could feel him trembling and loosened his grip but didn't let him go. Their faces were inches apart. The colonel's gaze slid to the stain on Jason's coat, the blood now seeping through the fabric and spreading like the petals of a blooming flower. His eyes said it all. Despite Jason's youth and health, they'd been almost evenly matched, and this could have gone a different way.

"I'd have dumped your body in the lake, next to that fool's secondhand finery," the colonel hissed. "And then I would have come back here every day just so that I could be here when your bloated corpse floated to the surface, your fish-eaten face no longer recognizable, and laughed, knowing I had won."

"But sadly, you didn't," Jason replied. His breathing was returning to normal and the wound no longer burned, the skin around the incision now numb.

"Is this the murder weapon?" Jason asked, nodding toward the dagger by his feet, the pistol still trained on the colonel's stomach.

"I don't have to answer your questions," Colonel Chadwick snapped. His breathing had slowed and the maniacal gleam in his eyes was replaced by a look of speculation, his gaze narrowing as if he were trying to figure out how to extricate himself from the situation. "You have no proof," he snarled breathlessly. "Even if you have the marriage certificate, as you claim to, it proves nothing."

"It proves that Caroline wasn't your son's lawfully wedded spouse and that his children were not conceived in wedlock. Margaret McDougal died only three months ago, and there's proof of that. Even if Constable Haze can't prove that you murdered your own grandson, the evidence is enough to destroy your family's reputation."

The colonel pinned Jason with a steely stare. "What do you want, Captain?"

"I want a written confession stating that you killed Alexander McDougal. I don't care what reason you give for the murder. Caroline and the children don't deserve to be punished for your son's callousness and your brutality."

"And what about Lucinda?" the colonel asked, his voice pleading. "She had little choice in the matter."

"Lucinda did what she did out of love for you. I will keep her name out of the proceedings as long as you comply with my wishes. You have until the inquest tomorrow. If you fail to confess, then Constable Haze and I will present the evidence, and I will also testify to the fact that you tried to kill me. Your family will be ruined, your grandchildren spurned by society. Everything you have worked for will turn to ash before your eyes."

Jason released the colonel's wrist, but not before kicking the blade out of the old man's reach.

Colonel Chadwick drew himself up to his full height, squaring his shoulders like a soldier on parade. "I understand, and I will do as you ask if I have your word as a gentleman that Caroline and the children will be spared. Lucinda was the only one who knew the truth. Caroline has no idea how close she came to losing everything she holds dear."

"You have my word," Jason said.

"Thank you."

Jason didn't return the pistol to his waistband until the colonel had walked away, leaning heavily on his knob-less stick as he hobbled down the path. Jason picked up the blade and followed at a safe distance, turning toward the stable block only after he'd seen the old man entering the house. Jason ignored the groom's stunned expression as he walked into the stables, a blade in his hand and blood on his coat.

"My horse, please," he said as civilly as he could.

"Eh, yes, sir. Right away, sir."

Jason mounted rather awkwardly and trotted out of the yard, breathing a sigh of relief once he was through the gates and alone in the sunlit lane. The wound had started bleeding again, a jolt of pain stabbing his chest every time the horse moved beneath him, but he gritted his teeth and stared ahead. He now knew what had happened, and how, but he could make no guarantee that Daniel Haze would survive his injury, nor did he trust the word of that old fox he'd just cornered. The next twenty-four hours would be crucial.

Chapter 29

Jason handed his hat to an open-mouthed Dodson and took the stairs two at a time, praying all the while that he wouldn't encounter Micah. He didn't, and he breathed a sigh of relief as he locked the bedroom door behind him and tore off his blood-stained coat and stripped off his shirt, tossing them on the floor.

"My lord? May I be of help?" Henley called through the closed door breathlessly, probably having raced up the stairs after being summoned by his uncle.

"I'm fine," Jason replied gruffly.

He cleaned the wound with cold water, disinfected it, then pulled out a wad of cotton from his medical bag and secured it with a gauze bandage. He then changed into a clean shirt, picked up his bloodstained clothes off the floor, tossed them into a laundry basket Fanny had placed there for his use, and descended the stairs. The ground floor was quiet as a church at midnight, the ticking of the drawing room clock the only sound disturbing the silence.

"Where's Constable Haze?" Jason asked Dodson, who had silently appeared at his side. Some days Jason felt as if he were wearing a cowbell to alert Dodson to his presence downstairs.

"I'm sorry, sir, but Joe and I transferred the constable to one of the bedrooms. He wasn't comfortable on the settee."

Jason was about to chide Dodson for moving his patient without permission, but bit back the reprimand. What was done was done, and Dodson had been right in his decision. The short, narrow settee was no place for a convalescing man. "Which bedroom?"

"The green bedroom. Third door on the right," Dodson clarified. "He's been asleep since you left, sir."

Jason returned upstairs and entered the room without knocking, startling the lovely young woman seated in a chair by the bed, her delicate fingers clasping Daniel's hand. She had dark hair and luminous dark eyes, but her face was as pale as her high-collared white blouse. She released Daniel's hand and sprang to her feet, clasping her hands before her as if throwing herself on Jason's mercy.

"My lord," she whispered. "Is Daniel going to get well?" she asked, her voice trembling with anxiety. "Please, tell me he'll get well."

Jason's gaze fell on Daniel's spectacles that had been carefully placed on the stand near the bed. One of the lenses was cracked and the wire rims were bent. For some reason, the sight of the spectacles nearly undid him, and he swallowed hard before replying to Mrs. Haze's question. He wanted more than anything to tell her what she so desperately wanted to hear, but he couldn't lie to her. In the long run, it might be the greater cruelty.

"Mrs. Haze, Daniel has sustained a serious head wound. There's no way for me to tell if the skull is intact. If he's merely concussed, then he will have a devil of a headache tomorrow, and experience nausea, dizziness, and fatigue, but he will begin to recover. If his skull has been fractured or if there's a hematoma, then he will develop swelling that might put undue pressure on his brain."

"What does that mean?" Mrs. Haze whispered, her eyes huge with terror.

"It means that we must wait and see. I will monitor Daniel throughout the night and will do everything in my power to help him through this."

"I need to be with him," Sarah Haze said, her expression determined.

"I will have a room made up for you so you can remain near."

"I didn't say *near*, I said *with*," she replied forcefully, bright spots of color appearing in her cheeks.

"Of course. I only meant that you'll have a place to retire should you wish to rest."

"Thank you, my lord. I'm sorry. I didn't mean to be rude. I'm just really frightened," Sarah Haze said, the fight going out of her as quickly as it had come.

"I completely understand."

Her lips moved, but no sound came out. She looked to be near collapse. Flouting convention, Jason approached her and put an arm around her, leading her to the wingchair by the hearth. "Please, sit down. Have you eaten?"

She shook her head. "I can't eat," she muttered.

"A cup of strong tea with lots of sugar," Jason said, as if prescribing a medicinal tonic. "Think you can handle that?"

She nodded. "Thank you, my lord." She looked up at him, her eyes swimming with tears. "I can't lose him. He's all I have left." Tears slid down her cheeks, but she made no effort to wipe them away. "I've been so stupid," she whispered. "So selfish."

"Daniel is as strong as an ox, and just as stubborn, from what I can tell."

"He hasn't been the same since—" She swallowed hard. "Since we lost our boy. Neither one of us has." Her voice was barely audible.

Jason laid a hand on her shoulder. "One can never fully recover from losing a child, but it will get easier in time, especially if you share your feelings with each other and don't close yourselves off in your grief."

She nodded miserably.

"I'll just examine your husband and then get you that tea," Jason said, turning away. Sarah Haze clearly needed a moment to compose herself, and he needed to check on his patient.

Jason performed a brief examination, waking Daniel for long enough to find himself on the receiving end of a bleary-eyed stare. Satisfied that Daniel's condition hadn't worsened while Jason had been out, he left the room and nearly collided with Micah in the corridor.

The boy looked excited, his eyes like saucers in his freckled face. "Were you going to shoot somebody?" Micah exclaimed. "I saw a Colt in your room just now. It hadn't been fired. I smelled it," he added. "It smelled like oil, but not a whiff of gunpowder."

"I wasn't going to shoot anyone. It was just a precaution. And what were you doing in my room?"

"Looking for you, of course. A precaution against what?" Micah demanded. "Where did you go this morning? Have you figured out who killed that man?"

"Yes," Jason admitted. "I have."

"I knew you would. You're like a dog with a bone when you're onto something."

"Thank you. I think," Jason replied, smiling at the boy.

"That's how I know you'll find Mary," Micah said, searching Jason's face. "You will find her, won't you? I know you will," he said quietly, as if trying to convince himself.

Jason put a hand on his shoulder. "Have you had your breakfast?"

"Hours ago. But I'll eat with you again, if you like," Micah offered generously.

"Come on, then."

Dodson appeared at the bottom of the stairs. "Breakfast, sir?"

"Yes, please. And we'd like some sausages," he said, surprised to feel Micah's hand in his own. "And please take a cup of strong tea with sugar to Mrs. Haze. Perhaps some toast as well."

"Yes, sir," Dodson said, and marched off toward the baize door with all the pomp and circumstance of someone who'd been charged with serving royalty.

Chapter 30

Jason spent the next few hours in a state of heightened anxiety, his mind continually returning to his conversation with the colonel. Short of killing the man, there wasn't much else he could have done, but he was afraid the colonel would blindside him by doing something unexpected, like a cornered animal who had little left to lose.

"May I go visit Tom?" Micah asked after lunch. He was still upset that their fishing trip had been canceled due to Jason's orders for him not to leave the house while he was gone.

"No," Jason replied curtly.

"Why not?" Micah whined. "I'm bored. And Tom will be mad at me. He was looking forward to going fishing and having a picnic. So was I."

Jason smiled, feeling contrite for being short with the boy. Of course, Micah was bored, and worried that his friend would be angry with him. "Tell you what. Why don't you ask Joe to bring Tom here? Would you like that?"

Micah nodded enthusiastically. "We'll be quiet, I promise. I know you have Constable what's-his-name to look after. Is he going to be all right? He's not looking too good, and his missus seems to need ministering to nearly as much as her husband."

"You just keep your friend from getting under my feet and I'll do the ministering," Jason said, amused by Micah's comments. "You are not to leave this house. Do you understand?"

"I understand. You know, you're beginning to sound just like my pa."

"I'll take that as a compliment."

Micah made a face at him and ran down the stairs and out the door, calling for Joe as he crossed the yard, while Jason returned to the sickroom.

229

The afternoon slid by quickly, with Jason insisting that Mrs. Haze have a rest in an adjoining bedroom while he sat with Daniel.

"How do you feel?" Jason asked when Daniel awoke and peered at him from the depth of the bed.

"Never better," Daniel quipped. "And you, Captain?"

"I'm all right, and I think you can start calling me Jason," he replied. "Are you in pain?"

"My head hurts like the dickens, and my vision is blurry," Daniel said miserably. "Can I have my glasses?"

"They're broken, I'm afraid. Do you have a spare pair at home?"

Daniel nodded, but immediately winced with pain and stopped moving his head. Jason was pleased to note that his speech wasn't slurred. Always a good sign in someone with head trauma.

"You'll have to go to the inquest in my stead," Daniel said. "Sadly, you won't have much to tell Magistrate Talbot."

"Actually, I have quite a lot to tell him," Jason said. He filled Daniel in on his encounter with Colonel Chadwick.

"That sly old dog," Daniel said when Jason had finished. He'd omitted the part about the colonel wounding him. Daniel didn't need to know that, not in his condition.

"I always thought Caroline Chadwick seemed wary of him; now I understand why. He's been raping her all these years," Daniel said with disgust. "She probably couldn't even turn to her husband for help. Robert Chadwick would have done nothing to stop him. Marrying Margaret must have been his one act of youthful rebellion, and he seemed to have regretted it as soon as it was done." Daniel's bloodshot eyes widened as he looked Jason. "Do you think he died of natural causes?"

Jason shrugged. "We'll never know, but given what I've learned about that family, anything is possible."

"I doubt Colonel Chadwick would have let Alexander live, despite what he said. I think that young man's fate was sealed the moment he told the colonel the truth of his parentage. As long as Alexander was out there, he could always demand more money, or threaten to sell his story to the papers. Imagine the scandal. The Chadwicks would never live it down," Daniel said.

"Do you think Caroline knows?" Jason asked.

"I hope not. I'd like to think he spared her that, at least. Imagine finding out your whole life has been a lie."

Jason nodded. Perhaps deep down, Caroline had already known that, having been married to an ineffectual, possibly impotent husband for twenty years, and having had to grin and bear her father-in-law's abuse. She might have been a willing participant, for all Jason knew, but he had no doubt that her willingness would have made no difference to the colonel, who was a man accustomed to taking what he wanted and disposing of what he didn't.

Satisfied that Daniel's condition hadn't worsened, Jason excused himself just after four o'clock and made his way to the church. The graveyard was bathed in the late afternoon sunlight and the smell of roses filled the air. It was so peaceful that for a moment Jason wished he could sit for a while and allow himself time to think about everything that had happened this past week, but he'd promised Katherine Talbot that he'd come by before Evensong, and there wasn't much time left before the villagers would start to file into the church for the service.

Jason pulled open the heavy door and groaned as a sharp pain tore through his chest. The wound Colonel Chadwick had inflicted would take some time to heal. Jason entered the church and stood silently at the bottom of the nave as his gaze adjusted to the dim interior.

Katherine was alone, humming quietly as she arranged flowers near the altar. She turned when she heard Jason's footsteps echo on the stone floor and smiled.

"You came," she said, as if she'd expected him not to show.

"Yes," Jason replied. She blushed prettily and he smiled, glad to feel something aside from worry and pain for even a short while. "Are you here all on your own?" he asked. He had no reason to think she wasn't safe in her father's church, but the events of this week were still fresh, even if the murder had had nothing to do with Katherine.

"Father's in the vestry, preparing for the service. I'm quite safe here," she added, correctly interpreting his question. "I heard about the attack on Constable Haze. Will he be all right?" she asked, looking up at him.

"It's too soon to say for certain," Jason replied honestly. "But I'm optimistic." Katherine's expression suddenly changed, her eyes filling with worry.

'What is it?" Jason asked.

"I found something this morning," she said. She extracted a folded piece of paper from the pocket of her gown. "It's quite…eh…damaging," she said. "I need you to promise me you'll be discreet."

"You have my word," Jason said. He held out his hand, and she placed the paper into it, her gaze never leaving his face.

Jason unfolded the document and scanned the contents. It was a marriage certificate made out to Robert Chadwick and Margaret McDougal, but it was different from the one he'd left in his desk. It was less ornate, for one thing, and the signature of the priest who'd officiated over the nuptials didn't have quite the same flourish, despite it being of the same name. "Where did you find this?"

"I'd noticed a smudge at the very base of the cross. Mrs. Dowd must have missed it when she cleaned it. I had to lay the cross on the altar in order to wipe the blood that had gotten underneath. I'd always assumed the base to be perfectly flat, since I'd never had reason to look at the bottom, but there's an elongated cavity at the center. The document was hidden inside." Katherine looked up at him, her brow creased with worry. "Does this mean what I think it does?" she asked, searching his face.

"Yes. This is what Alexander McDougal was killed for."

"He was Robert Chadwick's son?"

"He was. His only legitimate child, if this document is authentic."

"Why wouldn't it be?" Katherine asked.

That's a very good question, Jason thought, but decided to keep his suspicions to himself for the moment.

"I could see why someone would kill him to keep that a secret." Her gaze flew to his face. "Was it Harry, do you think? Did he kill that young man to protect his inheritance?"

"No, it wasn't Harry."

"Do you know who it was, then?" Katherine persisted.

"I do, but I'm not at liberty to say just now. We have to wait until the inquest."

"Will Constable Haze be able to attend?"

"I will present the case in his stead," Jason replied. "Will you be there?"

Katherine shook her head. "Father won't permit me to attend. He says it's unseemly for a young woman to be present when such shocking matters are discussed. But you'll tell me all about it, won't you?" she asked, her lips stretching into a beguiling half-smile.

"I will. Perhaps you'll join me for a walk after Sunday service?" he asked, hoping she'd accept, but Katherine shook her head sadly.

"I must return home to see to dinner. Father expects to dine precisely at one o'clock."

"I see," Jason replied, feeling sorry for this lovely young woman whose own feelings and needs seemed to be of no interest to her father. "When can I see you, then?"

"Perhaps I can manage to get away afterward. Father likes to take a nap after dinner. Normally, I just read or work on my embroidery, but I think a breath of fresh air would be beneficial."

"Fresh air has proven health benefits," Jason agreed, smiling down at her. "I strongly recommend it." He was about to tell her that he looked forward to seeing her again when the first members of the congregation started to arrive for the service.

"Will you stay for Evensong?" Katherine asked, looking hopeful.

"I'm afraid not. I mustn't leave Constable Haze unattended for too long."

"Till tomorrow, then," Katherine said softly.

Jason took her hand and brushed his lips across the pale skin. "Till tomorrow." He knew she was watching him as he walked out of the church.

Giving in to his earlier misgivings, he veered off the path and walked through the cemetery, finding an isolated spot. A stone bench stood beneath an ancient yew, so he sat down and leaned against the tree, his thoughts in disarray. What did the existence of a second marriage certificate mean? Was it simply a copy of the original made out on a different form? Was *this* the original? Why would Margaret McDougal have two marriage certificates in her possession? That seemed unusual. Had Robert Chadwick left his copy with her when he'd returned home from Scotland, and was a couple automatically issued one certificate each upon their marriage? This too seemed strange.

Jason took out the document and studied it in the sunlight filtering through the tree branches, searching for any irregularities that had nothing to do with the format. He didn't see anything, but then he was no expert and probably wouldn't have been able to spot a glaring mistake even if it had stared him in the face. But there was one thing he did know, and it applied to all people in all parts of the world. Conmen could be found in the bowels of any thriving metropolis, and Alexander McDougal had lived in Seven Dials, an area known for its criminal element, according to Daniel Haze.

Was it possible that the marriage certificate was a fake? How difficult would it be to forge a document no one was still alive to challenge? Perhaps Alexander had had several forgeries made and meant to use them to extort money from Colonel Chadwick or his father's widow for years to come, and it hadn't mattered to him if the certificates weren't identical in appearance. Either copy would serve his needs.

Jason sat up straighter, a new possibility taking shape in his mind. Had Margaret and Robert been legally married at all, and had Robert Chadwick truly been Alexander's father, or had this all been a clever ruse to extort money from a wealthy family? The only physical evidence that Margaret might have known Robert Chadwick came in the form of the old clippings Daniel had discovered in her Bible, but, in themselves, they proved nothing. She might have met Robert Chadwick in Scotland and developed feelings for him. Maybe she'd even had a brief relationship with him, but several people had described the man as being weak and ineffectual.

Would he have been rebellious enough to marry the daughter of a mine captain when he knew that his family would never sanction the marriage, all the more so because Margaret had been Catholic? Had marrying Margaret been Robert's one act of defiance, or had the marriage not taken place at all? Perhaps Margaret had been involved with someone else entirely, someone she'd married, or not, who had been Alexander's biological father, and the deathbed confession Charles Boyd had spoken of had never happened.

Colonel Chadwick had killed Alexander McDougal, by his own admission, but all the other facts Daniel had gathered were nothing more than conjecture. The story he'd pieced together might be true, or it might be a fairy tale invented by Alexander McDougal to free him from the clutches of poverty. It had rung true enough to convince Colonel Chadwick, and it had cost Alexander his life.

Jason stood and walked toward the lychgate, eager to leave the inhabitants of the graveyard to their peaceful slumber. The inquest was tomorrow morning, but they were no closer to the truth than they had been the day he'd examined the young man's body in the crypt.

Chapter 31

Jason returned home, stowed the second marriage certificate with the first, and went to check on Daniel. He was asleep, his face peaceful. Sarah Haze sat still as a statue, her shoulders hunched with fatigue. She turned her face a fraction, then smiled wanly when she saw it was Jason who had entered the room.

"Has he been sleeping the entire time I've been out?" Jason asked.

"Yes. He fell back asleep shortly after you left."

"Mrs. Haze. Sarah," Jason said softly. "Please, have something to eat and lie down for a while. I'll sit with Daniel. I will come and get you should there be any change, for the better or for the worse."

Mrs. Haze started to protest, but then thought better of it. "Do you promise?"

"You have my word."

She sighed with resignation and stood. She looked exhausted. "I think I will lie down for a few minutes."

"I'll have Mrs. Dodson bring a tray to your room."

"Thank you, my lord. You've been so kind."

"I'm not being kind, Mrs. Haze. I'm doing what any doctor would do in this case. I'm treating you both."

She nodded and left the room. Jason yanked on the bell pull to summon Fanny, then bent over Daniel to check his vital signs, which were much as before. He was pale and still, but his pulse was steady and his breathing even. Jason carefully examined his head, searching for swelling. There was some, but it was consistent with being hit on the head. If Jason was right, Daniel should begin to improve by tomorrow, and if he was wrong, Daniel might be dead within the next few days.

"Yes, sir?" Fanny asked as she came into the room.

"Please instruct Mrs. Dodson to send up a tray for Mrs. Haze and see if the lady requires any hot water or a nightdress to change into."

"Do you have a nightdress for her, my lord?" Fanny asked practically.

"She can use one of my shirts," Jason replied. The scandalized expression on Fanny's face made him smile. She clearly hadn't been in service for long if the whims of the gentry could so easily shock her.

"I'm sure that's most unorthodox, sir," she said, her cheeks suffusing with color once she realized the impertinence of her comment. "I—I'm sorry, my lord. I didn't mean—"

Jason waved her apology away. "No, you're absolutely right. Perhaps she can borrow something from Mrs. Dodson or from you."

"I will see to it, sir."

"Yes. Do that."

Jason waited until Fanny left before taking the chair Sarah Haze had vacated. He'd briefly considered waking Daniel, but then changed his mind. Sleep was the best thing for him, and he didn't think Daniel Haze could shine any light on the dark goings-on of Alexander McDougal's mind or on the doubts Jason felt regarding tomorrow's proceedings.

If Colonel Chadwick refused to confess to the murder, the burden of proof would be on Jason, but by presenting the marriage certificate to the magistrate, he would surely destroy the lives of four people. He didn't feel much sympathy for Lucinda, knowing what she'd done at her father's behest, but Caroline Chadwick and her other children didn't deserve the humiliation the revelation would bring. Harry and Arabella would lose any chance of making a decent match or retaining any of their friends, and Caroline would be shunned by society for the rest of her life. And if the certificate was false and the marriage between Robert and Margaret had never taken place, then he'd be perpetrating an even greater injustice against them.

Jason rested his elbows on his knees and pinched the bridge of his nose. A headache was building behind the eyes, something that always happened when he was tense. What was he to do? And how was he to deal with Lucinda? He didn't think the girl deserved to get off scot-free, not when she'd almost killed Daniel Haze, but knowing what he now knew of the colonel, he was convinced that she'd either been frightened or bullied into helping him. Perhaps Lucinda was a chip off the old block and was as cruel and manipulative as her father, but Jason didn't wish to take it upon himself to ruin the life of a teenage girl. He wanted to give her the benefit of the doubt.

Jason leaned back in the chair and closed his eyes, allowing himself a few moments of rest. He was tired, mentally and physically. And tomorrow would be a difficult day.

Chapter 32

Sunday, June 10

The dining area of the Red Stag was filled to capacity, everyone talking excitedly in anticipation of the inquest and stealing peeks at the body of Alexander McDougal, which was laid out on a long table by the far wall. He'd been washed and dressed with great care by Mrs. Etty, who sat at the foot of the table, but he'd been dead for nearly a week, a fact that was reinforced by the smell wafting from the corpse and filling the crowded room.

Several old-timers recalled a murder that had happened about thirty years ago, but the younger people weren't interested in the past, their attention fixed on a crime that had happened in their lifetime. There were several women present, but Jason didn't see Caroline Chadwick or either of her daughters. In fact, no one from the Chadwick family was present. Moll, who was leaning against the bar, caught his eye and winked at him.

A hush fell over the room as Squire Talbot entered, a leather folder beneath his arm. He looked stern and tired, the dark smudges beneath his eyes a testament to a difficult night. He took his seat at the table reserved for him and lifted his eyes to survey the crowd, a look of resignation on his ruddy face.

Jason sat in the first row of seats, his insides roiling with apprehension. He'd prepared two different versions, neither of which he was overly pleased with. In one, he intended to present the marriage certificate to support his claim that Colonel Chadwick had murdered Alexander McDougal to keep the secret of his son's first marriage from coming out. In the other, he planned to simply offer his word as proof that Colonel Chadwick had confessed to the murder of Alexander McDougal and present the murder weapon, which had been used against him as well. He'd cleaned and disinfected his wound again that morning, but it was still oozing blood and was clearly fresh, should Squire Talbot, in his role as magistrate, demand that he show proof of the altercation.

Neither statement was very convincing, in Jason's opinion, but either would tarnish the reputation of the Chadwicks irreparably. The only bright spot of the morning was that Daniel had woken and asked for something to eat. Hunger was always a sign of recovery, and the swelling on the back of his head hadn't increased during the night, which was the clearest indication that the trauma was external rather than internal. Jason had left the Hazes together, Sarah spooning boiled egg into Daniel's mouth and feeding him bits of toast dipped into the yolk, and Daniel gazing at her as if she were his angel of mercy. For a man who'd nearly met his Maker, Daniel had seemed surprisingly happy, so Jason had decided not to upset him by telling him about the second marriage certificate. He'd fill him in once he returned from the inquest, bearing news of the outcome.

"Good morning," Squire Talbot said as his gaze swept over the assembly. "Last night I received some news that pertains to this hearing."

The room became so quiet, Jason could hear a mouse scurrying behind the bar. Everyone leaned forward, eager to hear what Squire Talbot had to say.

"Yesterday evening, Colonel Chadwick took his own life. Before committing this ungodly act, he wrote a letter, which he addressed to me, confessing to the murder of Alexander McDougal."

"But why?" someone cried out. "Why'd 'e kill 'im?"

"It would appear that Alexander McDougal's father had known Colonel Chadwick in India and was in possession of some information that had given his son fodder for blackmail. Colonel Chadwick did not specify what it was he'd been blackmailed with. He confessed to killing Mr. McDougal in a fit of rage when they met to discuss terms and to trying to hide the body."

"'E must 'ave had an accomplice, guv," a man in the second row said. "No way the Colonel could 'ave disposed of the body on 'is own."

"Yes, I believe you're quite right, Mr. Todd, but in his confession, the colonel informed me that the person who assisted him did so under threat and had little choice in the matter."

"So, it were one of 'is servants, then?" someone asked.

"He did not offer up a name," Squire Talbot said. "In view of this new evidence, I rule that Mr. McDougal was unlawfully killed by Colonel Chadwick. Since the perpetrator is already dead, his soul is now in the hands of our Lord, Jesus Christ. May God have mercy on his soul."

"How'd 'e top 'imself?" Mr. Todd called out.

Squire Talbot glared at the man with distaste but answered the question, nonetheless. "He shot himself in the head."

"What 'bout the burial for the victim?" a woman sitting at the back asked.

"Colonel Chadwick has left explicit instructions for his family to pay for the burial and provide the stone for Alexander McDougal, since it appears that he had no living family of his own."

Squire Talbot rose laboriously to his feet and made his way to the door. He didn't look like a man who was pleased with the morning's work. Colonel Chadwick had been a neighbor and a friend, and his actions would leave a stain on his peaceful community. The room erupted in conversation as soon as the door closed behind him, everyone expressing their shock and dismay.

"Care for a drink, yer lordship?" Moll asked, appearing at Jason's side as if by magic.

"Thank you, no."

"Come now, my lord, surely ye ain't put off by the smell," she joked, wrinkling her nose in disgust. "Uncle will 'ave 'im moved right away. Rotting corpses are bad for business."

"Yes, I'm sure they are," Jason agreed.

"Moll! Get yer arse over 'ere," Davy Brody hollered.

"No rest for the wicked," Moll said, and pushed her way through the crowd toward the bar area.

Jason left the tavern and stepped out into the overcast morning. He was vastly relieved that he hadn't been called upon to give evidence and pleased that Colonel Chadwick had chosen to do the honorable thing for his family. Suicide was a sin in the eyes of the Church, but the manner of the death would soon be forgotten, and the family would be able to move on, none the wiser about who Alexander McDougal had really been or his reasons for coming to Birch Hill. Lucinda would be the only person who'd know the truth. Jason hoped that her grandfather—or rather, her father—had left her some sort of explanation or apology, but somehow, he doubted it. He was sure that the colonel's decision had been based solely on his desire to spare Lucinda and assure her future. To him, that would be apology enough.

"Tell me what happened," Daniel said once Jason returned home and came to see him, sending Sarah downstairs to have a well-deserved cup of tea.

"Colonel Chadwick killed himself last night. He left a signed confession, though, exonerating his accomplice and offering to pay for Alexander McDougal's burial."

"Big of him," Daniel said, wincing with pain. "Good thing, though, because we never would have been able to prove he did it."

Jason took the dual marriage certificates from his pocket and handed them to Daniel, who looked dumbstruck.

"Where did you get the second one?" Daniel asked, squinting at the document. "I wish I had my glasses," he muttered.

"Miss Talbot found it hidden in the base of the cross."

"What are your thoughts?" Daniel asked, now peering at Jason instead.

Jason shook his head. "I don't know, but I think there's a good chance they're fake."

"You mean this whole thing was a ploy to extort money?"

"I think that's very possible. What should we do with them?" Jason asked. He knew what he wished to do, but it was up to Constable Haze to make the determination.

"Leave them with me," Daniel said, his voice full of conviction. "I'd like to study them more closely once I feel up to the task."

Jason nodded. "Of course. My carriage is at your disposal should you need to go into Brentwood to order new spectacles."

"Thank you. I couldn't have done this without you, you know," Daniel said, his mouth stretching into a grin. "We might still have unanswered questions, but you've discovered who the murderer is and brought him to justice."

"We've brought him to justice," Jason corrected him. "We make a good team."

"That we do, Jason. That we do. Can I go home, do you think?" Daniel asked, his voice lifting with hope.

"Tomorrow, but only if you continue to improve. I don't think your head would benefit from the jolting of a carriage. Now, lie still and do as you're told, or I'll make you stay here for the rest of the week."

"Did anyone ever tell you that your bedside manner is appalling?" Daniel asked with an amused smile.

"No, you're the first," Jason replied.

"All right. I'll defer to your advice. And what do you plan to do for the rest of the day?"

Jason smiled. "I am going fishing with Micah."

Daniel chuckled. "You are the unlordliest lord I've ever met."

"And have you met many lords?" Jason asked, grinning with amusement.

"More than I care to name, in the line of duty, of course. Frightfully pompous old sods, one and all."

"Then I'm glad I'm the exception. If you'll excuse me, I must see Micah. I think he's feeling a little neglected."

Daniel nodded and closed his eyes.

Jason found Micah sitting on his bed and looking forlorn. "So, how did it go?" he asked petulantly.

"As well as could be expected. Colonel Chadwick blew his brains out last night." Jason winced at the crudeness of his words, but Micah's eyes widened with interest.

"Really? That must have been something. Who found him?"

"I don't know. It must have been one of the servants," Jason said, hoping it wasn't Caroline or one of the grandchildren. Especially not Lucinda.

"Are you sorry the old goat topped himself?" Micah asked, now inappropriately cheerful.

"Not really," Jason answered truthfully. *He had it coming,* he thought, *and not just for the murder of Alexander McDougal.*

A peal of church bells shattered the peaceful quiet of the morning, their joyful ringing summoning the parishioners to the Sunday service.

"I hope you're not expecting me to go to church," Micah said, adopting a defensive posture. He could be as stubborn as a donkey when his mind was made up.

"I don't, but if you like, I can ask if there's a Catholic church in Brentwood."

Micah shook his head, then stopped, a thoughtful expression crossing his features. "Can you? I'd like to go to Mass and pray for Mary's safe return."

"Consider it done," Jason said.

He turned away from Micah, needing a moment to hide his feelings. A wire from New York had arrived on Friday, but Jason had set it aside to be dealt with later, since no urgent reply was needed. It read:

Search for Mary Donovan fruitless. Suspending inquiries unless otherwise instructed.

B. Hartley

Jason had been planning to tell Micah when he returned home, but now he couldn't bring himself to do it. Let the boy hope for a little while longer, Jason thought ruefully. It was never too late to break his heart. He'd send a reply to Mr. Hartley, asking the inquiry agent to keep looking.

Turning back, Jason smiled at Micah, his heart turning over with tenderness for the boy. "What would you like to do today? Your choice."

"I want to go fishing."

"With Tom?" Jason asked, feeling a little hurt all of a sudden.

"No, with you. I have the worms all ready, and Tom has lent me his fishing poles." Micah was practically bouncing with excitement.

"I'll just need a moment to change," Jason said.

"Well, hurry up. All the fish will be gone by the time we finally get there."

Jason rolled his eyes in exasperation. "I'll be right down. Go get your worms."

Micah jumped off the bed and ran downstairs to pull on the wellies Dodson had provided for him and collect his tin of worms. He was ready and waiting by the time Jason joined him in the mudroom. "Let's go," he whined.

Micah skipped toward the river, his bright hair glinting in the sun that had appeared from behind the clouds. "You know, Captain, I'm beginning to like it here," he said as he found the spot he'd been searching for and set down his can. "We can stay for a while if you like. Dodson said the doctor's popped off, so maybe you can take over his practice. I know how you like to feel useful," Micah said, making Jason chuckle.

Jason didn't really want to take over Dr. Miller's practice, nor would he be invited to do so in England, where a surgeon wasn't considered to be a medical doctor, but more of a tradesman, due to a lack of a university education, and was addressed as Mister rather than Doctor. Jason had the education and the credentials, but he had no desire to set broken limbs or treat fevers and boils. He'd come out if called, but he did not seek to set up a practice, at least not in Birch Hill.

"Perhaps we will stay for a while," Jason said as he picked out a plump worm to bait his hook. "This place is beginning to grow on me."

Epilogue

September 1866

Daniel opened his eyes but made no move to get out of bed. Gentle fingers of sunshine caressed his face, and the heady smell of Sarah's roses wafted through the window, making waking up in his own bed even more delicious. Sarah was still asleep, a small smile on her lips as she dreamed. He'd let her sleep a while, he decided, his heart melting with love for her. They'd arrived back only yesterday evening, having spent a month in Scotland. A second honeymoon, Sarah had called it. The deliciousness of the word still sent shivers of delight down his spine.

They'd been a little awkward with each other those first few days after the attack, but once they'd returned home from Redmond Hall, their relationship had begun to blossom, growing stronger with each passing day. He almost had a mind to thank Lucinda Chadwick for bashing his head in. She'd unwittingly saved his marriage.

Sarah stirred in her sleep and let out a little sigh. They'd made love again last night, their hunger for each other renewed after years of abstinence. Daniel hadn't put his hopes into words, but he prayed that their trip would prove fruitful. A child would bring so much joy into their lives and give Harriet a grandchild to dote on in her old age.

Daniel smiled at the thought of Harriet. She'd been happy to welcome them back, and had filled them in on all the news, a torrent of words flowing from her mouth from the moment they'd walked through the door until they'd finally retired for the night. He'd barely paid attention to most of the things she'd said, but he'd listened attentively when she'd spoken of the Chadwicks.

An engagement between Harry Chadwick and Imogen Talbot had been announced only last week, before Caroline had closed up the house and moved the family to London for the upcoming Season. Harriet didn't think that Caroline ever took out an obituary for Colonel Chadwick in the London papers, a supposition supported by the fact that no one had come to the funeral besides the immediate family. Daniel could hardly blame her, given that she'd just come out of mourning for her husband and wouldn't want her daughters' introduction into society to be delayed by another year, especially since the colonel had committed suicide and hadn't died of natural causes. Caroline Chadwick was a woman on a mission. Perhaps that was what Arabella had been alluding to when she'd said that nothing would be the same and she'd be next. With Harry's future settled, Arabella would be next in line to marry, being the older sister.

"And Captain Redmond?" Daniel had asked.

"Still in residence at Redmond Hall. That boy of his has been running wild with John Marin's son. Needs a firm hand, if you ask me. I certainly hope Captain Redmond means to engage a tutor for him. Time that child learned something of value."

"I'm sure Captain Redmond has the situation well in hand," Daniel had said, trying to hide his smile. He'd been relieved to hear that Jason Redmond hadn't left. He looked forward to seeing him, and to sharing with him what he'd discovered while in Scotland.

No conscious decision had ever been made to visit Rutherglen, but some part of Daniel couldn't rest until he learned the truth of Alexander McDougal's murder and the dual marriage certificates, and so he'd proposed a stop in Glasgow on the way back. Sarah had wanted to do some shopping, so he'd left her on her own for the afternoon while he'd gone in search of the church listed on the marriage certificate. Some part of him had almost expected not to find it, but there it was, an old stone church perched on a hill overlooking the village. Daniel had walked through the graveyard, wondering if Margaret McDougal would have preferred to have been buried here rather than in London.

The priest who'd greeted him when he'd entered the church was no older than thirty and had been at the parish for only a few years, but he was a friendly fellow and eager to help with the inquiry. Father Michael had brought out the parish register from

1845 and they'd looked through the entries, searching for any mention of Robert Chadwick and Margaret McDougal. And there it was, on August 17 of that year, the date specified in the marriage certificate, a marriage duly recorded by Father Fergus, Father Michael's predecessor.

The marriage had taken place, and one of the certificates was valid. Daniel strongly suspected that Alexander had had a copy made and might have intended to hand it over to the Chadwicks, but changed his mind, possibly because he'd decided on blackmail instead once he saw which way the wind was blowing. For some absurd reason, it made Daniel feel better to know that Alexander McDougal hadn't been a conman bent on defrauding an innocent family. It was a shame he'd died, but at least he'd died while reaching for something that had been rightfully his.

Daniel stretched and tried to ignore the rumbling in his belly. He'd become accustomed to the hearty Scottish breakfasts and dreamed of the porridge he'd had every morning, flavored with butter, cream, and a dollop of honey, followed by eggs, toast, bacon, and fried mushrooms. Daniel slid out of bed, dressed quietly so as not to disturb Sarah, and made his way downstairs, hoping Cook had started on breakfast. He had just poured himself a cup of tea when there was a knock at the door, and a flustered Tilda appeared in the doorway, her eyes wide with shock.

"Ye're wanted, sir," she said.

"Who is it?"

"It's Matty Locke. Says he's been sent to fetch ye."

"Why? What's happened?"

"There's been a death, sir. Davy Brody reckons it's suspicious."

"Where's the victim?"

"Matty says Mr. Brody found her near the old abbey, sir."

Daniel set down his teacup and stood. He hated to admit it, but he felt a frisson of excitement and a deep pleasure at the thought of seeing Jason Redmond that very morning. He hoped he'd already been summoned to examine the body. A new case was about to begin.

The End

Please turn the page for an excerpt from

Murder at the Abbey, A Redmond and Haze Mystery Book 2

Notes

I hope you've enjoyed the first installment of the Redmond and Haze mysteries. There are several more to come.

This genre is a bit of departure for me, but I have always been a huge fan of Sherlock Holmes, and later, more modern British detectives, and wondered if I could pull off an exciting and atmospheric mystery. I hope I have.

I'd love to hear your thoughts. I can be found at irina.shapiro@yahoo.com, www.irinashapiroauthor.com, or https://www.facebook.com/IrinaShapiro2/.

If you would like to join my Victorian mysteries mailing list, please use this link.

https://landing.mailerlite.com/webforms/landing/u9d9o2

Excerpt from Murder at the Abbey

Prologue

The morning was cool and fresh, the cloudless sky promising the kind of day that made Davy happiest. There was just a hint of autumn in the air as the sun shone above the still-green trees and the pleasant smell of hay drifted on the light breeze, the golden stacks dotting fields like giant beehives. Davy reached for the leather flask that rested next to him on the bench of the wagon and took a long pull of ale. He'd left early, not bothering to eat, and now he was hungry and planned to enjoy a hearty breakfast of fried eggs, buttered toast, and a generous helping of beans.

Davy tensed as the ruins of the Benedictine abbey came into view. A tall arch, part of the eastern-facing wall of the church, still framed a bit of sky, its peak crumbling but stubbornly refusing to succumb to the elements, and several jagged columns lined what would have been the nave, their uneven tops rising from the earth like accusing fingers. A few low sections of wall and bracken-covered stone were the only remnants of the buildings that had housed the monks who had made this corner of Essex their home back in the thirteenth century but were driven out two hundred years later by an edict from Henry VIII. No one knew, or cared, what had become of the monks, but there were some whose land had once belonged to the priory that said they heard cries in the night and the mournful echo of the monks' chants. Others said that druids had worshipped at that very spot long before Christianity spread through the land and that their Pagan gods still haunted the holy place, angry that the old religion had been wiped from the face of the earth and hungry for vengeance.

Logically, Davy knew the ruins were nothing more than bits of broken stone, but he hated the place. Some part of him feared its malevolent atmosphere and had done since he was a small boy. He found himself holding his breath every time he drove his wagon past the moldering remains, desperate to get away as quickly as possible. Hunching his shoulders, Davy sucked in his breath as the wagon came to the bend in the road that afforded the clearest view of the abbey. He hadn't meant to look, but his gaze was drawn to the ruins, as always. He peered at the lush meadow before the church, curiosity quickly replacing superstition. Something was lying in the grass, something long and white. Davy pulled on the reins and the horse drew to a stop, instantly lowering its head to nibble at the grass beside the road. Davy jumped off the bench and cautiously approached, hoping he wasn't about to be lured to his death by some cruel Pagan deity.

It was eerily quiet, as if the ruins were holding their breath. Waiting. A woman lay in the tall grass, her fair hair spread about her head like a golden halo. At first, Davy thought she was asleep, but as he drew closer, he noticed that her eyes were open, her gaze seemingly fixed on the lone bird wheeling above the stone arch. Her arms were outstretched, and a paintbrush was held loosely in her right hand, her elegant fingers still wrapped around the polished wood.

Davy knelt next to the woman and took hold of her wrist, searching for a pulse, but there was none. He reached out hesitantly and touched her face. Her skin was still warm, as soft as a rose petal. He might have thought her some ethereal being had the acrid smell of vomit not assaulted his nose, destroying the illusion. The tip of one boot and the hem of her gown were stained, bits of her breakfast clearly visible on the expensive fabric.

Davy stood and backed away, studying the woman from a safe distance. There were no signs of violence that he could see, but why would a seemingly healthy woman just die? She looked as if she'd been struck down where she had stood. What had she done to anger God so? Davy took a step back, and then another. Before he knew it, he was hurrying back to the wagon, now terrified. He'd be damned if he'd hang around the old abbey with only a corpse for company. He grabbed the reins, startling poor Horace. The horse took off at a trot, the bottles of spirits Davy had purchased in

Brentwood clinking in their crates as the wagon lurched and trundled down the lane.

As soon as Davy reached the safety of the Red Stag, he called out to Matty, who'd come out of the stable to greet him. Normally, Matty helped Davy bring in the crates before seeing to the horse and wagon, but today, Davy had a different job for him.

"Matty, fetch Constable Haze to the old abbey. Tell him there's been a death. A suspicious one, I reckon. And be quick about it, boy."

Davy marched into the tavern, helped himself to a tankard of ale, then turned to Moll, who was watching him, her eyes wide with curiosity.

"What's 'appened, Uncle Davy?" she asked once Davy had drained the tankard and set it on the counter with a bang. "Ye look like ye've seen a ghost."

"A woman is dead. At the old abbey. Someone should tell 'is lordship."

Moll smiled prettily at the mention of Lord Redmond, the American captain who had arrived in Birch Hill only this June to claim his grandfather's estate. Lord Redmond was the oddest nobleman Davy had ever come across, but he had to admit that the man's medical skills had come in handy since Dr. Miller had passed three months ago. Lord Redmond didn't mind getting his hands dirty, nor did he treat only those of his own social class. He was a radical, to say the least, but Davy had a grudging respect for the man, and secretly liked him—as much as he could like any rich cove, that was.

"I'll send someone over," Moll said dispassionately. Women held little appeal for his niece, especially dead ones.

Davy helped himself to another pint, gulping it down despite the early hour, then went out to unload the shipment of spirits before someone with sticky fingers decided to take advantage of the situation and help themselves to a bottle of whisky or port. He had to make ready. News of the death would spread like wildfire. The Red Stag would be packed tonight.

Chapter 1

Friday, September 7, 1866

Daniel Haze lifted his hand in greeting when he saw the tall figure of Jason Redmond striding across the grassy expanse of the abbey grounds. He held his medical bag in one hand and tipped his hat with his other hand when he spotted Daniel.

"Good morning, Constable," he said. "Welcome back."

"Good morning, Captain," Daniel replied, surprised at how pleased he was to see the man, even if they were standing over a fresh corpse. They'd graduated to first-name basis when investigating the death of Alexander McDougal, but nearly three months had passed since they'd seen each other, and Daniel felt a little awkward using the captain's Christian name as if they were lifelong friends.

"How's the head?" Captain Redmond asked, referring to the injury Daniel had sustained during the investigation that had nearly cracked his skull.

Daniel's hand instinctively went to the spot where he'd been struck, but all he could feel was his hair, which could use a trim. "It's fine. Good thing I have a thick skull," he quipped.

"I'll say. How was your trip? Is Mrs. Haze well?"

Daniel felt heat rising in his cheeks. The trip to Scotland had been wonderful, a second honeymoon after years of grieving and hiding behind cool politeness, a reconciliation of hearts and bodies that had filled Daniel with the kind of buoyant hope he hadn't felt since before Felix's death. The loss of their little son had brought him to his knees, but it had nearly killed Sarah, who'd felt responsible for the tragedy and couldn't forgive herself for not being able to prevent it. It had been Daniel's injury that had brought them back together, reminding Sarah that she still had something left to lose and jolting her out of her impenetrable grief.

The captain smiled and nodded, his keen powers of observation telling him everything he needed to know.

With the pleasantries over, they turned their attention to the woman at their feet, taking a moment to study the scene and learn anything they could from the position of the body and the surrounding area. The woman was lying on the grass, her eyes wide open, as if she were simply daydreaming while watching the wispy clouds float overhead, an expression of surprise on her lovely face. An easel stood a few feet away, the canvas still in its place. A brown leather satchel lay next to the right leg of the easel, its flap thrown back to reveal tubes of paint, extra brushes, and a stained rag. Daniel could see no sign of a struggle or any evidence that anyone had been there at the time of her demise. A gold chain encircled the woman's graceful neck, an oval locket engraved with flowers and vines glinting in the morning sunlight, and a thick gold wedding band was still on her finger. Both items were valuable enough to fetch a good price if fenced, so robbery didn't seem to figure into her death. In fact, her death seemed natural, if untimely.

"I don't see anything that would lead me to believe this was a suspicious death," Daniel said. "Except for the paint palette, nothing looks out of place, but given its position in relation to the body, I'd say she dropped it when she fell. And the paintbrush is still in her hand, as if death occurred suddenly."

"Yes, I think you're right," Captain Redmond replied. "May I examine her?"

"Please."

Daniel watched as Captain Redmond squatted next to the young woman, studying her face for a moment before carefully turning her onto her side to see if she might have sustained a blow to the back of the head or her back. He then rolled her back and carefully checked her arms and legs before standing up and turning his back to the onlookers who'd gathered by the road and were craning their necks for a better look at what the two men were doing. News spread quickly in a place like Birch Hill, and those who could afford to take time away from their work or chores had come to see the scene for themselves, eager to have something to tell their friends and neighbors over a pint later.

"I can't examine her properly here," Captain Redmond said softly. "But she seems to have been sick before she passed."

"Of course. We'll need to move her somewhere private."

"I can use one of the outbuildings on the estate to perform a postmortem," Captain Redmond suggested.

"We'll need permission from her family," Daniel replied, speaking in hushed tones as if the woman could hear him.

"Do you know who she is? I haven't seen her around."

"I do. Her name is Elizabeth Barrett. Wife of Jonathan Barrett. His country estate is very near here. I think the land might have even belonged to the priory at some point but was sold off after the Dissolution of the Monasteries." Seeing the blank look on the captain's face at the mention of one of the most well-known events in British history, Daniel decided to stick to the more pertinent facts. "The Barretts reside in Brentwood for most of the year but visit their country estate every summer and usually stay through at least part of September. You wouldn't have seen them because they keep mostly to themselves while here and attend church in town."

"I see. Well, we can't very well leave her here until the family is notified. I can have the body moved to Redmond Hall for the time being."

"While I perform the unenviable task of informing her husband," Daniel finished for him.

"Precisely."

"You mean, you need to undress the woman completely in order to perform a thorough examination, and this will give you enough time to do that before Mr. Barrett refuses permission and claims his wife's remains?" Daniel asked, grinning at the captain, who grinned back.

"Take your time," the captain said. "I will need at least an hour."

Daniel sighed. "I'll be off, then. I'll give you as much time as I can."

"It's good to have you back, Daniel," Captain Redmond said, clapping Daniel on the shoulder.

"Thank you, Jason. I'll come and find you once I've delivered the sad news."

Jason Redmond tipped his hat and waved to his coachman, who'd been standing at the edge of the gathering crowd, watching the proceedings with a frown of distaste.

"Joe, let's get her into the brougham," Jason called to him.

Joe strode toward the woman's body and lifted it off the ground with a gentleness that surprised Daniel. He'd known Joe all his life and had always thought of him as something of a brute.

"I've got her, sir," he Joe quietly. He wrapped his arms around Elizabeth Barrett as if she were a child and carried her toward the carriage, shielding her face with his arm as if to protect her from the curious stares of the gawkers.

Jason opened the carriage door for him, and Joe settled the body on the padded seat, half-sitting, half-lying it to make it fit, then waited for his master to climb in before jumping on the box and setting off. He looked straight ahead as the brougham began to move, walking the horses at a sedate pace so as not to disturb the dead.

Chapter 2

It was with a heavy heart that Daniel approached Rose Cottage, as the Barrett country residence was known. He assumed it had been named after the flowers that climbed the brick walls of the Georgian manor, or perhaps it was a reference to the color of the brick that turned a shade of rose when lit up by the morning sun, as it was now. The window frames and door were painted a gleaming white that matched the white arbors, which were smothered with fragrant yellow primroses. It was a charming home, and within it lived a family that was about to be confronted with tragedy. Daniel lifted his hand and used the knocker to announce his presence, suddenly wishing he could just go home and spend the morning with Sarah instead of delving into the lives of people numb with grief and shock.

A young maid, who'd grown up in the village and attended Sunday services at St. Catherine's, opened the door and looked at him expectantly. "Constable Haze," she said, her brow furrowing with concern. "Is aught amiss?"

"Dulcie, please inform Mr. Barrett that I must speak to him," Daniel said.

Dulcie nodded and invited Daniel into the foyer. "Wait 'ere, Constable," she said. "I'll tell Mr. Barrett ye're 'ere. 'E's at breakfast."

"Tell him it's of the utmost importance," Daniel called to her retreating form.

Jonathan Barrett appeared a few minutes later, pointedly taking his watch out of his pocket and checking the time even though a grandfather clock occupied the wall directly opposite the front door and showed that it had just gone ten.

"I say, what is this about?" he asked, taking in Daniel's tweed suit and bowler hat and staring him down as if he were a cheeky tradesman who'd dared to come to the front door instead of using the servants' entrance.

Daniel used the opportunity to study the man, since he'd never seen him up close. Jonathan Barrett was around thirty and had curling brown hair that was cut short and swept back from his high forehead. His brown eyes were wide and thickly lashed, and his face was clean shaven, the sideburns neatly trimmed. He wasn't very tall, but he was lean and wiry and gave the impression of someone who possessed physical strength. Despite the early hour, he wore a crisp white shirt, a dark tie, and a well-cut jacket, and trousers.

"Mr. Barrett, I'm Parish Constable Haze. May we speak somewhere more private?" Daniel asked, hoping his hushed tone would convey the delicacy of his call, but Barrett ignored the request.

"I'm sorry, old chap," Jonathan Barrett answered irritably, "but I'm rather pressed for time. What was it you wanted?"

Daniel took a deep breath and plunged in. "Sir, I'm afraid Mrs. Barrett was found by the old abbey just over an hour ago."

"What do you mean, 'found'? She's not a stray dog," Jonathan Barrett snapped.

"She's dead, sir," Daniel said as gently as he could. "Davy Brody, the publican of the Red Stag, came across her body this morning."

Jonathan Barrett's mouth went slack, his eyes opening wide. "What? No, that can't be. Elizabeth is upstairs, asleep. She likes a lie-in in the mornings."

"There was an easel with a painting of the ruins and a palette of oil paints," Daniel said. "She appears to have been painting the ruins at sunrise."

Running a hand through his hair, Jonathan Barrett looked at him with all the shock and disbelief of someone who'd just been given the worst news of his life. "No," he whispered. "It can't be her. Not my darling Elizabeth." His eyes filled with tears. "Are you sure it's her?"

"I'm quite sure, sir, but I would be happy to wait if you'd like to check her room."

"Jonathan, what's going on?" A woman was coming down the stairs, her face full of concern. "What's happened?"

"Deborah," Jonathan moaned. "It's... It's Elizabeth. Constable Haze says she was found dead. By the ruins."

"No, that's quite impossible," the woman said, shaking her head. "Lizzie was perfectly well when I saw her this morning."

"You saw her?" Jonathan Barrett asked.

"Yes. I woke early and came downstairs to read a while. Lizzie came down just before sunrise. She was going to the ruins to paint."

"Miss...eh?" Daniel faltered, unsure who the woman was since they hadn't been introduced. Given her resemblance to Elizabeth Barrett, she was likely a sister or a cousin, but he didn't wish to presume.

"Mrs. Silver. Deborah Silver," the woman said helpfully. "I'm Elizabeth's sister."

Daniel nodded. Mrs. Silver had the same golden hair and blue eyes, but her beauty wasn't as delicate, her figure not as trim. "So, you saw Mrs. Barrett just before she set off?" he asked.

"I think we'd best step into the parlor," Jonathan Barrett said. "This is not a conversation for the foyer."

Daniel followed him into the parlor and accepted the proffered seat. Deborah Silver and Jonathan Barrett sat across from him, watching him as if they expected him to say it'd all been a mistake and he'd take his leave now.

"How did Mrs. Barrett seem?" Daniel asked Deborah Silver. It wasn't a very astute question, but he didn't want to open with a difficult or intrusive inquiry for fear of being asked to leave before he had learned anything that might be helpful. He'd seen that happen as a young bobby in London when he'd accompanied an inexperienced detective to question a witness in Seven Dials. The detective had instantly put the witness on his guard with his abrasive manner and could get nothing out of the man save his name and occupation.

"She seemed fine," Deborah said, shaking her head in disbelief. "She'd been itching to paint the ruins at sunrise but had overslept the past few days and missed her chance. She was drawn to that place. Lord only knows why. I always thought it sinister."

She pulled a handkerchief out of her sleeve and dabbed at her eyes. Jonathan Barrett patted her hand, and she rewarded him with a watery smile.

"How did she die?" Jonathan asked. "Did she suffer?" His voice caught and he looked like he was fighting back tears. "Was she set upon by someone who'd intended to rob her?"

"I found no signs of violence, Mr. Barrett," Daniel said, hoping to reassure the man. "Death seems to have come quickly."

The man nodded and averted his gaze, as if needing a moment to compose himself.

"Did Mrs. Barrett often go out alone?" Daniel asked.

"She didn't like to be disturbed while painting," Jonathan Barrett said sadly. "I thought she was quite safe so close to the house."

"Did no one help her with the supplies? Carrying the easel must have been difficult, especially for such a slight woman."

Jonathan Barrett instantly flared at the implication. "If you think I should have offered to help her, I did. I also suggested that she ask Dulcie, or one of the grooms, but she said she was quite capable of carrying her own things. I had the easel made especially for her. It's exceptionally light and the legs fold, making carrying it less cumbersome."

Daniel nodded in understanding, not wishing to incense the man further. Instead, he turned to Deborah Silver. "Did your sister have anything of value on her? Money? Jewelry?"

Deborah sniffed. "She always wore a gold locket, and her betrothal and wedding rings. I don't believe she took any money with her, only the easel and paints. She carried the supplies in a brown leather satchel. Was it still there?"

"Yes, it was," Daniel said, trying to summon forth the memory of Elizabeth Barrett's hand. "Did you say betrothal ring?"

"Yes. It was an oval sapphire surrounded by diamonds and set in gold," Deborah said, watching Daniel intently. "Was it not there?"

"No, I don't believe it was, but I can't say for certain. I would need to check."

"She must have been robbed," Deborah Silver exclaimed. "That's the only explanation that makes sense."

"But it doesn't explain how she died," Daniel pointed out gently. "As I have already said, there were no signs of violence or any evidence that a struggle had taken place. If, indeed, Mrs. Barrett had been robbed, she had not been hurt in the process."

"Then explain to me, Constable, how a twenty-six-year-old woman who's in good health dies suddenly and with no waning," Jonathan demanded, his grief turning to anger. "Someone must have attacked her, hurt her. She was such a gentle soul. Who would do this to her?"

"Mr. Barrett, I know this is extremely painful, but I must ask for your permission to perform a postmortem on the body, so that we can determine how your wife died."

Jonathan turned a mottled shade of plum. "A postmortem? Are you mad, man? Where is she? Where is my wife?" he cried. "What have you done with her body?"

"Sir, your wife has been taken to Redmond Hall. Lord Redmond is a surgeon. I've asked him to examine your wife's body for signs of violence," Daniel finished lamely.

"What? The American?" Jonathan Barrett sputtered. "You mean, you instructed him to see if she's been interfered with?" he thundered.

"Among other things."

"No! I won't have it!" Barrett raged. "I want her here, where she belongs. I will see to all the arrangements. I won't have anyone touching my Elizabeth." He buried his face in his hands.

"Dear God, how could this have happened?" he cried, looking up at Daniel, his eyes blazing. "I never imagined she wasn't safe. She liked to walk around the countryside. She loved it here," he wailed. "She loved this house. How could I have known this place would bring about her end?"

"Sir, we don't know what happened, which is why it's important to find out the facts."

Jonathan Barrett looked up at Daniel. His nose was red, and his eyes were swimming with tears. "I need to know what happened to her. I need to know if she suffered before she died. If she was scared," he added on a sob. "Please, find out what happened to her."

"Does this mean I have your permission to perform an autopsy?" Daniel asked.

"Of course not! You can find out in other ways. Do your job, man. Ask questions. Surely someone must have seen something. These villagers are busybodies, one and all. They're always hovering, watching," he babbled, sniffing loudly. "They'll know what happened. I'm sure of it." Jonathan Barrett suddenly sprang to his feet.

"Jonathan, where are you going?" Deborah asked, looking at him with concern.

"I'm going to Redmond Hall. I'm going to bring Elizabeth home."

"Shall I come with you?" Deborah asked.

"No, my dear. You stay here. I will be back shortly."

He glared at Daniel, who stood, sensing the interview to be at an end. He'd question both Jonathan Barrett and Deborah Silver again in the coming days, but for now, he'd allow them some time to deal with the shock. He was about to ask Mr. Barrett if he might get a lift to Redmond Hall but immediately changed his mind. The poor man needed time alone to come to terms with his loss.

Chapter 3

By the time Daniel arrived at Redmond Hall, it was nearly noon. Dodson, an old Redmond family retainer, opened the door and invited him in, smiling as if Daniel were a long-lost relative.

"It's nice to have you back, Constable," Dodson said as he took Daniel's hat and coat. "And you've returned just in time, it seems."

"Yes. We arrived back only last night," Daniel replied. "I believe the captain is expecting me."

"He's in the library."

Daniel was glad Dodson didn't feel the need to stand on ceremony with him. He was perfectly capable of finding the library on his own, having visited Redmond Hall several times in the past.

The door to the library stood open, so Daniel walked right in. Captain Redmond sat behind a desk, a thick volume open before him. A gas lamp cast a pool of mellow light on the text and the captain's dark head. He'd been reading but looked up when he heard Daniel's footsteps.

"Have you eaten, Daniel?" he asked without preamble.

"I've come directly from speaking to Mrs. Barrett's husband."

"You must join me for luncheon, then," he said, gesturing for Daniel to have a seat. "Mrs. Dodson always makes enough food to feed a family of six."

"Thank you. I will gladly accept your invitation," Daniel replied. He'd missed breakfast, on account of Matty Locke coming to fetch him to the ruins, and was ravenously hungry. "Where's Micah?" Jason's young ward was conspicuously absent, and from what Daniel knew of the boy, he never willingly missed a meal.

"Out with Tom Marin. I gave him the day off from his lessons, so they went fishing. Mrs. Dodson packed them a picnic lunch, but he'll turn up once he's hungry again," Jason said, smiling affectionately. He was very fond of the boy, their bond stronger than that of some fathers and sons.

Once, late at night, while Daniel was spending several days convalescing at Redmond Hall after being brutally attacked, Jason had told him about his time in the Union Army during the American Civil War and how he'd come to meet Micah Donovan, who'd been "the best damned drummer boy any regiment could ask for." He'd also spoken about his time at Andersonville Confederate Prison, where he'd spent nearly a year alongside Micah and his father and brother, who'd taken young Micah along when they had enlisted rather than leave him on the family farm in the care of his sister.

"It wasn't because they didn't trust Mary to look after Micah, but because Micah had worn them down with his pleas and promised not to get in the way. He'd offered to carry messages, help nurse the wounded, and generally make himself useful in any way he could," Jason had said, shaking his head with incredulity. "Imagine, taking an eight-year-old boy to war. Madness. But they did, and he was taken prisoner along with Liam and Patrick and wound up in Andersonville with the rest of us. He's eleven now, but he still carries the scars of those years, and will probably do so for the rest of his life." "What was it like?" Daniel had asked. And Jason had told him.

The place had been a hellhole, the Southern governor's ultimate goal to kill off as many Union soldiers as possible without firing a shot—unless they tried to escape, in which case they were often shot in the back. The lack of adequate food, sanitation, and medical assistance, combined with the unnecessary brutality of the guards, had resulted in the governor's execution for crimes against humanity, but his death had done little to comfort the families of those who'd been lost, nor would it provide a family for a boy who'd been left alone in the world. Jason had stepped into the breach, taking Micah into his home and treating him as he would a little brother. Or a son.

"Luncheon is served," Dodson announced with all the pomp of someone addressing the royal family.

"Please ask Fanny to set a place for Constable Haze," Jason said.

"Already done, sir. We assumed he'd be staying," Dodson replied smugly.

"Shall we?" Jason asked as he stood.

Daniel followed Jason into the dining room and took a seat, his stomach growling loudly enough for Fanny to hear. She did her best to hide her smile and served them consommé before discreetly leaving the room and giving the men a few minutes to speak privately before she returned with the main course.

"Has Jonathan Barrett come by?" Daniel asked once he swallowed a spoonful of soup. He found that dealing with death did nothing to diminish his appetite.

"Been and gone. He's taken his wife's remains," Jason replied. "He didn't even ask to see me; he simply demanded that Dodson direct him to the body. He had his coachman to help him, so I decided not to intervene. The man was in no mood to speak to me—not that I can blame him. I caught a glimpse of him from the window. He seemed distraught."

"He is. Did you have enough time to examine the body?"

"Not as much time as I would have liked, but enough to make a determination as to the cause of death."

Daniel leaned forward in his eagerness to hear what the captain had to say.

"I believe Elizabeth Barrett was poisoned."

"Poisoned? Are you certain?"

"I am."

"Could she have taken the poison herself?" Daniel asked. There'd been no evidence of another person's presence at the scene, and given the abbey's reputation for being cursed and haunted, he thought it might appeal to an unhappy young woman—if Elizabeth Barrett had indeed been unhappy—as a place to commit suicide.

"If you were to kill yourself, would you do it in a place where you weren't likely to be discovered for some time? Left to the elements and animals, who wouldn't take long to start feeding on your remains?" Jason asked. "Besides, why bring an easel and paints and begin painting a picture if you're about to top yourself? I can't pretend to know what Mrs. Barrett had been thinking at the time of her death, but that sort of behavior doesn't seem consistent with a suicidal person's state of mind."

"I suppose you're right," Daniel said. "Have you any notion which poison was used?"

"Cyanide."

"How can you tell just by looking at her?" Daniel asked, genuinely perplexed.

Jason finished his soup and leaned back in his chair, looking thoughtful. "Generally, cyanide will kill within a few minutes, if the dose is strong enough. The victim would experience weakness, confusion, headache, dizziness, and vomiting. I can't be sure that Elizabeth Barrett experienced any of those symptoms, not having been there at the time she ingested the poison, but there were traces of vomit on the hem of her dress and her shoes, and a small amount was still present in her mouth. The fact that the vomit on the dress and shoes hadn't had a chance to fully dry means she was sick shortly before her death. She dropped the palette, which tells me the symptoms came on quite suddenly, and her pupils were dilated. She appears to have staggered backward, possibly in her confusion."

"That's hardly conclusive evidence," Daniel argued.

"You're correct. However, when I bent over her and opened her mouth to check for vomit, a scent of bitter almonds was clearly discernable. That particular odor is synonymous with cyanide poisoning. I wouldn't have smelled it had I not opened her mouth and brought my face close to hers. It would have gone completely unnoticed."

Daniel was about to comment when the door opened and Dodson entered, carrying a platter of roast chicken surrounded by potatoes. He ceremoniously deposited the platter on the table and asked if he should carve. Fanny appeared a moment later, bringing a dish of vegetables and another flagon of wine. As soon as they retreated to the kitchen, Daniel returned to his line of questioning.

"Where would one obtain cyanide?"

"One would either purchase it or make it," Jason replied. He speared a potato and popped it into his mouth.

"How would one make cyanide? From what?" Daniel asked, taken aback by Jason's answer.

"Cyanide is found in many common fruits. It can be made by crushing cherry stones or apricot pits."

"There's lethal poison in fruit?" Daniel asked. He was inordinately fond of fruit, and this news came as a shock.

"Yes. Each pit contains a miniscule amount. You'd need quite a few pits to obtain enough cyanide to kill someone," Jason replied calmly.

"And how would one go about extracting the poison from a pit?"

Jason shook his head. "That's what I was trying to figure out when you came in. I was reading up on poisons. Unfortunately, the method of extraction wasn't specified. I'd need to find a more descriptive guide or consult someone with practical knowledge."

"Such as?" Daniel asked.

"Such as a knowledgeable chemist. Would you know of such a person?"

"Can't say that I do," Daniel replied.

"Have you ever purchased a poisonous substance?" Jason inquired.

Daniel thought back to the last time he'd visited a chemist with the express purpose of buying poison. It had been when they'd lived in London and Sarah had thought she'd seen a rat in the kitchen of their rented lodgings. "I bought rat poison from an apothecary in London."

"Did you have to sign a register when you purchased it?" Jason asked, tilting his head to the side as if considering something.

Daniel thought back to the day he'd purchased the arsenic. It was more than three years ago now, and the memory was hazy at best. "I can't recall."

"There's no chemist in the village, so the nearest place to buy poison would be in Brentwood. Are there many chemists in Brentwood?" Jason asked.

"There are several. I suppose I'll have to speak to them all in due course. But before I do, I need to figure out why someone would wish to kill Elizabeth Barrett," Daniel said. "What would they have to gain by her death?"

Jason took a sip of wine. "Were the Barretts happily married?" he asked.

"I wouldn't know. Why do you ask? Do you think Jonathan Barrett had something to do with it?"

"I have absolutely no basis for making such an accusation, but killing an unsatisfactory wife is a lot cheaper and less public than divorcing her."

"The man appeared to be genuinely shattered. I know nothing of their marriage, but I didn't get the impression he thought of Elizabeth as unsatisfactory."

"Do they have any children?" Jason asked.

"No, they do not."

"How long have they been married?"

"I don't know for certain, but if I had to guess, I'd say about seven years. I recall seeing them together before Sarah and I left for London." Daniel paused to consider what Jason was insinuating. "Are you suggesting she was barren? Would that be a motive for murder?" he muttered under his breath. A man might be driven to get rid of a wife who couldn't provide him with an heir, but Elizabeth Barrett had been only twenty-six. Surely there was still time for her to conceive, unless her husband knew for certain that she never would.

"She wasn't barren," Jason said, interrupting Daniel's reverie.

"How can you be certain?"

"She was with child. About four months along, I'd say."

"Have I missed lunch?" Micah Donovan burst into the room, interrupting Daniel's exclamation of surprise. "I'm starving."

"Have you washed your hands?" Jason asked calmly. Any English parent or guardian would have instantly banished the boy from the dining room, but Jason didn't seem too annoyed by Micah's lack of manners.

"Of course I have. I washed my face too," Micah replied, smiling smugly.

"Ask Fanny for a clean plate," Jason said.

Micah bounded over to the bell pull and yanked it with all the determination of a professional bell ringer. Daniel thought the narrow strip of damask might come right off in his hand, but it withstood the assault. A moment later, Fanny bustled into the room, a place setting balanced on her tray.

"Fanny, I need a plate," Micah announced.

"I know, Master Micah. I heard ye come in," Fanny said affectionately. "Got it all 'ere for ye." She set a place for Micah. "Would you like some consommé? I can heat some up."

"Neh. I'm all right with the chicken," Micah replied, already reaching for the platter and spearing a leg with his fork. He helped himself to some potatoes and peas and snatched a roll from the breadbasket.

Jason poured him a glass of water. "Drink. Your lips are chapped, which means you are not drinking enough," Jason admonished the boy.

Micah gulped down some water and began to eat.

"I'm sorry, but our discussion will have to wait," Jason said. To speak of Elizabeth Barrett's fertility in front of the boy would have been highly inappropriate, even if the boy in question behaved like a little savage. Perhaps Daniel's mother-in-law had been correct when she'd mentioned only last night that the child needed to be taken in hand.

"Tell us about your trip to Scotland. I was very pleased to receive your letter," Jason said. "It cleared up the question of Alexander McDougal's true parentage once and for all."

"Yes. Too bad the proof came too late for poor Alexander. Had he tried to stake his claim through legitimate means, he might still be alive today."

"There's nothing you could have done, Daniel. Alexander's fate was sealed long before you or I even heard of him," Jason replied.

"I hear the Chadwicks have decamped to London," Daniel said as he resumed eating.

"Yes. It will do them all good to be away from here after what happened."

"Can we go to London?" Micah asked suddenly. "I'd like to see the British Museum and the zoo." He'd finished his meal in record time and was eyeing a bowl of fruit positioned at the center of the table.

"I don't see why not," Jason said, smiling at Micah indulgently.

"Can I invite Tom?"

"If his parents have no objection, we can take Tom along," Jason replied.

Micah clapped his hands in glee. "Oh, it will be grand. I can't wait to tell him."

"Don't tell him anything until I ask his father for permission," Jason said. "Now, if you're finished with your meal, go and read for an hour."

Micah made a face of distaste but didn't argue. He snatched a pear from the fruit bowl and left the room after bidding the adults a good day.

"I must find him a tutor," Jason said. "I've been teaching him myself, but it's not working out too well. He needs a firmer hand."

"Have you considered sending him away to school?" Daniel asked carefully.

Jason shook his head. "Micah has suffered enough loss to last him a lifetime. He deserves to be in a place where he feels safe and happy, and I can't imagine he'd feel comfortable among highborn English boys who'll forever see him as the son of an Irish farmer. Besides, he's not ready to be on his own, and to be perfectly frank, I'm not ready to part with him."

"I quite understand," Daniel said. He pushed away his plate with a small sigh of satisfaction. "I'd best go now if I hope to catch the magistrate at home."

Jason nodded. "Daniel, there's something else. I didn't get an opportunity to mention it before Micah came in, but when I examined Mrs. Barrett, I noticed signs of recent intercourse."

"How in the world could you tell if she—? Never mind. I really don't need to know," Daniel said, feeling surprisingly embarrassed to learn this fact about the deceased and to be discussing something so private so openly.

"Do you think she was raped?"

Jason shook his head. "There's nothing to suggest she was forced. Her clothes weren't in disarray, nor was there any bruising or tearing. Likewise, her arms and wrists showed no evidence of being pinned down."

"Nothing untoward in a woman having relations with her husband, then," Daniel said.

"Who's to say it was with her husband?" Jason asked, a smile of amusement tugging at the corners of his mouth.

Daniel tried to cover his discomfort with a cough. "Is there any indication that it wasn't?"

"That I couldn't tell you. You'd have to ask him that."

"Are you mad? How could I ask Jonathan Barrett if he's had relations with his wife? That would be impertinent at best, deeply offensive at worst."

"Whom she had relations with might be at the root of her murder," Jason said, completely unimpressed by Daniel's dilemma. "Were she having an affair, her husband would be the obvious suspect in her death, more so because the paternity of the child would be called into question."

Daniel sighed heavily, suddenly wishing he were still in Scotland. "Yes, of course. I will question Jonathan Barrett again, but first, I must speak to Squire Talbot. As the magistrate, he'll have to be made aware of the situation. I just hope this time he allows me—us—enough time to investigate the crime properly," Daniel said, watching for Jason's reaction. Would he wish to get involved with another murder case? Would he be as eager to help as he had been the last time? Daniel didn't think he could solve this case without the captain's help.

"We did all right last time," Jason said with a smile. "We got Alexander McDougal the justice he deserved. How shall we proceed?" he asked.

Relief washed over Daniel, and he smiled at the captain. "I will begin by questioning both Jonathan Barrett and Deborah Silver, Elizabeth Barrett's sister, again."

"And I will speak to Davy Brody," Jason said.

"Why? What can he possibly add?" Daniel asked.

"He can tell me when he came upon Mrs. Barrett's body. That will narrow down the window of time during which she was poisoned. It's always helpful to have a timeline of events."

"Yes, of course," Daniel agreed. Deborah Silver had said that Elizabeth had left shortly before dawn. Davy Brody's testimony would give them the approximate time of the murder.

That was something, he supposed, given that at the moment, they had nothing to go on at all.

"Captain, I nearly forgot. Did you happen to notice if Elizabeth Barrett was wearing a sapphire ring with diamonds?"

"She wasn't. I looked at her hands quite closely to check if her nails might have been broken during a struggle or if there might be blood beneath the fingernails if she'd happened to scratch her attacker."

"And was there?" Daniel asked.

"Nothing but traces of blue paint."

"So, there must have been someone there with her," Daniel said. "She had been wearing the ring when she left the house, but she was no longer wearing it by the time we arrived on the scene."

"Might Davy Brody have taken it?" Jason asked. "He was the only person to have seen the body before we did."

Daniel considered the question. "I wouldn't put anything past Davy Brody—he's always been a shifty character—but if he were going to rob a corpse, why leave the locket and the wedding band?"

"Perhaps he didn't think them valuable enough," Jason suggested.

"Both were made of solid gold. How could they not have been worth stealing? They would have fetched a tidy sum, were he to fence them to one of his London mates."

"Would you like me to ask him, or would you prefer to put that question to him yourself?" Jason asked.

Daniel was about to tell the captain not to ask about the ring but quickly changed his mind. He and Davy Brody had been friendly once, a long time ago, but relations had been strained since Daniel had reported Brody to the excise men for his smuggling activities, a charge that had resulted in a hefty fine and the loss of a substantial income for Davy, who'd used the cellar at the Red Stag to store the contraband. Daniel had only been doing his job, but he wouldn't expect Davy to understand that or forgive what he saw as the ultimate betrayal. Even if Davy had pertinent information to share about the death of Elizabeth Barrett, he wouldn't share it with Daniel out of sheer spite.

"Go on and ask him," Daniel said. "He'll never admit to taking the ring, even if he had taken it off her finger, but you're a good judge of character. You'll be able to see if he's lying."

Jason nodded. "All right. I'll let you know what I discover."

Printed in Great Britain
by Amazon